JUST BUSINESS

THE TAKEOVER SERIES BOOK TWO

ANNA ZABO

To Lori. Thank you for the love, encouragement, and occasional prodding. This Eli's for you.

CONTENT NOTES

This novel contains descriptive on-page consensual kinky sex, including bondage and pain play. Instances of 'sub drop' and 'top drop' are depicted. Safe words are used.

Characters consume alcohol socially.

Mental therapy is discussed.

Eli has PTSD from a car accident that resulted in deaths, and experiences flashbacks and a brief moment of suicidal ideation. The accident is described briefly.

Justin is recovering from an abusive past relationship.

Justin's sister is former military and lost her legs while on duty.

There are instances of homophobia based in religious pressures directed at Eli by his parents. Some amount of reconciliation also occurs (but is not complete).

CHAPTER ONE

When the Grounds N'at doorbell jingled, Justin White flipped his textbook closed and sent a silent thank-you to the universe. Watching paint dry would have been more exciting than reading about financial statistics, so any distraction was welcome at this point. That his two favorite customers walked through the door? Even better.

Well, more like favorite customer and his icy sidekick. Where Sam was warm and outgoing, Eli was a wall of indifference. He had no idea how those two worked together. It didn't matter, really. It was Sam he was focused on, not Mr. Wet Blanket.

Justin slid off his stool and tucked the textbook under the counter next to the folder that contained his cover letter and résumé. Sam grinned at Justin and held up two fingers before settling in at their usual table. Eli didn't even glance his way—just leaned his cane against the wall and took a seat.

As usual....

Justin started their regular drinks—a large cappuccino

for Sam and a medium Americano for Eli—with room for cream.

Had they hired someone today? He foamed the milk while watching the coffee drip out of the machine. Sam had been looking for an office assistant for at least a week. Justin had planned to hand over his résumé yesterday, but Eli had done the equivalent of cock-blocking, and had dragged Sam away to some meeting just as Justin had taken a breath to speak.

He stole a glance at the two men. Sam sat with his back to Justin. As usual, the face Justin saw was Eli's. Not an unpleasant view, to be honest. If Eli had any warmth in his body, he'd have had his pick of the coffee shop patrons—male or female. Classic Hollywood beauty—tall, with long, lean features, like something out of an old film. Despite a limp, Eli moved with an elegance that made his halting steps look graceful. And, of course, there was the cane—which varied from Victorian to futuristic steampunk—along with thin black leather gloves he peeled from his hands every time he took a seat.

Justin finished up the drinks and placed them on a tray with a little carafe of half-and-half. Résumé now or later? Later. See which way the wind blew today—if he understood their schedule correctly, this was the postinterview chat. He lifted the tray and headed over.

"...honestly, how hard can it be to find someone competent?" Sam leaned back in his chair.

Eli's smile—if you wanted to call it that—was a thin thing, indeed. "Not hard at all. Problem is, you're looking for someone beyond competent."

Justin stepped up. "Excuse me, gentlemen." He slid the edge of the tray onto the table and set their drinks out. Not normal practice, but these two weren't commuters who wanted their joe in a cup to go or students who were happy to nurse a mug for seven hours of free Wi-Fi.

"Thanks, Justin." Another grin from Sam.

Justin answered Sam with a smile of his own, then met Eli's gaze. A little shiver trickled down his spine. Eli's gray eyes seemed to bore into Justin through the loose, dark curls that fell over them. Natural black, too—not the dye Justin used in his own.

"Half-and-half." He set the small glass pitcher next to Eli's Americano.

"Thank you." Deep voice. No smile.

Justin nodded and stepped away.

He always had to catch his breath when Eli looked at him like that—as if ticking off all the things wrong with Justin's appearance. But he'd heard enough to know the opening for the job was still there.

Office assistant pay wasn't great, but it had to be more than the coffee shop, and there was no one better to learn how to run a business from than the owner and CEO of S. R. Anderson Consulting. Time to put to use some of the dreck he'd been learning down at Carnegie Mellon for the past two years.

The way things were going, he would need the extra income. Given his bills and Mercy calling every couple of weeks to ask for help, what else could he do? Her disability checks weren't covering her needs, even with the VA's care, and you didn't abandon family. It wasn't like their parents could help. Hell, he should probably send them some cash, too, if he had any to spare. None of them would be in this bind if he hadn't fucked up so royally.

Justin's heart thudded. Should he hand over his résumé now?

Later. They still had to pay. He wiped the tray down,

cleaned the espresso machine, stole another look over—and met Eli's gaze again. *What the hell?* Justin shivered and looked away. Thank God one of the hipster undergrads came up for a refill. Kept him from glancing over into those cold eyes again.

By the time he finished serving the dude and cleaning up the cups left in the dish bin, the familiar scrape of chairs and the regular *thump* of Eli's cane sounded against the wooden floor.

Sam in front, of course, but Eli not far behind.

"Great coffee, as always." Sam handed his credit card over.

Justin rang them up and handed the card back with the receipt. "My pleasure."

Sam and Eli turned.

Now or never. "Mr. Anderson?"

Sam spun back, curiosity in his face. "Yes?"

A horde of elephants stomped in Justin's stomach. "Are you still looking for an office assistant?" Somehow he kept his voice steady. Professional.

"I am." Sam shifted back. Eli's cane tapped against the floorboards.

He wasn't sure when he'd grabbed them, but there the résumé and cover letter were, in his hands. He held it out. "I'd like to apply."

Oh, he'd surprised Sam. And holy fuck, Eli's brows were up in his hairline, too. Mr. Emotionless... wasn't.

Sam took the papers and read the cover letter right then and there. Flipped the page. "You're attending the Tepper School?" Sam looked up.

"Part-time. I graduate in the spring." Nine more months.

"Who's your advisor?" Eli demanded in that clipped voice of his.

Justin squared his back and met Eli's dark stare. "Don Miller."

Eli's lips parted ever so slightly. Another crack in that façade. Probably because Professor Miller only took on the best. *That's right, you smug bastard.* Yes, Justin dressed like a goth artist. Fit in well at the coffee shop and annoyed the fuck out of his classmates. Didn't mean he wasn't good. The grin and the shrug were a bit of theater, but Justin couldn't help throwing that at Eli. "I'm more than a pretty face, you know."

Sam laughed and Eli... blushed. Ever so slightly, but color touched his cheeks. Goose bumps rose on Justin's every limb. Eli's stare wasn't so cold now, nor indifferent. He couldn't put a name to it at all.

"I guess we'll find out whether that's true or not," Eli said.

"When are you free?" Sam folded the papers.

"I have tomorrow off. My classes aren't until the evening."

"Then you have an interview at nine tomorrow morning."

Relief—pride—ripped through Justin even as his heart threatened to gallop out the door. "Thank you. I'll be there."

"Good. See you then." Sam turned and headed for the door.

Fuck yes! He would nail this! He would—

"Justin." Eli hadn't moved, his gloved hands folded over the silver handle of his walking stick. "Don't be late."

Fucker. "Don't you worry. I always come right on time."

That icy exterior vanished entirely. Eli held Justin's gaze and *smiled* before he turned and followed Sam.

Justin sank onto his stool because his legs didn't want to work. He couldn't tell if the emotion behind the curl of Eli's lips had been amusement or malice.

He shook himself. Didn't matter. *Bring it, asshole.* He'd ace this interview. For himself, for Mercy, and for his family.

Eli Ovadia climbed the stairs to Anderson Consulting and, for once, his leg didn't scream at him when he reached the top. That smart-mouthed barista was one of Don's students? Unexpected. Either Don was growing soft, or there was *quite* a bit more to Justin White than dark clothes, black nail polish, and too much eyeliner around those blue eyes. A pretty face, indeed.

I always come right on time.

Now, *that* would be interesting to test, to have Justin's lithe body under his. A different ache settled into his core.

Too bad Justin's personality was everything he hated in a man—snarky, smirking, and too full of himself. A hot mess.

Would be fun to break a man like that. Eli shook himself. Get your mind out of the gutter.

Yet... there was something familiar about Justin, in his nervousness and determination. Those stunning eyes.

Just a bit like Noah, that wicked grin.

Eli stopped and sucked in air. He wasn't even sure what Noah would look like now, had he lived—but certainly not like Justin White. Still, the fear and hope that rode under Justin's skin was so like Noah before the car crash.

There was the tingle in the back of his skull, the one that signaled the memories creeping back. He really did not want to deal with those right now. Eighteen years, countless hours of therapy, and that night *still* haunted him. He took another breath and focused on his gloves, the silver of the airship that topped his cane, and pushed Noah back into the past, the only place he still lived.

Eli shook himself and headed for Sam's office. It was Mr. White he should be dwelling on, not the past. He took a seat in one of the guest chairs then placed his cane against the other. "You're going to hire him."

Sam leaned his elbows on the desk and tented his hands. "Is that a prediction or a challenge?"

Eli couldn't help the chuckle. They'd developed an almost a symbiotic working relationship over the past eight months spent building the firm. Sam had a vision and the determination to achieve it, plus a list of contacts a mile long. They already had companies clamoring through the door, begging for help.

Someone had to be the brakes that kept Sam from leaping too far into the unknown. Like succumbing to the pity stories of too many companies that couldn't be saved. Or hiring a *barista* as an office assistant, even if Don Miller was his advisor. Even when there was grit underneath the eyeliner. Eli took off his gloves and draped them over his thigh. "He's abrasive."

Sam snorted. "So are you."

"Not in the same way."

"True. He makes people roll their eyes. You scare the shit out of them."

Eli leaned back and indulged in a smile. He'd made the last two interviewees pale and stammer with his blunt questions. "Better to weed out the slackers early." And he enjoyed that aspect of this job. Probably more than he should, but Sam didn't mind his kink when it benefited the business.

"Not sure Justin is a slacker. His résumé reads well. The cover letter is professional. Even the paper's nice." Sam flicked the folded pages across the desk. "And it took balls to hand it to me."

Eli retrieved Justin's résumé and scanned it once more, paying attention to the dates. "He's older than he looks." Two years younger than Eli, judging from graduation dates. Undergrad at Stanford in Management Science and Engineering. MBA at Carnegie Mellon. Makeup or no, Justin had a head on his shoulders.

And, yes, balls. He hoped Justin was late tomorrow, even by thirty seconds. "Work experience isn't bad, before now." Three decent companies in California before slumming it at Grounds N'at in Squirrel Hill.

"Why does he want this job?" *And why do I want him to have this job?*

"He's been listening to us. Knows I want more than a receptionist. He's willing to make less if he gets to work for *the* Sam Anderson."

No fault there. A chance to work with Sam had been one of the aspects that had attracted Eli to becoming Sam's CFO. Sam *was* the best, and he didn't blink at Eli's other... hobbies. "Wonder if he'll take that chipped nail polish off before the interview?"

Sam waved the question away. "If that's your only concern..."

Hardly. Still. "I like things neat." Justin White wasn't *neat*, even if he was tempting and evocative with his jagged hair, high cheekbones, and brash mouth that just begged to be tamed. Eli shifted in his chair. "He's... messy."

Sam laughed. "It's a wonder you and Michael were ever friends."

That snapped Eli's thoughts away from Justin. He'd been friends with Sam's lover, Michael Sebastian, since their undergraduate days. "Michael's messiness has always been carefully cultivated."

A man as tall and as broad as Michael could be—and often was—intimidating. The clothes Michael chose were more suited to a tropical bar, but it relaxed folks, set them at ease. Eli had seen Michael in other outfits, as well—and watched men fall to their knees at Michael's commands. "He chooses the effect, regardless of which look he picks."

Sam's eyes were not nearly as blue as Justin's, but still penetrating. "Oh, don't I know that." Soft words. "I'm willing to bet Justin is just as aware of his appearance."

The temptation. The carrot. "What's the wager?"

"Dinner for two. Winner's choice."

"Done."

They shook over Sam's desk. Sam leaned back, his smile slight but sly. "He'll leave the nail polish. On purpose."

Eli picked up his gloves and cane and rose. Not even a twinge in the leg. A good day. "Why would he do that?" *It wouldn't cultivate a professional appearance.*

"To fuck with you."

Not the answer he'd expected. Eli spoke through a suddenly dry throat. "With *me*?"

Sam grinned and rotated slowly to face his monitor. "Hard to miss your... contempt, Eli."

Sam had considered another word in that pause, Eli was sure. Pinpricks trickled down his legs. Still, he grunted. "It's not contempt."

Sam looked over, his eyebrow lifted in a manner that reminded Eli of Michael. "Oh?"

He waved the question away. "I'll be in my office."

As Eli crossed the hallway he rolled Sam's words around in his head. He dropped the gloves on the corner of his desk, and leaned the cane against the wall.

Sam had noticed something in Eli's behavior. Troublesome. Very troublesome. If Sam had, chances were Justin had as well.

Worse, he wasn't exactly sure what signals he'd given off. Eli ran a hand through his hair and sat down. There was raw potential in Justin. But his attitude, his flippant manner... Eli wanted to channel that. Put it to use in so many ways entirely inappropriate for an office environment. Well, being unbalanced was new... but intriguing. Eli adjusted himself through his pants.

Tomorrow would be very interesting, indeed.

CHAPTER TWO

Justin stood in the coffee shop bathroom and adjusted his tie before checking his watch. Eight thirty.

Would anyone be up at the office now? He'd considered showing up at seven and sitting by the door until Eli arrived, just to see his face.

Don't be late.

He wasn't a child; far from it. He didn't need a rich asshole telling him what to do or wear. He'd had enough of that with Francis, when he'd blown it at his previous company. Justin took a breath to settle his nerves. He so needed this job.

Brian gave a low whistle when Justin stepped out into the shop proper and more than a few of the normal morning crowd whipped their heads around to take a second look.

Well, good. That's what he wanted; the surprised look, the parted lips. With any luck, the transformation would impress Sam—and put Eli in his place.

Really think you're going to be able to do that?

His pulse ticked up a notch. *Focus on the CEO, not his sidekick.*

"Dude," Brian said between customers. "You look awesome."

That coming from a straight guy. "Thanks." He forced a smile onto his face. Time to head upstairs. "I'll let you know how it goes."

"You'd better." Brian's gaze lingered a bit too long before he shook his head and went back to slinging coffee.

Justin took the stairs up to S. R. Anderson Consulting and forced his heart rate and his cock down. Walking in with a hard-on wasn't the impression he wanted to make. Professional but unique—that was the idea. They'd seen him in Grounds N'at, knew that version. Time to shake things up.

Justin brushed a bit of fuzz off his lapel. Thank goodness the thrift stores also got in unsold clothing. The suit had been a *find*.

Last step. Justin looked up—and met Eli's gaze through the glass door to the office.

Holy shit. That smirk. Those gray eyes. Didn't help calm Justin's dick down at all.

The bastard pulled a pocket watch out of his vest—of course he was wearing a three-piece suit—and made a show of checking the time before he opened the door for Justin.

"I'm not late." Justin brushed past Eli, aware of how warm he was. Hard, too. For this guy? Please.

"No, indeed. Seems you've come just a bit prematurely."

Justin bit back the *fuck you* before it came out. Blowing the interview before he even saw Sam wouldn't help him or Mercy. "Do you always meet candidates at the door?"

"Yes, actually." Eli didn't have his cane and didn't make any move farther into the office, so Justin planted his feet and folded his hands behind his back. Kept him from fidgeting.

Which was good, because the predatory once-over Eli gave him sent ice straight to his feet and nearly had him on his knees. *What the hell?* Hadn't felt that impulse in ages, not since he'd left Francis and the Scene behind in California. "You the receptionist?"

A low chuckle rattled Justin's bones. "Chief financial officer. I like knowing what we're spending our money on."

Eli was the CFO? *Oh hell.* He schooled his expression. "I'm worth every penny."

Wrong, wrong thing to say, because the flash of teeth Eli gave Justin wasn't anywhere close to a smile and it sent a bolt of lust straight to Justin's balls. "You don't get to decide that." He nodded toward the inner office. "Follow me."

The cane wasn't just for show, it seemed. Without it, Eli's steps were more halting. An injury to his left leg? Something around the ankle? Not that Justin would ask. He suspected Eli wouldn't answer anyway. Mercy didn't talk about hers, though not having legs anymore was pretty visible to anyone with a brain.

Justin rolled his shoulders. He could do this. He'd done it before.

They stopped at the first office—a double office, but the first room was empty except for an assistant's desk. The inner office was spacious, decorated, and contained Sam. He glanced at Justin before shifting to Eli and lifting his eyebrow.

"Justin's arrived for his interview." Now he knew what Eli's amused tone sounded like, as if his heart weren't hammering fast enough.

"Good morning."

"Thanks, E. Justin, please take a seat."

Eli retreated—to wherever CFOs retreated to. Justin didn't care. He focused on the chair Sam had indicated and sat.

"Do you need anything before we begin? Water? Coffee?"

"You have coffee up here?"

Sam laughed and the knots in Justin's back loosened. "No. I'd have to run downstairs."

"I'm fine, thanks."

"Good." Sam took out a copy of Justin's résumé. "Then let's just jump in, shall we?"

Sam wasn't kidding. His questions came, one on top of the next, digging through Justin's work experience, his schooling, his thoughts on management and the work environment. After a half hour, Justin regretted not asking for water. His throat hurt from talking.

Sam leaned back and crossed his arms. "How do you feel about LGBT rights in the workplace?"

"Strongly in favor of them, seeing as I'm gay." Justin folded his hands into his lap. "Why shouldn't I have a photo of my boyfriend on my desk?" Justin shifted his gaze from Sam to the framed photo next to Sam's monitor—a portrait of a brown-haired man in sunglasses and a garish shirt, lifting a margarita.

Sam's chuckle redirected Justin's attention. "Why not, indeed?"

"I don't even mind working with straight people."

That got him a bark of laughter. "Good, because we have a few here."

He didn't ask who. Part of him hoped Eli was one of them. The other part shivered. Why the hell was he thinking about that asshole? Because he was Sam's CFO.

That he looked stunning in a three-piece suit had nothing at all to do with it.

God, he so needed to find the Scene in Pittsburgh, especially if he got this job. Nothing like a forceful man in a business suit to fuck with his head. Or get him angrier than hell, especially after what that fuck Francis had done to him.

"If I took this position, would I be working for you exclusively?"

Sam sat forward. "Not entirely." Now he knew what Sam sounded like when very amused. "You'd report to me, but some of your work would be directed by Eli."

Of course. "I can handle that." *Fake it until you make it.*

That sly smile didn't fade. "See what you think after you interview with him."

If that wasn't a wet blanket... or an inferno. *Please let that man be straight.* "Is that who's up next?"

"No. The engineering team. Eli's always last, so the candidates can fall apart afterward in peace."

He must have blanched, because Sam's grin widened. "Kidding. Mostly."

"I don't think he likes me."

"See what you think after you interview with him."

Fair enough.

"Come on. I'll introduce you to the people who work the real magic." Sam rose.

Justin followed Sam deeper into the office, into an open space of desks, monitors, whiteboards, sticky notes plastered on a wall... and a Ping-Pong table.

Very nice.

Four engineers sat at a round table in the center of the space. Sam introduced them all before vanishing to the front of the office. "He's all yours" were his parting words.

One of the four—Jen—handed him a bottle of water. "Surviving?"

"Yes. And thanks."

"Sam makes you talk yourself dry."

Another of the team—Fazil—snorted. "Better than what Eli does."

Justin choked on the water. Not much, but enough for a ripple of amusement to move through the team. He cleared his throat. "What does Eli do?"

"Grills the shit out of you. He's..." Fazil shrugged.

The blond—Adam—finished that thought. "Merciless and tough."

"Unforgiving." The fourth member spoke. Sertab, if Justin remembered the intros correctly. "But fair."

"Don't let them psych you out," Jen said. "He's not a monster."

No, *monster* wasn't the word Justin would use. *Intense.*

"So," Adam drawled, "why here?"

Just like that, he was off and running again. By the end of the group interview, his head spun. Too many questions, too much laughter. Some of the conversation went over his head—he hadn't been into computer science—and was honest about that.

"Dude doesn't have to know programming. Just respect it," Jen said to Fazil.

"Ping-Pong?" That from Sertab.

"Yes, though you'll all probably beat the pants off me."

Approval. Good. They shuffled their papers and Fazil stood. "Ready for the endgame?"

Eli. Justin shrugged and rose. "I'm not worried." Bravado and skill was the only way to survive in business.

Fazil led him to a large office across from Sam's. No

assistant's space. *Thank goodness.* Eli swung around in his chair. No smile. "My turn at last."

"So it would seem." Justin stood inside the doorway.

"Good luck." Fazil zipped away.

Eli pointed to one of the chairs behind a small table in the center of the room. "Have a seat, please."

Well, here we go. Justin squared his shoulders and did as told.

WELL, NOW, WASN'T JUSTIN A PICTURE OF STRESS AND tension in his suit. How delightful. Eli took the seat across the table from Justin and folded his hands. He owed Sam a dinner for two.

Everything about Justin's outfit was calculated, down to the blue shirt that matched his eyes perfectly. The gray of his jacket and vest contrasted with the black of his tie, the latter matching his unnaturally dark hair. Somehow, that ragged cut looked perfect with the clean, crisp cut of the suit.

Justin had left the chipped polish. It fucked with Eli exactly as Sam suggested it might. What he wanted to do was bend Justin over the table between them and find out if he really did come right on time. Instead, Eli crossed his legs and leaned back. "Why is someone like you working in a coffee shop?"

Justin took a breath. "Because CMU is fucking hard."

"Yes, I know." Eli pointed a thumb over his shoulder in the direction of two diplomas from Carnegie Mellon. Hard to miss, given their obnoxious size.

What a pretty blush Justin had. "Oh." He cleared his throat. "Tepper School?"

"I was one of Don's students." Justin met Eli's gaze. No eyeliner. Justin's eyes were far bluer than Noah's had ever been. A tingle in Eli's leg was a reminder of the past he could not forget. He didn't need that now, not during an interview.

"I know my shit." No warble in Justin's voice. No fear, or at least none showing. *Good.*

"You think you do. Time will tell if your ego matches your ability." Eli tapped his good foot against the underside of the table. "You didn't answer my question. Why the coffee shop? You could do better."

Anger softened Justin's voice down to the level of a lover's. "Fuck you."

If only. "That's still not an answer, Mr. White."

Justin drew a breath and rose from his seat. He pressed his hands flat on the table and leaned over, his whole body trembling in his fury. "Seriously. Fuck you. I've done my time in corporate America. Short hair. Clean-cut. Straight, conservative male. I don't want to live like that." He drew in a breath. "Downstairs, they don't care how I dress or who I screw, as long as I can brew a good cup and keep the customers happy. Nice change of pace. You should try it sometime."

"Check your assumptions." Eli stood then spoke low but with the force that usually buckled men's knees. "Sit down, Mr. White."

Justin did, lips drawn into a circle, his eyes wide. Surprise and beautiful obedience. *Good God.* If Sam hired Justin, Eli would have to be careful not to walk over every line he desperately wanted to cross. What the hell was it about Justin? He was just another candidate.

Justin exhaled, the anger all but gone. "I'm sorry. That was way out of line."

Very. Seemed he'd hit a sore spot. Eli waited.

Justin's conviction returned, but without the fury. "I'm not an idiot, nor a freeloader. I do know my shit."

"You still haven't answered my question."

There was the anger and pain again. "Yes, I could do better." He dropped his hands into his lap. "But I want the best. That's why I'm here."

Now, that was a proper response. "Much better. Thank you." Eli settled into his chair. "Do not make me get up again."

A tremor shuddered through Justin.

Working with this one could be exceedingly fun, or utterly frustrating. Given how hard Eli's cock was, probably both. "Now tell me about your work with Don."

After the outburst, Justin spoke calmly and without the rancor that he'd carried. By the time he'd finished explaining his studies and capstone, Eli understood why Don Miller had taken on this hot mess. The *potential* in Justin, the intelligence. Focused, he could take on the world. Undoubtedly, Don had seen that, too. A perfect fit for Sam.

Why hadn't Justin gone further at his age? Eli doubted it was Justin's sexuality or style choice—but something had derailed Justin White. Oh, to pick the man apart and discover what. Sadly, his methods wouldn't be appropriate.

Working together would be an interesting challenge, for both Eli and Sam, and very likely for Justin, too.

Eli softened his tone. "Thank you, Justin. That was nicely done."

Praise spread a different kind of flush over Justin and his shoulders relaxed. "Is that—are we done?"

"There are some HR housekeeping details. My department, too, for the moment. Something Sam's assistant will take over." He'd very nearly said *you*. Eli rose, crossed to his desk, and picked up the application for Justin to complete, plus the list of benefits.

"I'll give you some time to fill this out." He handed the papers and a pen to Justin.

"Thanks." The shake in Justin's voice played along Eli's nerves. He was far too hard—probably noticeably, too. But Justin focused on the papers in front of him.

Pity.

Eli made his way to Sam's office and leaned against the doorframe. When had he gotten so breathless? *When Justin sank at your command.* No. Before that. Long before.

Sam gave him a once-over. "Looks like he made quite an impression on you."

Of course Sam would notice what Justin had missed. "He's an interesting man."

"Engineering adores him." Sam tapped his pen against his desk.

Ah, so he thought Eli would say no. A banner day when he could surprise Sam. "Of course they do. He's edgy and charming."

"You don't want me to hire him."

Eli laughed. "Actually, he's perfect."

The pen stopped moving, as did Sam. "What?"

"Hire him, Sam." Eli pushed himself off the doorframe. "And you won that bet."

Sam placed the pen down on desk. "Close the door, Eli."

His turn to be surprised, but he did as Sam asked.

When he turned back, Sam was very much the CEO and less the friend. "What did you do to him?"

Fire burned in Eli's veins. He did not like where this was heading. "What I do to every candidate, Sam. I asked questions."

"You've never come from an interview with your cock tenting your pants." Sam's voice was surprisingly mellow, and that stripped the anger from Eli. "What did he do to you?"

"He yelled at me." Turned him on. Reminded him of Noah. It wasn't the look or the suit—though he'd seen Noah in one often enough. Standard issue for yeshiva. Eli shook his head.

Sam's eyebrows rose into his hair—he'd definitely picked up Michael's mannerisms.

"It was justified. I pushed. You're right about him having balls." Eli leaned against the door. "He's exactly the person you've been looking for."

Sam was silent for long enough to make Eli's skin itch. "Can you work with him, despite your attraction?"

Eli snorted. "Of course." One thing he did have control over was himself.

"Good."

And just like that, they hired Justin White.

HALFWAY DOWN THE STEPS TO THE FIRST FLOOR JUSTIN stopped and gripped the railing. He couldn't tell how that had gone. Brilliantly? Horribly? Sam liked him well enough, and so did the engineers. Pretty sure Eli didn't. If he weren't such an asshole, he'd be hotter than sin. Imposing. Commanding. The last time Justin had obeyed without thought, he'd been naked and wearing Francis's collar. And fuck if he needed Eli to remind him of *that*.

How dare Eli imply that Justin was a lazy shit because he worked at a coffee shop while studying at one of the hardest schools in the country? Chances were Eli's parents had bought his education. There was nothing rags to riches about him. Justin had gotten into school both times on merit. He'd also excelled at the corporate job he'd shoved in Eli's face, before he'd thrown it all away at Francis's feet while Mercy was fighting in Iraq.

Are you pissed off at Eli or Francis or yourself?

Yes and no. Confused. He was used to disdain from someone like Eli. Not... niceness. Eli's praise and gentleness once the hard questions had been answered had been unexpected and screwed with his mind and body. Hadn't helped that Eli had seen him to the door.

I expect you'll hear from us soon, he'd said.

Guess you'll not be doing the post downstairs.

Not this time. He'd looked directly into Justin's eyes and wet his lips with his tongue. *Pity, that.*

Like sex on ice. Justin shivered. He didn't want to walk into the coffee shop sporting an obvious bulge.

Out one door and in the other. Brian opened his mouth, but Justin cut him off. "Gotta go, man. Drank too much water." He grabbed his change of clothes from behind the counter and hightailed it toward the back.

Thank fuck no one was in the men's room. The wood against his back was as hard and unforgiving as his cock. He could *not* be seen like this. Only one solution, really. He had to change out of his suit. No one would notice if he took a bit more time.

He dropped trousers and boxers, and wrapped a hand around his dick. He hadn't been this turned on in ages. All because of a man who probably hated him. Justin braced against the wall and stroked.

Eli might be an ass, but he also had long, elegant fingers that looked good in black leather. Justin could imagine Eli's gloved hand wrapped around his cock, jerking him off, his tall, hot body pressed against Justin. That deep voice whispering in his ear. *You think you're something, don't you, Mr. White? I suppose we'll see.*

Fucker would probably get a kick out of ordering him around. Justin shuddered and bit back a moan.

Don't you dare come yet. Not until I say.

He was close. Panting. Thank God the fan rattled so loud. He grunted and worked his cock faster.

Warm lips pressed against the back of his neck. Hot breath against skin. "Come."

Justin moaned as semen coated his hand and hit the back of the urinal.

Fuck. Fuck. Every nerve felt like fire. Did he really just jack off in a men's room thinking about Eli? The evidence was right there, white and sticky on his hand. *Shit.*

Worse. That had been hotter than anything he'd imagined in a while.

Jesus. I am desperate. He flushed away the evidence, cleaned himself up, and changed back into jeans and a t-shirt. Black with a stylized raven on it. All his other classmates wore suits or business casual to class. He couldn't abide by the dress that reminded him how he'd fucked that life away with Francis.

He stuffed his dress clothes into his backpack. He'd outshone everyone. His grades were fantastic. Don praised his work. He could rise above it. Again. This time, he'd help Mercy, too.

Justin opened the door and flicked off the light. The smoky, acrid smell of coffee swam down Justin's lungs as he stepped out into the shop. He grabbed a table near the counter and stuffed his backpack onto the seat.

A few customers sat at the tables, but none were distracting Brian. "So how did it go?"

"Good, I think." Justin stepped behind the counter and started making a cappuccino. The adrenaline would wear off, and he still had an evening of classes ahead. "Pretty sure Sam liked me. Engineering did, too. But..."

"But?"

"I don't think I impressed the CFO."

"Is that the tall guy with the cane?"

"Yeah. Eli." He scratched the back of his head. "I kind of yelled at him."

"Dude—"

The bell on the shop door rang—and speak of the devil. Cane, gloves, but no jacket. Just his shirt and vest, which did nothing to hide the long lines of Eli's body and everything to stir up Justin's blood again. He held a large envelope. Probably outgoing mail.

"Shit," Justin muttered. He set about frothing his milk. Really needed to find a fuckbuddy. By the time Justin finished making his drink, Eli was at the counter.

"I thought you had the day off."

"I do." Justin picked up his drink. "I'm kind enough not to make my boss work for me." He nodded at Brian. "But he'll happily take *your* order." Looking away was hard, but if he stared at Eli's canted lips, he'd need another trip to the men's room. He slid into his chair.

Eli remained at the counter and ordered, but when he got his drink he tucked his mail under his arm and headed straight to Justin's table. Despite not wanting Eli to sit, Justin moved his backpack. Eli placed his cup down—a latte?

Jesus. Eli never ordered one of those. "Isn't that a little risqué for you?" The quip slipped out before he could shut his brain off.

Eli's chuckle took Justin's breath from his lungs. "I like to live life on the edge."

"If that's your edge..." This time, Justin clamped down on the rest of his words.

Eli merely smiled and handed him the large white envelope he'd been carrying.

What the fuck? Justin took it. Opened it. Slid out the papers— *Holy shit.*

It was an offer letter. Thirty minutes hadn't even passed.

A quiet laugh from across the table made Justin look up. Eli's smile lit up his whole face. "Well, that certainly was worth the hand delivery." He sipped his latte.

Justin's hands shook. Hell, his whole body vibrated. "How—I mean—"

"There are only six of us, Justin. Doesn't take that long to make a decision."

Justin pulled the letter out, got to the salary, and his mouth dried up. The offer was for far more than an assistant should receive. By several tens of thousands. That would solve—a whole host of problems. Bills. Debt. Mercy's needs. Maybe allow him some cash to send to his folks.

"I do hope you're worth every penny."

His own words, thrown back. "Don't you worry about that." Justin shoved the letter into the envelope. "When are you expecting an answer?"

"I know your answer." Eli leaned back and crossed one leg over the other. "We'd like the signed paperwork within a week."

"That's presumptuous."

"Is it?" Eli stripped off his gloves, the leather stretching to reveal the flesh beneath.

Justin didn't answer Eli. He wanted the job. They were

handing him more money than such a position should pay. He placed the envelope on the table, wrapped both hands around his cup, and sipped, the sharp taste of the coffee clearing his mind and wetting his mouth. "Why me?"

The gloves hit the table. "Sam likes you. Engineering likes you."

"But you don't."

Eli ran a finger around the rim of his mug. "Assumptions, Mr. White."

Those words sank straight into his bones and tightened his balls. What *would* those fingers feel like on his lips, in his mouth? *Stop it.* "You didn't seem impressed."

"You have potential. Untamed talent." Eli picked up his cup. "I'm interested in seeing that harnessed." There might have been a grin around that last word, but any expression vanished when Eli's lips met the rim of his cup.

Harnessed. Justin stared at Eli's gloves. He didn't know whether to despise Eli or flirt with him. "Is there a dress code?"

"Other than requiring clothes? No." Eli put his cup down. "Engineering tends to dress casual. You've seen how Sam and I dress." He gave a light shrug. "You'll be interacting with customers on occasion, but you'll have warning."

"So if I came to work dressed like this"—Justin gestured at himself—"you wouldn't throw me out?"

Eli smiled and there was warmth to it, enough that Justin's own cheeks heated in response. "I prefer the suit on you, but no, I wouldn't throw you out. Sam wouldn't blink, either."

He preferred... *Shit.* Not what Justin wanted to hear. *I am so not having fantasies about this man.* He took a breath.

"Thank you. I need to read this fully. I'll let you know in a day or two."

"Of course." He glanced over at Brian. "I'm guessing your current employer knows you've been interviewing?"

Behind the counter, Brian was trying very hard to look like he wasn't listening to every word. "Yeah. He knows."

Eli finished his coffee and stood. "Let us know when you can start." He picked up his gloves and grabbed his cane. "I look forward to working with you, Justin."

Hearing his name from Eli again drove the air from his lungs. The memory of his orgasm and why he'd come so fast sent a tremor through him. "Can't wait."

"Neither can I." Eli's grin was sharp. Wicked. *Sexy.* He turned and headed toward the door.

Well, shit. He had a job. And another raging boner for Eli. Justin drank his coffee. Turned on by a control freak. Not good, if his past was anything to go by.

Working for Sam Anderson might be more difficult than he thought. He touched the white envelope. For what they were offering, he damn well would excel at this job, Eli or no Eli.

CHAPTER THREE

A WEEK AND A HALF AFTER HE'D HANDED JUSTIN THE offer letter, Eli let Justin, backpack and bike helmet in hand, into the office as an employee. The eyeliner was back, highlighting his intense blue eyes, along with black jeans and a dark blue t-shirt, a toned-down version of his Grounds N'at outfits. Justin had added a black cord tight around his neck as an accent.

Leather, from the looks of it. How hard would it be to tuck a finger under that and *yank*? Eli let his gaze linger as Justin shifted from foot to foot.

Justin licked his lips. "Going to come out here every day to let me in?"

"Only today." He handed over a keycard. "Please don't lose that. They're a pain to replace."

Justin looked at the card for a moment before sliding it into his back pocket. "Wouldn't want to cause you any extra work." A lilt to that, and a sly grin.

Oh, Justin was going to be quite the handful. "Given that job is now yours, you'd only be causing yourself pain."

"Self-flagellation isn't my thing."

Eli turned toward the inner door. "Oh?"

"It's no fun whipping *yourself*."

Eli stumbled at the thought that chased after those words—Justin's naked back stretched out and open, the weight of a flogger in Eli's hand, the smell of the leather and flesh—and caught himself against the doorframe.

"Shit, are you okay?" Justin gripped his arm at the elbow and helped Eli upright, sending lightning into Eli's veins.

He'd never been so grateful for his injury. "Yes. Sometimes it gives out when I least expect it." True, though certainly not in this case.

Justin let him go.

In the faint reflection of the glass door, questions chased across Justin's features, but he was good enough not to ask. Eli pulled the door open and answered anyway. "I was in a car accident when I was fifteen. My leg was crushed."

Yes, Justin certainly had a very lovely blush. "I wasn't—I didn't—" He stood rooted to the floor.

That wouldn't do. Nor would grabbing that tiny cord and leading him down the hall. Eli gripped Justin's shoulder, savoring the tremor that ran through Justin, and squeezed. "It's the question everyone asks. I'm not offended." He gave Justin a little push. "Come on."

This time, Justin moved and Eli followed. And there was the tempting expanse of Justin's back, in a tight t-shirt. "We'll start at your new desk."

As Eli expected, Justin remembered the office layout, and strode forward toward the office he'd be sharing with Sam. When they reached the room, it was as it had been—empty. "I didn't know what supplies you'd need. I'll show you where we keep them."

"Thanks." He dropped the bag and helmet on the desk,

and peeked into the adjoining office. "No Sam?"

"He's dropping his partner, Michael, off at the airport."

"Mr. Margarita on the desk?"

He didn't even bother to hold back the laugh. "Yes, that's Michael in the photo."

"He looks..." Justin shrugged. "Not the kind of guy I'd expected Sam Anderson to date."

"What *did* you expect?"

A flush crept up his neck. "I don't know." He ran a hand through his too-black hair. "Someone more like him? A business guy? Not..." He gestured at the office. "Jimmy Buffett."

If Justin only knew. Eli stepped in, closer than he should, but the office *was* small. "There you go with your assumptions," he murmured close to Justin's ear.

Eli longed to put a finger under Justin's slack jaw and push his mouth closed. An unexpected warmth grew in Eli's chest.

Propriety, Eli. He stepped away. "Michael Sebastian is the vice president of research and development at Sundra Networks."

"Oh." Justin cleared his throat. "So no Sam?"

"It's just the two of us at the moment."

"No one else? I mean, engineering?"

"They'll be wandering in soon, I'm sure."

"Good." Justin sucked in a breath. "I mean—not that you aren't—shit."

Oh yes, Justin wore nervousness well. Parted lips, rapid breath. Hard cock, judging from the impressive bulge. "Lost your words?"

"No coffee this morning."

Now, *that* was a surprise. "There's a rather fine coffee shop below us."

"I know." There was that spark, the defiant glare. "I used to work there, you might recall."

Eli said nothing, just folded his arms.

Justin's shoulders sagged. "I was going to stop. But... it's weird going as a customer. No hopping behind the counter, you know? Having Brian wait on me when I know perfectly well how to make what I want."

Another interesting trait. Was it not being allowed to do a task he was capable of? Or did Justin resent being waited upon? "Change can be hard."

Justin held Eli's gaze. "Sometimes it's worth the pain."

Yes, Justin, but are you? "Let me show you where we keep the office supplies."

AFTER ELI SHOWED JUSTIN THE SUPPLY CLOSET, AND where the free pop resided in the kitchen, everyone else trickled in—but for Sam. Eli left Justin to engineering, thank goodness.

Justin was intelligent. Mouthy. A charmer. His interactions with the engineering team had been instructive. Open and energetic, but calculated in many ways. A smile here, a laugh, a gesture to ease nerves, to pave the way to friendship.

How much was Justin playing Eli? A game of power? Eli settled into his desk chair and let that thought cascade though his blood. Don's lessons flooded back. *The Art of War*. Etiquette. When to bend to an opponent and when not to.

Those had all been on business—Eli had learned other lessons elsewhere that had been as instructive about human nature. As much as he wanted to apply *those* to Justin... he wasn't about to take his boss's assistant home, tie him down, and flog him.

Those little quips were likely Justin attempting to be edgy.

Time to call Lyle and go to a party. He needed an outlet to sate his inappropriate lust. Sam hired him to be a professional, not a fool.

Eli sighed and opened the Sanhex Equipment folder and settled into finding every reason they shouldn't take on this account. Sanhex was huge, but kept losing market share because of incompetent leadership, financial decisions, and marketing. That would be hard to change, but if Sam could, the business that would bring in would be astounding. A soft rap against his open door startled Eli out of his research and his gut lurched. Justin?

No, it was Sam. A very tired, relaxed, *glowing* Sam. Eli huffed a laugh. Must have been a good send-off.

"Don't give me that look." Sam's words held no bite.

"Wouldn't dare." Eli pushed back from his desk. "How long is Michael gone this time?"

The smile faltered. "Two weeks. Well, sixteen days. Training, a conference, then customer meetings."

Meaning Sam would need distracting, preferably by work. "I've been going over the Sanhex proposal."

"Good. I expect you've already listed seventeen reasons why we should say no."

Eli glanced at his monitor. "Only twelve. But I'm not finished."

There was Sam's grin. Good.

"Of course you aren't." Sam nodded toward his own office. "How's Justin doing?"

"Hopefully Sertab's got his laptop set up."

"If she's finished, you can train him on expense reports,

since I know how much you *love* doing mine." Sam gestured for Eli to follow.

A good task for Justin to start with. Not just Sam's reports, but everyone else's, too. Better for Justin to handle that particular pain. Plus, it introduced Justin to the staff and the companies they were working with. A gentle ramp-up. Eli rose and grabbed his cane. Gave him something to do with his hands, least he reach for something entirely inappropriate. Like Justin.

Sertab sat at Justin's desk while Justin leaned over, both his hands on the desk. "...and to launch the VPN, click this," she said.

Justin's t-shirt had ridden up, and what a fine view that provided. "That's easy enough," Justin said.

Eli planted his cane against the carpet. Too tempting to thwack that band of flesh.

Sertab leaned back. "If you have any problems, let me know." She looked over her shoulder. "Hey, Sam."

"Morning." Sam glanced at his watch. "For a little while yet."

Justin righted himself, his expression shifting from smooth and confident to parted lips and reddening cheeks when he saw Eli. Nice, but certainly Sam caught that.

"All settled in?" Sam gestured at the laptop.

"Tech's done," Sertab said. "Rest is up to you guys." She stood and paused at the door. "Justin, Ping-Pong starts at four thirty, if these guys let you loose."

"You know what they say about all work and no play," Justin said.

She laughed and was gone.

"Somehow, I doubt you're ever a dull boy." Eli couldn't resist.

Justin froze.

Sam choked, trying not to laugh. "E, behave." He pointed at his office. "In. Both of you."

Eli felt Justin's stare burrowing in between his shoulder blades as he entered Sam's office. Still, the line had been too good to pass up.

Sam rounded his desk and took his seat and swallowed a hiss on the way down.

Someone had fun last night. Sore ass. Back, too, given Michael's tastes. He stole a glance at Justin—yes, he'd noticed Sam's wince as well.

Very interesting.

"You'll have to forgive Eli. He's not one to pass up an opportunity for wit."

"I'm not sure that qualified as wit," Justin said.

He *should* have laid his cane across that ass. "Considering what I had to work with—"

"Considering," Sam said, "that you're going to be training Justin this afternoon, can we keep the blood loss down to a minimum?" Sam grinned.

Justin relaxed. "Truce?"

Eli stared down at Justin. "No bloodletting and a truce are two very different things. Unless, of course, you want to conce—"

"Challenge accepted." The timber of Justin's voice took Eli's breath away.

Sam coughed. "If you two are finished?"

Justin didn't speak. Eli nodded.

"Good." Sam explained what he expected of Justin and which tasks Eli would oversee—those dealing with finance. "Eli will hand over HR duties to you, if you're up for that."

Justin sat up straighter. "I am. But—" His Adam's apple shifted his little leather necklace. "I have two semesters left. Classes. My capstone."

"Taken into consideration. We're seven people. I don't anticipate hiring more at the moment, so there should be enough downtime. If there isn't, tell me, and we'll work something out."

"Thanks." Justin let out a slow exhale. "Good to know."

"And yes, Ping-Pong is fine," Sam said. "Even Eli takes a break once in a while."

The look of incredulity. Justin must have practiced that one for ages. "But not for Ping-Pong." Eli tapped his leg with his cane.

"Then what?" Curiosity in Justin's voice.

"Macramé."

Justin laughed, though. "You've got to be kidding me."

"Not at all. I find tying knots into rope very soothing." Especially when wrapped around limbs and torsos.

Justin's smile faded as color rose up his neck. *Yes, Justin. Imagine that for a moment.* "And speaking of knotty issues, I need to go finish taking apart a proposal." Eli turned his attention to Sam. "If you no longer need me?"

"No, thanks, E."

Eli rose and turned from Justin, partly to cover his arousal, but mostly because Justin wore a look that made Eli want to stroke his cheek. "Door open or closed?"

Sam also had an interesting expression, one that said he would pay Eli a visit later. "Open's fine."

Eli crossed the hall to his office.

Challenge accepted. They would both see how that went.

WHEN ELI LEFT, JUSTIN COULD BREATHE A BIT EASIER. He looked up at Sam. "Macramé?"

Sam shrugged. "You'll need to ask him."

That didn't help the movie playing in Justin's head, the one where Eli wrapped rope around Justin's hands. As if Justin would let him. "He hates me."

"No." Sam folded his hands into his lap. "Eli rarely speaks to those he dislikes. He certainly doesn't banter with them."

Well, shit.

"Do you have a problem with Eli?"

Fear leached into Justin's bones. "No." He couldn't afford to lose this job, especially on the first day. "He's—he seems cold. Sometimes." When he wasn't setting Justin on fire with quips and smoldering looks.

"He expects a lot from you." Sam leaned forward and rested his hands on his desk. "I do as well, for that matter. Eli is exacting, even with me, but fair. You'll see."

That sounded like a dismissal. "So after lunch, training with Eli?"

"Yep. That covers it."

The bathroom fans up here were as silent as owls' wings. No chance of jacking off. "Guess I should grab lunch."

"Wise plan."

Justin stood. *Hours with Eli. Wonderful.*

———

THE FORTY-FIVE MINUTES THAT JUSTIN SPENT EATING Middle Eastern food with engineering blew past far too fast. When they returned to the office, his coworkers disappeared into the back, leaving Justin at the mouth of the lion's den.

Justin steeled himself and knocked on the doorframe.

A small startle, a final glance at the screen—checking the time, Justin realized—then Eli swung around and smiled. "Right on time."

That sent a shiver down Justin's spine. "I did tell you."

"So you did." The smile didn't diminish. "Get your laptop and cord. I'll show you the tasks on your computer. Kill two birds, as it were."

When he returned, Eli was carrying a chair from the center table to his desk, his face twisted in pain.

"If you'd waited, I could have—"

The words died in Justin's throat when Eli looked up. A fleeting glimpse of deep anger and pride, which vanished under what Justin had assumed was cold indifference.

A mask. Same one his sister wore sometimes. *Shit.* Car crash when he was fifteen. Meant Eli had been living with his leg for half his life or more. *You're a fuckhead.*

Eli straightened. "I've told everyone in the office this—including Sam—and I will tell you. If I want your help, I'll ask for it. If I don't, then I don't want your help. Is that clear?"

"Yes." Justin clutched the laptop to his chest, which hurt like hell. He knew that look, had seen it on Mercy. "I'm sorry, that was rude of me."

Eli patted the chair. "Come sit. I'm not mad, just..."

"Frustrated?"

Another sharp look from Eli.

Justin held the computer tighter. "My sister lost her legs in Iraq. I should know better."

A look of understanding and compassion. "Justin, sit down."

For once, the command didn't rankle. Justin sat and placed the laptop on the desk. "I wasn't thinking."

"No, you weren't." No rancor. Eli slid into his own chair. "Is not thinking going to be an ongoing issue?"

Justin couldn't help the flinch. "Don says I have a habit of leaping before seeing whether there's ground underneath. Good sometimes..."

"...but not others." Eli chuckled. "Yes, that's Don." He paused. "You did fine with approaching Sam. Surely that was premeditated?"

"Oh, when I want something, it's easier."

"Good. That's a starting point, then."

"For what?"

"Giving you incentive to think."

Holy fuck, the edge to that smile and bright flash of teeth. Every minute with Eli was like working in goddamned free fall.

Eli nodded toward Justin's laptop. "Open that thing, and I'll show you how to do the most hellish job in the office."

Training with Eli wasn't that bad. Expense reports were tedious and boring, but they gave a glimpse into the work Sam did. Justin drove the process as much as he could, Eli walking him through the steps.

"You do this for engineering, too?" Justin stretched, popping a few vertebrae in his neck.

"I tried having them do their own, but I ended up redoing them." Eli tapped absently on his desk. No gloves. Those sat to the right of Justin, the faint odor of leather washing up from time to time.

"It's not going to scale well."

"Oh, don't I know that." Eli stretched his arms over his head—and shit, the man had muscles underneath the sleeves of his shirt. Smelled good, too. A scent clean and deep—sandalwood? "Theory is, when we're big enough for it to matter, we'll have better software, training, and staff."

"But for the time being it's not worth the struggle?"

Eli lowered his arms. "Exactly." He tapped Justin's computer. "Think you can repeat that?"

"Yeah. It's straightforward enough, if you have the right paperwork."

"Good." Eli picked up a stack of files from farther down his desk and dropped them on Justin's open laptop. "Enjoy. I certainly will."

Walked right into that. "Been putting those off for a while?"

"I always do, for as long as I can. Thank you for getting hired before the quarter ends." Eli's grin was infectious.

Justin couldn't help the laugh. "Now I know the true reason you didn't veto me."

That earned him a chuckle. "Back to your own office."

Justin stood and gathered his laptop and his newly acquired files. "I'll make sure I come by every five minutes with a question." He gave Eli his slyest smile and fled for the door, but not before Eli's reply caught him.

"You do that, and I'll turn you over my knee and tan your bottom."

It took every ounce of control Justin had not to spill the laptop and the files all over the hallway. He made it to his desk, but barely.

He would *what*?

Justin looked across the hall and Eli smiled back.

Maybe he shouldn't have made that "challenge accepted" crack after all. More than anything, he wanted to test Eli's threat. Every nerve in Justin's body begged for release.

Bent over those knees? That hand on his ass? Justin

collapsed into his desk chair. An hour more of work. Then three hours of lecture.

Would Eli really...?

There went any hope of concentrating in class.

As the day wore on, every time Justin looked out the office door, Eli was there, across the hall, most of the time intently working, thankfully. But the last time Justin looked, right before five, he met a wicked smile. Eli casually held up a ruler—an old-fashioned wooden one.

Goose bumps rose on every inch of Justin's skin. There must be a sign on Justin that pointed out every one of his buttons, because Eli pushed them *all*. The casual way Eli slipped his gloves on after he'd set the ruler down stiffened his dick even more. Justin turned away, because if he looked much longer, he would forget to breathe—and, fuck, did his balls hurt. Biking would be a torment. Maybe the pain would take the edge off the mind-boggling amount of heat and desire and *Eli* swirling in his head.

"Mr. White."

That didn't help. "Yes?"

Eli stood in the doorway, gloved hands on top of his silver-capped walking stick. "How are you coming..." Eli paused, just long enough that Justin knew the word choice had been intentional. "...with the reports?"

"It's been quite frustrating, actually."

Eli raised an eyebrow. "Oh?"

"I'm lacking quite a lot of information." Justin let his own pause sink in. "You were right about needing the correct paperwork."

"If you ask, you'll usually get what you want." Eli tapped his cane on the carpeting. "See you tomorrow, Justin."

"Good night."

Then Eli was gone.

Justin lowered his head until his brow met the edge of the desk. He was pretty damn sure Eli wasn't straight. "Fuck."

A very quiet chuckle came from the inside office.

Holy shit. He'd forgotten about Sam. *Oh, fuck. Hey, Mercy, I got a new job. Lost it on my first day, too.*

Justin lifted his head and pushed back from the desk. Time to get out of here and down to campus. Get his head screwed on straight or this would be the shortest job he ever had. He grabbed his backpack and bike helmet and steeled himself to say good-bye to Sam.

If Sam was angry, he didn't show it. He looked up from the paperwork and smiled.

"I'm heading out. Class tonight."

"Have a good one."

"Thanks." Justin headed toward the outer door, but Sam called his name. He peeked back into the office. "Yes?"

"You're doing fine. Very few people can hold their own against Eli."

Justin wet his lips and searched for something to say. There wasn't anything, just heat radiating from his face.

"Have a good class, J."

"Thanks."

This time, Justin escaped the office and unchained his bike. He had no idea what to make of Sam's comments—other than whatever game he and Eli were playing didn't upset the boss.

He didn't know whether to be relieved or terrified. Last time he'd flirted like this, he'd ended up in Francis's trap. No job. No money. No freedom. Justin swallowed bile. Eli *had a job*, at least. That put him in an entirely different category. Justin pushed off and pedaled toward campus.

CHAPTER FOUR

THERE WAS AN UNWRITTEN RULE ABOUT PITTSBURGH weather that in October, when the leaves crunched under foot, there would be one day with clear blue skies and temperatures in the seventies. Eli glanced up. That day had arrived right on schedule and had made the entire office itch to get out—even Sam.

After an obnoxiously long telephone conference, Sam offered Eli lunch and lured Justin along with the promise of buying. Engineering had scampered out earlier. If Sanhex hadn't been such shits, the whole office might have gone out together, though Eli didn't mind the smaller group.

Justin stood out against Sam's suit, with his rock t-shirt, leather wrist brace, and ripped blue jeans. His casual clothes had grown on Eli, especially when he could admire Justin's ass as they walked up Murray Avenue. One benefit of his leg—which ached like hell, despite the good weather —was that his pace was slower than Sam's or Justin's. He'd let them take the lead.

Sam said something and Justin laughed. Eli smiled and the pain in his step faded a bit.

Justin had settled in nicely the past few weeks. He'd managed to wheedle all the necessary expense paperwork out of Fazil in a matter of days, rather than the two weeks it usually took Eli. Even Sam had coughed up missing information for Justin after a single inquiry.

Perhaps the pretty face helped, even with straight-as-sin Fazil. Or the offbeat demeanor. Certainly Justin's fine features still drove Eli out of his mind. Not that he'd let Justin see that. Instead, he left his ruler and his gloves on the edge of his desk—and didn't Justin stare at those every time he entered the room or walked past.

Was it idle curiosity? Hard to tell—Eli had certainly met plenty of men who talked the talk and ran the fuck away when an actual flogger and a set of cuffs came out. If Justin was a submissive, he was likely a horribly bratty one. Every one of Eli's nerves sang at that thought.

They reached the top of Murray and Sam stopped outside of the Silk Elephant. Thai tapas. Perfect for lunch.

"One of Eli's favorite places." Sam held the door open for both Eli and Justin, the bells on the door clattering pleasantly.

"You like things hot?" A quirk to those lips.

Sam wore a poker face. Badly, but that was Sam for you.

The hostess smiled. "Welcome, three for lunch?"

Eli nodded, avoiding Justin's question. "Yes, please."

"We're clearing off tables right now. Won't be more than a few minutes."

"Excellent."

They waited by the door while the staff worked. By the looks of things, they'd arrived just at the end of the lunchtime rush.

The bells on the door chimed, sounding the arrival of more patrons. Eli paid the ringing no mind until a man's voice sounded at Eli's back, as musical and cutting as he remembered. "Do you ever wonder what became of our son?" In Ladino, of course, so Eli would understand but no one else would.

Splinters of glass cut their way up Eli's spine. His parents still lived in the area, but they'd all managed to carve out an existence that excluded one another. Not today, though, because here they were. If they still kept strict kashrut, they shouldn't have been here.

"Maybe he would have grown into a fine man and not a..." His mother's voice soft voice trailed off, but the missing word drove the stabbing straight into his skull. Monster. Fag. Whore. Disobedient son. He'd heard those and more.

Air. He needed to breathe. Unclench his jaw. Not think of Noah's smile or the blood or the sound of metal crumpling or Rachel's cut-off scream or Milka sitting next to him in the car as it turned and bent and shattered. His friends, his love: gone, all gone.

"He certainly wouldn't have kept the company of miscreants. That one is as painted as a prostitute."

Justin and his eyeliner. White haze ringed Eli's vision, but everything else became sharp, including the beating of his heart, the ache in his leg, and the rage clawing through his chest. Eli spun, cane scraping against the floor.

"They're my coworkers, actually." He spoke English through years of bile and pain. He couldn't navigate the heat in his heart and mind to even attempt Ladino. "My CEO and his assistant."

The nearby banter in the restaurant quieted.

"E—"

He ignored Sam's voice, his tug at Eli's sleeve, and stared into unflinching eyes the same color as his own.

"Is that any way to speak to speak to me?" his father said, but then he'd always been strict with Eli.

"You shouldn't be so rude." So much worse to look at his mother. At one point, she'd actually loved him.

Justin pulled him away from the memories that lurked, the ones that might drag him under again. "The table's ready."

Eli managed a shuddering breath. "I'm dead to you. How can the dead be rude?" He put his back to them and followed Sam and Justin to the table.

Both men were quiet. Eli's fingers shook. He shouldn't have lost it, should have just ignored the taunting. But the hole in the center of his being, the one filled with loss, betrayal, and dishonor, hadn't quite healed over. He needed to ignore the prickling at the backs of his eyes, too.

Eighteen years.

"E…"

"Don't start with me, Sam." The words snapped out like a whip. Justin flinched.

Sam tilted his head. No anger. No condemnation. "Wouldn't dream of it. You know we have your back."

The tension in Eli's shoulders eased. The waiter brought water, and a long sip of that helped as well. He blinked until his eyes stopped watering, until the storm in his head quieted. The voices, the screeching of tires, and the rending metal faded.

Justin wrapped his hands around his glass, his blue eyes wide. "Are you all right?" Concern and a total lack of snark. Eli hadn't thought that possible.

"Yes." Eli paused. "I will be. Give me a moment."

Justin nodded and searched his water for several heartbeats. "What the hell had you in a meeting until twelve thirty, anyway?"

Sam sat back. "Sanhex wants assurances that we'd succeed in turning their mess around."

Justin flipped open his menu. "But you don't do that. No consulting firm can."

"Exactly, and we won't. It's a big legal black hole. But they wouldn't take that for an answer." Sam gave the menu a cursory glance before setting it aside. Probably lamb curry. Sam had his habits and only Michael could break them.

Eli stared at the menu, but the words didn't make sense. Somewhere behind him—he'd purposefully put his back to the rest of restaurant—his parents sat. Whatever they ate, the protein would likely be tofu—they might not be so strict anymore, but he doubted they'd dropped kashrut completely, so eating out meant vegetarian. Funny how they could bend the rules for themselves, but not for their own *son*.

Eli closed his eyes. There was the pull to order something pork or shrimp... and the resistance not to. The desire to rebel. The need to not react. His hands shook more, which made holding the menu hard.

Justin's voice broke through the pounding of blood in Eli's head. "Do you know what you want?"

"Yup," Sam said. "Beef Massaman curry."

Eli opened his eyes. "Not lamb?" Even to his own ears, his voice sounded stretched and thin.

Sam shrugged. "Michael's tired of leftover lamb. Suggested I try something else."

Bingo.

Eli tried the menu again and this time, he could read it, but his lungs and chest hurt. Noah's smile. The EMTs draping a sheet over his face. Noah's mother's tears when she visited Eli in the hospital. He hadn't been able to visit shiva or go to the funeral. Eli shut the menu. *Why am I not free of this? When will I be free of this?*

"Eli?"

Justin so rarely said his name. Eli turned toward that voice and blinked until his vision cleared.

"Yes?"

"I was thinking of ordering some tapas. Want to share? I always order too many." Bright eyes. And yes, eyeliner. But Justin was no whore, not anything close to it.

Nor was he Noah. Very much not Noah. *I want this man far too much.* "That—would be fine, yes."

A kindness.

"Anything you don't like?"

"No." Not anymore. "And yes, I like things hot."

Justin blushed high on his cheeks. The waitress came to take their order before Eli could say anything else to make Justin's color rise more.

Justin ordered six plates—which was more than enough food. Some vegetarian, some not—including shrimp and pork toast. Eli ate bits of everything, including stealing a bite of Sam's curry.

"I'll tell Michael."

Eli shrugged and let the smile come. "Go right ahead."

Sam chuckled and shared some with Justin, too. They would never finish all the food on the table, so Michael would end up with a nice selection of leftovers. Enough to counteract Eli's snitching his food.

The days of Michael correcting Eli were long since over, though he was pretty sure Michael still kept count of infractions.

The vestiges of bad memories sank away. He was who he was, regardless of his parents' wishes or actions. The accident that had unveiled it all had been an *accident*. His therapists had warned him that the event would always be there, but he did not have to—would *not* let it rule him.

Justin cleaned his fingers on a napkin. "So you turned Sanhex down?"

Sam laughed. "Oh, no. They agreed to our terms once Eli had a chance to grab them by their neckties and put them in their places. Figuratively speaking." He winked at Justin, who blushed again.

"Would have been more interesting to do that in person," Eli said, watching carefully.

That had the desired effect on Justin—dilating pupils, hitched breath. What he wouldn't give to sit down and have that conversation with Justin, the one he was never going to have with a coworker other than Sam.

Especially not one he *liked.*

Sam lifted an eyebrow.

"Anyway," Eli said, "I explained exactly why we would not be contracting our time the way they wished and exactly why they *would* sign on with us. Their own report had enough fodder that I stuffed their own words back down their lovely little throats until they choked on them."

Justin croaked.

"Figuratively speaking."

"E can be very commanding."

Oh, now was Sam getting into the teasing? Eli returned his attention to Justin.

A strange expression—part desire, part need—passed over Justin. It wasn't sexual, though. "You make the executive end of business sound a lot more exciting than the textbooks."

The waitress came with the check for Sam to sign and a box with Michael's leftovers. Sam looked over the slip, added a tip, and signed. "It's certainly more fun *when* it's exciting," he said. "But the books don't completely lie." He rose.

Eli followed suit, as did Justin. "So what do you do when things are as dull as drying paint?" Justin said.

The restaurant was blessedly devoid of Eli's parents. "Make our own fun," he said.

They made their way to the door. Justin pushed his fringe of hair from his eyes. "Ah yes. Macramé. You'll have to show me your knots sometime."

Sam nearly dropped Michael's leftovers. Both eyebrows were in his hairline when he glanced at Eli.

"They're rather *lovely* knots, Mr. White."

Sam opened the door. "Out, both of you. We have work to do."

They both obeyed—but not before Eli caught sight of just how tight Justin's jeans had become. *Excellent.*

"I'M HEADING OUT, J." SAM STOPPED IN THE DOORWAY to their office, holding the leftovers from lunch. "Have a nice weekend."

"Thanks. You too." Justin was still full from lunch—and a bit breathless. Too many bits of information about Eli rattled around in his head.

Sam nodded before he vanished down the hall.

Justin shook his head to clear it. The weekend needed to be about Financial Engineering. Plus, he'd planned to meet with his capstone group. The management game was heating up and they had to up their strategy if they wanted to win. Or at least have their company survive.

Justin exhaled, saved the spreadsheet he'd been staring

at, and closed the laptop. Time to head to campus. He grabbed his bicycle helmet and bag.

The whole building rumbled. *Shit, no. Really?* He peered through the door into Eli's office and out the window. Black sky. Sheets of rain. Eli studied the window, hands poised over his keyboard.

"Fuck!"

Eli started and whipped around. No anger—just shock.

Damned if it didn't look good on him, the tinged cheeks and wide eyes. "Sorry. It's just..." He held up his helmet.

Eli folded his hands into his lap. "Not the best timing."

"I'm supposed to meet with Don at six." And soaking wet was not really a look he liked, outside of a pool or hot tub.

Eli studied the clock on his laptop before closing the machine. "Would you like a ride down to campus?"

Yes. No. That close to Eli? *Fuck.* "Sure, that would be great."

Eli looked like a cat when a bird hopped by. That thought zapped through Justin, raising goose bumps. Like everything else he refused to think about, he pushed it out of his head.

Work. Classes. Bills. Mercy.

Eli pushed it right back in when he stood and pulled on his tight leather gloves—slowly—before grabbing his jacket. "You're in luck. I normally walk, but I have errands to run this evening."

"You live that close?"

"On Wightman. A few blocks." He grabbed his cane—steampunk today. "It helps, the exercise."

One of the few times he'd acknowledged the injury. "That's good. I mean, the exercise." God, what a dumb thing to say.

Eli pulled something from behind the door. "My car's on Hobart. Did you bring... ?" He held up an umbrella.

No. He hadn't. "It's only a couple of blocks."

He wasn't sure which was worse, the rain sheeting against the window behind Eli, or that raised eyebrow that seemed to say, *Are you really that much of an idiot?*

"Come on," Eli said.

Justin tossed the helmet back onto his desk and slung his messenger bag over his shoulder and across his chest. Eli shut off all the lights before they descended the stairs. Big fat drops plopped mockingly against the sidewalk.

"The umbrella will fit two," Eli said. "If you don't mind getting close."

Just what he needed, to be pressed against Eli. It was either that or get soaked in two seconds flat. "I don't mind."

"Good." Eli stepped out and raised the golf umbrella with the touch of a button. "Come here."

A command. Like every other time, Justin obeyed without thinking, heart hammering against his ribs.

"Hold this." Eli handed him the umbrella and wrapped his free arm around Justin's torso. "Do *not* get me wet."

Every nerve fired from the grip of Eli's hand at his waist. It was a wonder Justin could walk. But he did, at the pace Eli set, down the street a few blocks to Hobart.

Thankfully, Eli's car, a blue Audi, was one of the first ones parked along the street. Justin wanted lean into Eli, kiss the tantalizing skin above his shirt collar. Eli unlocked the car and steered Justin to the passenger door. He loosened his grip. "Take the cane, give me the umbrella, and get in."

They made the exchange. Justin opened the door and sank into the seat. Eli closed the door. A moment later Eli settled into the driver's seat, tucking the umbrella against the door. "Nicely done."

The praise sent a shiver down through Justin. "Thanks for the lift."

Eli chuckled, but didn't say anything more. They rode in silence up Murray, and past where they'd eaten lunch, where Eli had lost his shit. Sam had pulled Justin aside after lunch and explained that those two had been Eli's parents. They'd been dressed conservatively and Eli's father had worn a kippah.

Different thoughts rattled through Justin's head. Eli's shell-shocked expression, the tremble in his hands. The inward focus on something horrible. He'd seen those in his sister, too—though Eli had pulled himself back together far quicker than Mercy could after an episode. PTSD from the accident that had fucked up Eli's leg. But there was more there, much more.

Justin glanced out the window as they crawled past Wightman—biking would have been faster, had the weather not been shit. Traffic was horrid this time of night. He stole another glance at Eli. "You're Jewish."

Eli gave him a quick look. "Yes." A pause. "Figured my name would have been a clue."

His first name, sure, but... "Ovadia sounds—I don't know—Spanish, or something."

A chuckle. "I'm Sephardi. Family's from Portugal. *Ovadia* is Hebrew, though."

"Well, I guess that's my one new thing learned for today."

"God help you, if it is. Don't you have a class tonight?"

"Yeah. Financial Engineering."

Eli's face twisted and Justin laughed. "Good to know I'm not alone there."

"Last thing I should do is discourage you from your studies." Eli's smile was small but warm.

Traffic freed up and they moved faster now, rolling down Forbes toward CMU. "Where do you want to be dropped off?"

"University Center is fine." He glanced at the dashboard clock. "I want to get a soda before Don and class, or I'll never make it through."

Eli nodded. Soon—too soon—they pulled into the UC turnaround. Eli put the car into park.

"There's a smaller umbrella in the door pocket."

Justin glanced down. So there was, one of those ones that folded up into a tiny thing.

"Take it."

"I'll be fine."

Now Justin remembered why he'd thought Eli the ice king. "If you'd rather Don see you as a drowned punk rat, I could have let you bike in the rain."

Justin grabbed the door handle. "If I'd known you'd be an *ass* about it—" Before he could yank open the door, Eli put a hand on his shoulder and—for fuck's sake—it stilled him.

"I was *teasing*, Justin." Gone was the mask, and what lay behind was far more complicated. "Please take the umbrella. I have the other, and it's not like you don't know where to find me to return it."

The anger evaporated. "I—sorry. I get..." He took a breath then blurted out what he'd wanted to say for weeks. "I'm not an idiot."

"I know. Believe me, I have never thought you to be one."

Justin had no idea how to respond to that. So he

watched Eli, who blushed ever so slightly. "Take the umbrella."

Pride. Justin's pride said no. He pulled the umbrella out of the door and into his lap. "Thanks."

Eli squeezed his shoulder. "Thank you. For this afternoon." Gray eyes held him in the seat. "I know what you did and I very much appreciate it."

Ordering for him. Pushing the conversation in other directions. Keeping Eli present. "My sister," he said, his heart suddenly in his mouth.

Eli nodded. "You mentioned her before."

"I couldn't just..." He shrugged. *I couldn't leave you like that. Caught in the past.* "Did they disown you because you're gay?"

Eli scrubbed a hand over his stubble. "Yes. Though it was mutual. I left when I turned eighteen."

Justin's legs itched. "I didn't mean to pry."

Eli waved the words away. "It's a tiny company, Just. We all get to know each other too well eventually."

Just. The itching turned into a tingle and went straight to his head. Before he could reply, a flash of red and blue and the distinctive *bloop* of a police car made them both jump. Eli rolled his eyes and looked much younger. "Damn campus cops. You better go."

"Yeah. Thanks." Justin opened the door and popped the umbrella before climbing out. "See you on Monday."

Eli's wave and smile when Justin closed the door made his ribs ache. The Audi pulled away. Eli Ovadia wasn't just hot—he was *nice*, too.

Shit. Shit. Shit. So many thoughts rolled through Justin's brain as he wandered into Entropy, the little convenience store in the UC, and grabbed a Diet Coke. *Nice.* Eli was nice—and complicated. Human.

Hot. Commanding.

"Fuck."

Someone next to him whipped his head around. "The hell, dude?"

Justin shook his head. "Sorry. Talking to myself."

The guy let him be. He paid and headed to Don's.

While it wasn't pouring so hard—the rain hadn't let up. He would have been soaked through, even though he took the more convoluted path through the maze of buildings to get him close to Hamburg Hall. Right before he left the Gates Center, his phone vibrated.

That was odd. So few people texted him. He pulled it out and didn't recognize the number, but the content— Justin's hand shook.

Figured you should have my cell. If the weather's bad
after class, call. Or if you need a lift to get your bike over
the weekend. —E

It made sense that Eli had his number—he'd put it down as a contact. Likely Sam had it as well.

But now he had Eli's. When he could make his fingers stop shaking, he typed a reply.

Thanks. Will let you know.

No reply to that. The clock on his phone told him he had exactly eight minutes before he needed to be at Don's office. Time to move.

Besides, Justin doubted Eli would approve of his being late.

Though the text from Eli had burned itself into Justin's skull and rain still came down, albeit gently, he didn't call. Trudging through the back streets of Oakland in the dark seemed the better idea. He sure as hell wasn't going to show Eli where he lived. *Welcome to my shithole basement apartment. Don't mind the mold and the Goodwill furniture. Make yourself at home.*

Yeah. No. Given Eli's car, his expensive suits, and that he lived on Wightman, Justin could only imagine the wrinkle of his nose.

But his place was cheap and gave him somewhere to put his head at night. Justin opened the basement door and pulled mail out of a box that barely hung from the shingles. Never mind that the apartment broke a billion codes. You got what you paid for.

He closed the door, dropped the umbrella onto the tile, took two steps, and tossed his bag onto the kitchen table.

Class had gone well and his meeting with Don even better. *You're much more focused this term, Justin. Working with Anderson looks good on you.* They'd talked about the capstone project, Don picking at his ideas until Justin's fingers cramped from typing notes so fast. So many things to consider. He'd need to get with his group and discuss strategies, but it was all good and doable, and *Don Miller* thought he was on the right track.

Justin exhaled and sorted through the mail.

Boom. Liquid nitrogen poured over his enthusiasm. Bills. Electric. Gas. And the latter in an envelope with red lettering. *I thought I paid that! I could have sworn...*

He pulled out his laptop and sat down. A few minutes later, he swore at the ledger on the bank website.

No. He hadn't. Worse, rent, his credit card bill, and the money he'd sent to Mercy pretty much had emptied his account until he got paid again. Where he was going to come up with one hundred thirty-five dollars and twenty-seven cents? He had a little more than that in checking, but then there was the whole *eating* thing.

He looked at the numbers again.

Guess it was ramen and crackers for a while. Plus whatever was in his student account at CMU.

He'd gotten ahead, too. Then Mercy had called.

I need help again, Justin. And I can't ask Mom and Dad...

His folks didn't have anything. Only he did, or so he said. He'd sent the cash because he would not let his big sister get tossed out on her own. The woman was a goddamned hero.

Shit. Justin stood up, toppling over his chair.

He couldn't ask Sam for a raise. They were already paying him more than the position required. He twisted his hands in his hair. Still paying for his time with Francis. Still not free of that man.

He'd extended himself after he'd left LA. Too much shit on his credit card. He knew his debt load, knew how much he needed to get out from under it, and had pared down everything he could.

Except Mercy needed him, and there was no cutting her off.

Justin picked up his chair, took three steps, and sat on the edge of his bed. Yup, Justin White. Stellar employee. Star MBA student with an eye for business and finance. Forty thousand dollars in debt because he'd been stupid and reckless and fallen for the wrong guy while his sister had been off getting blown up in Iraq.

He dropped his head into his hands. If only Don could see him now. Or Sam. Or Eli.

When Monday came, it was as if Eli had never driven Justin to campus, as if they'd never spoken in his car. The brusque, snarky Justin marched into the office in the morning. He returned the umbrella but didn't look at Eli, just muttered his thanks before slinking across the hall.

The gut-punch of emotion made Eli's body ache. He hadn't expected Justin to call him over the weekend. But he didn't understand the reversal of any hint of a friendship between them. Couldn't shake it off.

Eli closed the door to his office. Seeing Justin at his desk, hearing his laugh when he spoke to Sam, but seeing that scowl and curled lip directed at him? No. The stabbing in his chest increased until breathing hurt.

Too much to handle, especially on the heels of dealing with his parents. He'd called Dr. Brohmer on Saturday to fill her in on the flashback—it had been a long time since he'd had one this bad—and while she hadn't insisted, she'd strongly suggested he make an appointment soon.

He'd resisted. A small thing, that episode. *You're going to be fragile for a few days, Eli. Off balance. The appointment won't hurt.*

Except they did, every time. They helped, too, but he hated the stretched, thin feeling after he'd spilled his emotions. Even if they'd been doing this for how many years?

He eyed his door. Whatever had caused Justin's return to snarl, in all likelihood, had nothing to do with Eli. But a part of Eli felt shunned. Rejected. In his own office, by the same man who'd been kind to him, someone he'd started to think of as a *friend*. Banished from his community, all over again.

Eli picked up the phone, called Dr. Brohmer's office, and made the appointment.

He kept the door shut for the rest of the morning. Just before lunch, Sam knocked and opened, but only enough to slip inside. He leaned against it, arms down, fingertips pressed against the wood. "Are you all right?"

Eli considered how to answer the question—and that act of doing so was answer enough. "Not exactly, no."

"Friday?"

Sam knew him well enough to understand the issues with his parents, and what Sam *didn't* know, Michael did. "A bit of that, yes."

A nod. "We've been worried."

"We?"

"The office."

Oh now, come on. Sam shrank ever so slightly when he gave him *that* look. "The office? Engineering hardly knows I'm here."

"They know you're here, E." Sam exhaled. "But mostly me. And Justin. We're... concerned."

He couldn't keep the skepticism out of his voice. "Justin?"

Sam gave him an odd look, one he couldn't interpret for the life of him. "You know what he did for you, yes?"

Eli found himself on his feet because his sudden anger needed an outlet. "Sam."

Sam pushed himself off the door and planted himself in front of Eli. The disappointment written in Sam's face, the hurt in his eyes, ripped through Eli and sank claws into his shame and fear.

He ran a hand through his hair. "Yes. I know, and I thanked him for it."

Sam's stance softened. "He's a good guy, E."

"I know that." He reached for his gloves and cane. "I need a break from his growling today, that's all." So many other things he wanted to say. *I like him, Sam. He's funny and bright and I haven't felt like this for anyone in years and I want...* a touch. A kiss. To discover what Justin's skin tasted like, the timbre of his moans. Eli shook his head. "When I come back from lunch, I'll leave the door open." He met Sam's gaze. "Have I ever let you down?"

"No." Sam spoke gently. "Have I?"

"Never."

Sam nodded and reached for the doorknob. Paused.

"Yes, I made an appointment, Sam Randell Anderson."

Sam gave him a grin before slipping into the hall.

Eli grabbed his coat off the back of his door, swallowing the lump in his throat. Working for Sam was like working for family—and he'd thought he'd never have any kind of family again. Eli shrugged his coat on and opened the door. There Justin was—all blue eyes, black hair, and eyeliner. Eli met that gaze, his lips suddenly dry.

Sam had told the truth. Worry, concern, and an apology were all wrapped in Justin biting his lip.

Eli turned away and headed out for lunch. Liking someone *and* wanting them—too dangerous. Too many pitfalls. He couldn't control others, not all the time, but he damn well had mastery over himself.

CHAPTER FIVE

FOR ONCE, JUSTIN WAS THE FIRST PERSON AT THE office. Then again, it was six thirty in the morning, early enough that Brian had waved him into Grounds N'at and let him make a cup, just like old times. Didn't let him pay, either, which was nice.

Nice. That was a state of being Eli had apparently forgotten. Given Eli's dark stares and acerbic replies every day since Monday, Justin figured he'd show Eli he could get to work before nine fifteen.

And Justin could turn down the heat in his apartment a bit earlier. Save some money. Justin tossed his bike helmet and bag down by his desk.

Eli was running cold again. Freezing was more like it. An hour without Eli scowling at him would be grand. From kindness and confessions in Eli's car to stony stares in the office. Typical, but he had enough of his own troubles. Another e-mail from Mercy and one from his parents. A call from a collections agency. Last thing he needed was to deal with Eli's moods.

Eli brought down the whole office. He'd never closed

his door—except on conference calls—until this past week, and everyone noticed. The wall he'd thrown up was horrible. Deafening. More than anything, Justin wanted to know how he could to turn Eli's tap back to warm—or at least tepid. Everything he'd tried—banter, wordplay, even turning things slightly sexual—had fallen flat. When Justin pushed, Eli closed down.

Even Sam was on edge and worried—though he'd relaxed a great deal when Eli had left early yesterday.

Justin picked at the black polish on his nails. The weekend was almost here. He could make it to that. Perhaps Monday would bring an entirely new Eli to the office, or at least the return of the one he'd worked with before this week. He'd liked that guy.

The current Eli reminded him too much of Francis. Justin had nearly lost himself slotting himself in between Francis's moods and demands.

Justin fired up his laptop and fell so deep into figuring out the intricacies of flying Jen and Fazil out to La Crosse, Wisconsin, and housing them for a week within the tiny budget that had been set by Sanhex that he wasn't aware of anything else until Sam strode through the door at eight thirty.

"Morning, J. You're here early."

"I wanted to get these travel plans nailed down." Justin glanced at Sam and caught sight of Eli's office—which was occupied. When had Eli come in? Didn't Justin even rate a *good morning* or *hello* anymore? His chest tightened. "I know Fazil's getting itchy for the details."

"Fantastic. I know the budget is tricky."

Nearly impossible. Then again, Sanhex was in pretty dire straights, so no wonder they held their purse strings so tight. "It's a challenge, yeah."

"If anyone can work it out, it's you." Sam continued into his office.

At least someone thought that. Justin looked into Eli's office, expecting a delivery from the scowl-of-the-week club. Instead, Eli limped along the cabinets, a small stack of files in his hands, until he vanished from Justin's view. Pain had etched every line of Eli's face, been written into every step. Sorrow, too.

Justin's insides somersaulted. *What did I do?* He wanted Eli's smile, the one he'd glimpsed right before Eli had driven away that night that seemed far too long ago.

Good God! You are so hung up on this man.

Time to do something about that, because mooning after Eli was about as safe as dancing naked on porcupines. And while he *liked* pain from time to time, he hated needles with a passion. He needed to drown Eli out.

He switched over to his private e-mail. There were no restrictions on Internet usage—Sam had even dragged everyone in to watch a particularly funny video Michael had sent him—but Justin hesitated wasting too much time surfing or e-mailing. He fired one letter off.

> Hey, Kelly. You said you could hook me into the Scene? I really could use a night of fun and frivolity… anything coming up in the near future?
>
> —Justin.

It had been a long time since he'd been in the LA Scene. Before Francis, playing had helped his work. Hopefully, here it would focus him, too.

THE OFFICE REMAINED SUBDUED AND QUIET, EVEN when engineering arrived. After lunch, Justin managed to find flights and hotels that wouldn't break the budget and finished the travel arrangement puzzle. Sanhex squeezed the line on this and Justin had even received a terse e-mail from Eli stating that they could add a bit from their budget if the numbers were proving too hard to work with.

Like fuck he'd ask for that. He wasn't about to let Eli think he couldn't perform a task handed to him.

Now he had. Justin sent the arrangements to Sam and Eli for approval. Sam's reply came back immediately.

Fantastic job! Yes. Approved.

Justin smiled at his reflection in the screen. *Victory!* He leaned back in his chair.

Eli's response came a few minutes later, dousing ice water over Justin's joy. He nearly didn't open the e-mail

Impressive, Mr. White. Approved.

Short and to the point. Justin couldn't help turning his head and peering across the hall. Of course Eli watched him, but those lips that had been so recently turned down quirked up into a small smile. Justin nodded and turned back to his screen, breathless. A smile—and for him. Justin swallowed. His throat felt raw, but every muscle eased, far more than when Sam had praised his work.

Justin closed the browser and rose. He reached for the ceiling, arching his back, and several vertebrae popped. *Thank God.* Time for a soda and maybe Ping-Pong. When he turned, he expected Eli to be watching him, but no.

Eli stood at his cabinets with another handful of files,

his posture entirely wrong. One hand white-knuckled the top of the cabinet while Eli lowered himself down to his knees—but he winced and the papers spilled onto the floor. Eli pulled himself up and pounded a fist against the top of the cabinet. "Fuck!"

Justin stared at the spilled files and crept closer to Eli's door. A tumult of emotions played across Eli's face and Justin's chest constricted. Eli exhaled a breath that sounded suspiciously like a sob. "Fuck," he repeated, though this time the word was filled with pain. The helpless look on Eli's face—

Justin must have made a sound, because forlorn morphed into furious. "What the hell do you want?"

Face hot, Justin gripped the doorway and searched for something, *anything* to say. He knew that *Let me help you* would be snarled away, but there had to be something else. Other words.

Eli turned. "Please leave, Justin." Hard edges over every syllable.

"Look," Justin said, sounding far stronger than he felt, "you and Sam hired an assistant for a reason. Get your money's worth out of me."

Eli scraped his nails across the top of the cabinet, the sound eating into Justin's brain. His heart slammed against his ribs. *Shit*. Shit.

After a long, painful moment of silence, Eli pushed off the cabinets. "Then get your ass in here and *assist* me." Eli hobbled back to his chair and sat. "You can start by picking those up." The tension melted from Eli's body.

Good. He'd managed to find the right words around Eli's pride. He'd done that with Mercy from time to time, too. But Mercy was his sister and Eli was... a coworker. A friend? Who the fuck knew?

Justin knelt and carefully picked up the files. While they'd strewn their contents onto the rug, they'd done so in an organized enough way that he could scoop up each one and hand it back to Eli.

"Well done." Soft voice, full of the warmth that had been lacking all week.

Justin sat back on his feet. "What now?"

"If you wouldn't mind a little more time down there, I have these"—he held up the files in his hands—"and those left." Eli waved to a much larger stack. "All of them go into the bottom cabinets. And I can't—" His voice cracked.

Justin examined the fluff on the carpet, rather than the deep anger on Eli face. Mercy got like this when her injury held her back in unpredictable ways. He let Eli find his balance.

Eli sighed. "My leg hurts too fucking much to kneel today." He handed a file to Justin. "Far cabinet, two-thirds of the way in. You'll see the company name."

Justin shimmied over, opened the cabinet, and filed the folder.

Eli held out the next one. "Closest to me."

Stand or crawl? Well, if he had to get up and down, his knees would give out, too. He crawled on all fours to Eli and took the file.

"Halfway down." Eli's voice fell like a caress.

Justin opened the drawer and found the location, his blood thrumming in his ears. He pushed it closed, and looked up. Fuck if it wasn't the burning-hot Eli staring back, a smile touching his lips. Those gray eyes were as impenetrable as storm clouds, though.

"Does you leg get like this often?"

"No." Same soft voice. "Only when I do something stupid, like walk to Strip District and back."

Even Justin would feel that in the morning. Had to be four miles from Squirrel Hill, one way.

His expression must have been readable because Eli laughed and shrugged. "I had a lot on my mind." He handed Justin three folders. "All of these go in the far cabinet, second drawer up."

With Eli's laughter spinning down his body to his balls, Justin shuffled on his knees as ordered. When he crawled back, it was Eli's mouthwatering expression that burned Justin's veins.

Being on his knees for Eli felt good. Inappropriately good. There really wasn't a way to hide just how turned on he was.

"You're doing very well, Justin." Eli handed him another stack. "I'm quite pleased."

Justin's whole body shook and he stifled a moan. That was not the kind of praise a coworker gave. Justin gripped the folders.

"Middle cabinet." Eli shifted in his seat—and the bulge in Eli's pants wasn't the kind a coworker should have for another, either.

"Justin." A little force in Eli's voice.

Every nerve in Justin's body lit up. "Sorry." He moved to the cabinet and filed the folders, slowly so he could catch his breath. *Man, Kelly better come through with a party, because this is ridiculous.*

Still, he savored the burn in his body and the tightness in his balls when crawled back to Eli. Hadn't felt that in ages. If nothing else, he'd have a spectacular orgasm when he got home.

He sat back on his heels and waited. No way Eli could miss the outline of his cock pressing against his jeans.

Sam's voice sounded in the hall. "Justin, where— Oh." Sam tilted his head.

God, Justin's face felt like he'd been shoved into an oven. Sam couldn't miss the erection, either. Oh hell.

"E, why is my assistant kneeling at your feet?"

A chuckle. "He's helping me file."

Sam shook his head.

"I promise I'll put him back where I found him. In one piece, even." Oh, the grin that wrapped Eli's voice.

Sam laughed. "Well, good." And then Sam smiled at him. "J, when Eli is finished with you, stop by. I want to go over the Lumendaris expense report."

"Sure, Sam." His voice sounded normal, not the moaning mess it wanted to be.

Sam slipped back across the hall.

A cough redirected Justin's attention to Eli.

"Ready to continue, Mr. White?" One raised eyebrow.

Like fire down his back. Thank God Eli wasn't wearing his gloves, or Justin would have been a groaning puddle. "Sure, Eli."

Another stack of folders. Another order. Yet another shower of sparks from his head to his balls.

Well, he *had* wanted a warmer Eli. He'd gotten his wish.

ELI HELD OUT ANOTHER STACK OF FILES. "FAR CABINET, bottom drawer. Right side."

Justin took the folders, his fingers brushing Eli's hand. The touch seared a path down Eli's nerves. "Yes, Eli."

His name on Justin's lips spun Eli's head around like a shot of tequila. He stilled the impulse to grab Justin by the shoulders and kiss him.

Justin's jagged hair flopping over his eyes, his mouth parted with exertion made up for a hellish week of snark, innuendo, and punk posturing. Eli wasn't blameless for the wall that had gone up between them, but Justin got under his skin. In good and bad and *wicked* ways.

The secrets he wanted to pour out into Justin's ear. The trust he wanted to give. The things he wanted to do to that fine, slim body. All of it dangerous and heady. At least his leg hurt less now. His cock, on the other hand...

He wasn't alone in being turned on, however. The bulge in Justin's jeans gave away what kneeling at Eli's feet cost him.

Was Justin a submissive? Certainly acted like one, down to the little shudder when Eli ordered him across the floor. But a reaction didn't mean Justin was into the Scene—just that he was turned on. In any case, whatever was between them should go no further than this. Opening himself up to another was like handing them Pandora's box. Eli didn't wish that on anyone.

Justin filed the folders and came crawling back. "Any more?"

"Just two stacks." Pity. He could watch Justin on all fours all day. Given the desire carved into Justin's trembling body and the need written in those blue eyes, Justin would have obliged.

There was more in Justin's expression—a relaxation not born of any submissive kink, but from relief overcoming worry. That pulled at Eli's heart. Beyond the delightful vision of Justin on his knees was the truth of why he knelt there: Justin *cared*, and without the pity Eli loathed and rejected.

"Third cabinet down. Bottom drawer. Middle. Make sure you have the right place. Lots of Smiths."

Justin's smile stole the air from Eli's lungs. Justin had managed to twine his way around Eli's rejection of help and give assistance anyway. Eli knew why—Justin's sister. He didn't talk much about her and Eli didn't pry, but he knew enough. Went to war with legs, came back without. Guilt stiffened Eli's muscles.

Where did he get off complaining when he still could walk? He wasn't a hero. He'd been a kid in the wrong car on the wrong night—and survived when no one else had, including his first boyfriend.

And when *that* relationship had been revealed, his parents had screwed over Noah's parents, all under the guise of doing the right thing. Bitterness rose into his mouth.

"Eli?"

Breath left him. His office, files in hand. Justin sat on his heels, anxiety overtaking relaxation and arousal.

"Sorry. Lost in thought."

Justin pressed his lips together and a flicker of sadness lit in his eyes. All Eli wanted to do was cup Justin's cheek and stroke his frown away. *Not for me. Don't worry about me.*

He gripped the file tighter. "Thank you for this."

A flush rose in Justin. "It's nothing."

It was everything. Eli handed the last stack. "This one's easy." He kicked the nearest cabinet with his good leg.

Justin shuffled sideways, opened the cabinet, and slid the file home. Eli tried not to notice the way Justin's arms trembled when he pushed the cabinet shut.

Justin clasped his hands together at the small of his back. "Is there anything else I can do for you, Eli?"

That stance spoke of training. *Shit.* Not what Eli needed to know. "No, thank you. I should return you to Sam."

"In one piece." He sounded disappointed.

Eli couldn't help the smile. "This time."

Justin parted his lips and leaned forward. Every inch of Eli's skin crackled with energy. All he needed to do was lean down and if Justin sat up, they might meet lip to lip. From Justin's wide eyes, flush skin and thrumming pulse, he knew it, too. They hung there until they both moved away.

Justin climbed to his feet, dick thick in his jeans. "If you need me to file anything else…"

"I'll let you know." Eli nodded toward the door. "Sam's waiting."

That seemed to wake Justin out of a haze, out of the subspace.

"Right." He licked his lips and headed for the door.

"Justin?"

Hope blazoned across Justin's body. "Yes?"

"Would you mind closing the door? I have a call I need to make."

His expression crumpled. "Sure."

To see Justin deflate like that hurt down to Eli's bones. Had he been that unforgiving this week? "I'll open it when I'm done. I promise." Keeping it closed had been a mistake. Whatever happened now, he wanted Justin as a friend, even with the snark and the eyeliner.

"Good. I mean—"

Eli pointed at the door. "Sam. Go."

Justin grinned. "Yes, Eli." He left, closing Eli's door behind him.

God. Eli pressed his hand against the length of his cock and stroked. Wasn't the first time Justin had left him hard. Probably wouldn't be the last—but he needed another outlet, one that wasn't so complicated and full of pitfalls.

You could ask him out. For a moment, he even considered it, but no.

You may find relationships hard, his therapist had said. Both true and false. The affection he had for Sam and especially for Michael ran deep and had come without hardship. Even the subs he played with, he was fond of them. But fuck if he wanted his heart wrenched out of his chest and used as a bargaining chip.

He'd been right about Justin. So very *messy*. He'd sunk straight into Eli's soul. But why *this* man?

Because he's not afraid of you in the same way Noah never feared you. Eli scrubbed his face, rotated to his desk, and woke his computer.

One e-mail from Sam. No subject.

I have no issues with it.

Eli did. Eighteen years of issues. He picked up the phone and punched out a number he knew better than his own.

"Hello?" A deep voice on the other end.

"Lyle. It's Eli."

"E. Good to hear from you." A pause. "Does this mean you're going to grace us with your presence this weekend?"

"If you'll have me, yes." Lyle's parties always provided a distraction and an outlet.

"You know my home is always open to you."

"Oh, I know. And it's been a while. I've been... busy."

"So I hear." Another pause. "Will it just be you?"

Straight into the important questions. "Yes. Though I do intend to play. I'll figure out with who when I get there."

"Excellent. It's always a treat to watch you. I'm sure you'll have no end of choices."

"I'm sure. Thank you, Lyle."

After a few more pleasantries, he hung up. *There. All set.*

There were always willing subs at Lyle's. Finding the one he wanted... That was another story. *You know who you want.*

That temptation sat across the hall. Eli rose, wincing at the stiffness in his leg. Not as much pain. That walk last night—what *had* he been thinking?

He flinched. The accident. The deaths. His parents. Noah. Justin. All tumbling in his head.

Eli sighed, shook out his leg, and hobbled to the door. Opening it would calm Sam as well.

Justin sat at his desk, focused on his screen, absently biting his lip. He typed something, clicked the mouse. He looked over and gave Eli an unsure smile.

The way things had been this week, Eli couldn't fault that. Eli nodded and returned to his desk.

Lyle's party would relieve his physical needs. He'd work out the emotional ones. Eli lowered himself into his chair. Perhaps less painfully next time.

FRIDAY COULD NOT MOVE FAST ENOUGH FOR JUSTIN, nor anyone else in the office, it seemed. Even Sam was twitchy for the weekend. Everyone was upbeat—just ready to get the hell out of the office.

Especially Justin. Kelly had come through and in spades. An invitation to pretty much the best BDSM party in town. Some guy out in the western suburbs. He'd be able to get Eli out of his head, or at least get dominated hard enough to overshadow thoughts of him.

No coldness from the other room today. Might as well be July in Arizona, given the heat coming off Eli. Didn't help that he wanted to walk into Eli's office, shut the door, and kneel at his feet. Not even to suck his dick, though that fantasy had played itself out a few dozen times. No, kneeling before Eli felt *right*.

He's your coworker. And there wouldn't be a better job than this, not for some time. That's why he needed Eli gone from his brain. Helping Mercy mattered. He'd fucked up with Francis. Playing was fine, but not anything beyond that. Especially not with someone with fistfuls of money.

Sam stalked out of his office, jacket in hand. "Lunch."

Only eleven thirty and not a dollar in Justin's wallet. "Have a good time."

"You're coming with me. The whole office. My treat."

Justin locked his computer and grabbed his coat. "Magic words."

Sam left only his chuckle behind as he marched to the back of the office. When Justin peeked into Eli's office, the master of the house—so to speak—had a look of curiosity.

"Apparently Sam's taking us all out to lunch."

"How very kind of him." Eli rose, took a glove from the edge of the desk, and put it on his left hand. The leather slid down Eli's elegant fingers and molded to the back of his hand—as if the glove had been tailored to fit exactly those fingers. Sleek and slim. God, how he wanted that hand—covered in leather—around his dick.

How could putting something on be so hot?

Eli smiled. "Something wrong, Mr. White?"

"No, I..." he stammered... and was saved by Sam leading the troops out of the back. Thank *fuck*. He turned away from Eli and hoped his arousal wasn't too noticeable.

Sam paused at Eli's door. "Justin fill you in, E?"

"Oh yes. Rather nicely, too."

Goose bumps rose all over when Sam glanced Justin's way. But if Sam understood the double meaning in Eli's words, he showed no sign. "Let's go."

Justin matched his pace with Eli's when the others surged ahead. Eli's leg must not have been bothering him much, but he would never match Sam's frenetic pace, and to leave Eli alone seemed... rude.

Sam, of all of them, should have known that. Justin shoved his hands into his jacket and grunted.

"It's fine. He's too full of energy today," Eli said. "Better he burn it off a bit."

He glanced at Eli. Sam's back was getting progressively farther away. "We don't even know where he's going."

"Doesn't matter. He'll realize what's he's done and either come back or wait for us." Amusement in Eli. Obviously, this wasn't the first time Sam had left him in the dust. "Might think he's used to keeping up with Michael— that man has legs a mile long—but it's who Sam is. Always moving forward."

Mr. Margarita. "Michael's taller than you?"

"By two inches." Eli's expression turned distant. "And broad all over." He shook his head. "I'm all length."

Everywhere? Justin's face warmed. "Bulk isn't everything."

There was that stunning grin. "Indeed."

He picked up Eli's good mood, but sobered after a half a block. "I'm sorry about this week."

"Which part?"

Not yesterday. God, he'd replay that in a heartbeat. "The beginning. I was—I don't know what I was."

"Yes, you do." Eli spoke without malice. "Or you wouldn't be apologizing for it."

He couldn't argue with that. He'd been a brat. "You weren't exactly Mr. Sunshine, either."

"No, but when am I ever?"

Justin coughed a laugh, but the answer was right next to him. Today. Eli was bright as the sun and full of cheer.

They made it to Forbes Avenue, but none of their coworkers were in sight. "Eli, I—" *Like you. Want you. Need you.* Nothing seemed the right thing to say. "Can we manage friends?"

Eli placed both hands on top of his cane. "We're already there." No smile. No frown, either, just light and warmth. Justin wanted to cross the space between them and kiss Eli. Hard. Now. He shifted his weight. Eli stepped forward.

A shrill whistle, the type one might use to call a dog, startled them both. "Eli!"

Eli hissed and whipped around and the mood shattered.

Sam waved from outside of Uncle Sam's Sandwich Bar. Good God, but that man excelled at inopportune timing. Or the right timing. Last thing Justin needed was a *relationship*. Especially one with the CFO where he worked and not when he needed every cent that job brought in. "Guess we should go."

Eli stared at Sam. "I suppose we should." Eli set the pace once more, but tension reigned in him.

They entered the crowded shop. Sam stood near the door. "We snagged a table near the back."

"Good." Eli focused all of his attention on Sam. "Don't you ever whistle for me like that again, Sam." Though friendly in tone, the force behind that order—and it was nothing less than that—rattled Justin.

Sam, too. He took a half step back, a flush rising on his neck. "I—" Sam straightened. "My apologies, E. Won't happen again."

"That's all I ask. Let Justin and me order, and we'll join you."

Sam nodded, handed Eli a twenty, and headed toward the back. The hairs on Justin's neck stood up. Had Eli just ordered Sam around?

Eli must have read him like a book. "Sam's my boss and my friend, but that was a little much, even from him." He stepped up to the counter and ordered a steak and egg sub.

Justin followed, opting for the cheesesteak and fries. The whistle had been harsh. Still, it had kept Justin from doing something very wrong. He glanced sideways at Eli. Or very right. *Fuck.*

Eli paid the cashier. Justin took his slip, checked the time, and counted the hours until Kelly would pick him up for that party. Better to find someone else to flog or fuck his brains out. He didn't need attachments. Far too close to entrapment, and given the way he reacted to Eli, he might do anything for him.

He would not walk down *that* road again.

CHAPTER SIX

THE HOUSE WAS OLDER, VERY LARGE, AND SECLUDED. Kelly eased her Honda up the long drive and parked next to a BMW in the expansive driveway. "Lyle only holds a party every couple of months, so it can get crowded depending on who accepts."

"Crowded is fine," Justin said. Better to find someone to help him get the image of Eli's commanding face from his mind. Strip the sound of Eli's voice from his ears.

"The usual paperwork. No alcohol. Sex is fine with protection."

Made sense. This far out from the main road and surrounded by lots of nothing, not like the neighbors would complain. They climbed out of her car. The path to the house was well lit, and the night warm for October. Good, since the blue silk shirt he'd chosen to wear was thin, but it clung to his body and was easy to peel off, if needed.

They were greeted at the front door by a tall man who defined the term *silver fox*. Dark hair, with just a hint of gray. Dark suit, too, over a white shirt. Classic and masculine. "Kelly, so good to see you again, and you've brought a guest."

Kelly's smile was large and relaxed. "Master Lyle, this is Justin. An old friend from California.

He's new to the Pittsburgh Scene."

"But not to the Scene," Justin added. Lyle held out his hand and Justin took it. A firm shake before Lyle let go.

Master Lyle made Justin's breath catch in the way all Doms did, but did nothing for his dick. Handsome, yes, but there wasn't that spark, that fire. There needed to be if he was going to get Eli out of his head.

Lyle gestured down the hall to a table with forms. "The necessary evils."

And legal protection, if something happened. He'd been to parties with waivers before, and to those without. He read over the text then signed. Nothing unexpected; nothing Kelly hadn't told him about.

When done, they both fell in step behind Lyle. "New in town?"

"Been here about two years, but I'm in grad school."

"Ah," Lyle said. "Yes, that will eat your time." They stepped into the biggest room Justin had ever seen. "I'm glad you've had a chance to join us."

"Me too." A small stairway led down into the main space. The room swirled with mingling people. Some couples, some more. Dressed to the nines—or not at all. "This is what I need, I think."

Lyle chucked. "If you're looking for anything in particular, don't hesitate to ask. I know everyone here. He stepped back and gave Justin an appraising look. "Men rather than women?"

"Yes."

"Perhaps Master Carmichael or Master Theo." Lyle rubbed his chin. "Master E is here tonight, as well."

The floor became far less solid under Justin's feet and the air thin. No way in hell.

"Master E?" Kelly rose up on her toes and peered into the main area. "He's incredible to watch. Intense. You'd love him, Justin."

"Perhaps I should introduce you?"

"I..." Justin scanned the room. "I don't..." His breath caught when he spotted the dark curls, the long line of his torso, and the cane. Eli laughed at something said by the man next to him and flicked a glance up.

That glance became a stare followed by one of Eli's cock-hardening smiles. Justin's heart nearly beat its way out of his chest. "Shit."

"I see you've already met," Lyle said.

Oh God.

"Just?" Kelly's voice was higher than normal. "You *know* Master E?"

Eli moved toward the stairs, the crowd parted, and holy fuck, he was wearing black leather pants. The white button-down was no different from the ones he wore at work except there was no tie and the top two buttons were undone. The vest was far more elaborate. Dark brocade that shimmered with gold. It matched the handle on his cane. Black gloves.

Utterly Eli. Down to the lifting of a single eyebrow when he reached the foot of the stairs.

Justin's feet moved on their own, taking him down each step until he stood before Eli.

"You know Master E?" Kelly asked again.

Eli tipped his head slightly. "Justin and I work together."

"Ah." That from Lyle.

"Wow," Kelly said.

God, the way those pants clung to Eli's legs and over his package. Justin's own jeans were skintight—and his cock pressed against the confinement. "I... What... We..."

It took one gesture—a single finger pressed to Eli's lips—for Eli to silence him. "Lyle, is there somewhere Justin and I can talk in private?"

"The deck off the east hallway. There may be some folks outside, but I assume you can change that."

Eli's chuckle twisted around Justin's nerves. "Unless you object, Justin?"

"No." Because they did need to talk. *Holy fuck.*

Eli crooked a finger. "Then come with me."

Following Eli was like a drug.

"Breathe." Eli wasn't even looking at Justin, and yet he *knew*.

Justin pulled in a breath. All around them, people moved out of the way. Deferential nods for Eli and curious looks that stroked over Justin. Some tinged with envy.

Everything fell into place. That afternoon in the office. Hell, every day in the office. Of course Eli was a Dom. What else could the man be?

Your CFO.

Yes, that. They reached a sliding glass door, which led out onto a deck that would have been huge had it not overlooked a sprawling terraced patio that made the deck seem downright cozy. As Lyle said, there were a few people on the deck. Justin walked to the railing and gripped it since his legs were about ready to give out.

Eli. Master E.

How the hell was *that* supposed to work? What if Sam found out?

Except Sam's words echoed in Justin's brain. *E, why is my assistant kneeling at your feet?*

Hell. He really didn't want to think about what that meant. He stared at the patio beneath them. Somewhere, water trickled.

Eli murmured behind him. The sliding of the glass door opened and closed and Justin knew they were alone.

He shivered, but it had nothing to do with the night breeze and everything to do with the distinctive sound of Eli's cane against the wood decking. "Justin."

He couldn't move. Couldn't *think*.

"Turn around, please."

He could obey, though.

Eli rested both gloved hands on top of the golden head of his cane. "You should know that I'm not entirely surprised to see you here."

Justin's heart wanted to race its way out of his chest. "Was I that obvious?"

Eli moved closer. "Obvious? Yes and no. It's hard to judge when someone is merely trying to be edgy." He stopped inches from Justin and leaned his cane against the corner of the railing. "That afternoon in my office, however..."

God, his dick *hurt*. Next time, looser jeans. "That's why I'm here." The railing bit into his back. "After that, I needed... wanted..." Discipline. Orders. To feel Eli's hands on him.

"What you need is to start finishing your sentences." Amusement, but also annoyance. So very Eli.

"That's hard with you right in front of me."

"You poor thing." Eli purred the words—and stepped in closer.

Justin's pulse thudded in his ears. "I don't know what the fuck to do."

In the diffused light of the deck, Eli's eyes appeared black. "May I touch you, Justin?"

"Yes." He exhaled the word. *Please, please touch me.* He'd figure out how bad of an idea this was later. All he wanted was—

Eli traced his gloved hand against the side of Justin's neck.

That. Eli's touch. Every nerve shook. When Eli tucked two fingers under his leather collar and yanked him forward, he moaned. That was swallowed by Eli's mouth.

Eli kissed like the devil himself. Hot, demanding, possessing. Tongue forcing past lips, that leather-wrapped hand tighter around his neck than Justin's collar. Body pressed in against his.

Justin groaned and opened to Eli. If he had any doubt about Eli's attraction, that was dismissed by Eli's leather-covered bulge grinding against Justin's.

If Eli kept doing that, he was going to come just from the friction and Eli's mouth on his.

Eli broke the kiss, but didn't pull back. He rolled his hips. "A little hot under the collar, are we, Mr. White?" His lips brushed Justin's with every word.

"So are you." What he wouldn't do to have Eli kiss him again.

Eli nipped his neck and the scape of his teeth tightened Justin's balls. "Care to do something about it?"

God yes. But he could not afford to lose his job. Eli gripped his neck and cupped his ass. "I—need to think."

"Do you?" Eli opened up a space between them—thank God. Another minute would have had Justin moaning in ecstasy.

"We're coworkers."

Eli stroked his thumb along Justin's jawline before pressing it against his jugular. Not hard, but enough to turn Justin's legs into jelly. *Fuck.*

"So?"

"So, what do we do?" It came out as a whisper.

Eli stepped back. "As I see it, you have two choices. You can go back into the house, find another man to give you what you so obviously want from me, and have your friend take you to your home and life will go on as it has for the past two months." There was a hard edge to Eli's voice.

"Or?" Justin pushed the word out between his lips.

Eli tugged at his gloves. "Because of you, I came here tonight to tie a man up, flog him, and fuck him. If you want to be that man, you better get on your knees *right fucking now.*"

Justin let go of the railing and sank. There was no other option. Everything else—Sam, Mercy, the job—fuck if he knew. All that mattered was Eli.

Eli stepped in and took hold of Justin's chin. "That's what I thought."

God, his grip was strong. A hard edge to every one of Eli's words, too. "Still need to talk," Justin whispered.

"And so we shall." Eli didn't loosen his grip. "Right after I come down your throat."

Oh fuck. If that didn't make his entire body shiver. He let out a small moan.

Eli released Justin's chin and stroked his cheek. The warm soft leather of Eli's glove slid over Justin's skin like silk. "Assuming you agree, of course."

"Yes, please."

A smile, finally. "Very good."

Every inch of Justin's skin felt like a live wire, just from Eli's touch, his promise of what was to come.

Another caress of leather against Justin's cheek. "Hands behind your back, like in the office." Eli tipped Justin's head back and looked him in the eyes. "If you need me to stop, raise a hand."

Doubtful he would—but a good sign. Justin did as told, settling into a wider stance—as much as his tight jeans would allow.

"Well, isn't that a pretty sight." Eli undid his belt buckle and the top button of his pants before stepping forward. "Use your teeth on the zipper."

The scent was intoxicating. That deep, rich smell of tanned leather. Justin pressed his mouth against Eli's hard length under leather, ostensibly hunting for the zipper.

Eli threaded his hands into Justin's hair, curled his fingers, and *yanked*. Oh *fuck*, that hurt so good, like lightning from his head to his feet. He panted against Eli's thigh.

"The *zipper*, Mr. White." Gravel in Eli's voice.

This time, Justin searched for and found the piece of metal. He caught it between his teeth and pulled it down, each tooth clicking as it released and split open to reveal dark curls against pale flesh and the root of a very hard cock. Justin kissed the shaft. He leaned backed as Eli freed himself from his pants.

Stunning. Not overly thick or long, the perfect size to slide down Justin's throat. Eli was cut, of course. The smooth head was wide and beaded with moisture. Justin licked Eli's slit and was rewarded by a gasp from Eli. He pulled the head into his mouth and pressed the underside with his tongue.

This time, Eli moaned and tightened his grip on Justin's

hair. "This is a fine way to keep that mouth of yours quiet."
He pulled out and thrust in. "How much can you take,
Justin?"

Justin flicked his gaze up and met the devil's smile. *Just
you wait.* With Eli's next thrust, he opened his throat and
let the cock slide in deep. Eli tilted his head back and the
sound he made—half groan, half shout—sent pinpricks over
Justin's skin.

"You love this." Eli drove forward until Justin's lips slid
up to the root. "Don't you?"

God yes. Especially when Eli held him there, his cock
thick and full in Justin's mouth and throat until Justin
struggled to breathe and his eyes watered.

Eli pulled back, giving Justin just enough time to snatch
a breath before sliding in again. Over and over, until Justin
couldn't tell their grunts and moans apart. Hard, even
strokes plowed into Justin's throat. The sharp sting of his
scalp—Eli must have tightened his grip—only made Justin
relax as his balls tightened. He hadn't ever come from giving
a blow job, but he wasn't exactly *giving*, not with Eli in
control. Heat sparked down every limb and Justin's whole
body shuddered. He moaned around Eli's shaft.

"Don't you dare come," Eli panted the words. "You
don't get to come yet."

Every nerve fired at once when Eli thrust deep into his
throat and he flew. The pain in his balls, his throat, the
tightness of his lungs demanding air, the bliss on Eli's face
as he looked down—pushed him higher until time stretched
thin and took all the pain and turned it into heaven. Tears
ran down his cheeks.

That steady rhythm faltered and the pull on Justin's
hair became almost unbearably tight. Eli came with a
guttural cry that seemed to echo through the night. Heat,

salt, and musk flooded Justin's mouth and he swallowed as much as he could before his lungs had him gasping for air.

So *good.*

Eli's grip in his hair slackened and he leaned on the deck railing, sheen of sweat on his face, his breath coming in gasps.

Justin pressed his head against Eli's leg and panted. After a minute, Eli chuckled. "That was—very well done." Eli caressed his cheek and he couldn't help nuzzling the gloved fingers. The gravel in Eli's voice, his breathlessness— to have made this man crack and come? Heaven. Justin forgot how much his balls ached, how much his knees hurt. It had been some time since he'd given head like that.

Eli placed a finger under Justin's chin and pushed up until Justin found himself staring into Eli's amused face. "Tears?"

"Happens sometimes when I can't breathe." Or when he was completely blissed out of his skull. "That was rough." His throat ached, dusting his words.

"Too rough?"

No. It had been *perfect.* "Did I raise my hand and ask you to stop?"

Eli's amusement deepened, as did his voice. "Don't get cocky with me, Mr. White."

Like *that* would stop him.

Then reality slammed back in. "Oh God, what are we going to tell Sam?"

"Sam?" Eli ran a finger up Justin's chin and held it before Justin—some of the semen that had leaked from his mouth. Justin sucked it off the leather. "Do you mean the man watching us through the glass door?"

What? Ice ate its way up into his brain and he looked over at the door.

Holy shit. There were quite a few people watching them. Embarrassment crept over Justin like an itchy blanket. And there was Sam.

But not Sam from the office. No, this Sam's button-down hung open and a chain swung between clamps on his nipples. Behind him stood Michael—not Jimmy from the photo, but an imposing man tailored into a suit, a man who made everyone else at the door seem insignificant.

Justin looked back at Eli. Fucker was grinning from ear to ear, even though his cock still hung out of his pants.

"Sam's kinky?" That... actually explained a lot.

Eli's laugh was full and real. He tucked himself back into his pants. "Sometime, ask him how he met Michael." He glanced at the door. "Or ask Michael. Might be more... educational."

He wasn't sure he wanted to be educated by Michael. Eli, however... "We really need to talk." Preferably before fear settled into his chest and the little voice in the back of his head took over.

"Yes, we do." He collected his cane. "Can you stand?"

Maybe. God, he hoped so. Justin grabbed the railing and hauled himself to his feet. Yup. Standing. "Looks like it."

Eli pulled him into a kiss that nearly took his legs out from under him again and drove away all doubt that this was *right.* Hot, demanding, seeking. Everything Eli did curled Justin's toes.

"I am proud of you, Justin." Eli ran a finger over Justin's lips. "Such a lovely mouth you have."

Bastard. He sucked Eli's finger.

The hard head of Eli's cane stroked against Justin's bulge. "And you didn't come."

"Not yet."

"You won't. Until I tell you, yes?"

"I'll try not to."

Eli's fingers were under the leather, pressing against Justin's throat. "You'll do more than try, Justin. Do I make myself clear?"

He moaned. "Yes. Very clear."

"Good."

ELI TUGGED AT JUSTIN'S COLLAR, DELIGHTING IN THE tremble that followed. No mistaking the way Justin had opened to him, obeyed him, and taken his dick—the passion for surrender was truly there under Justin's snark. The thrill of finally touching Justin, of ordering him, of pounding that lovely mouth pushed Eli away from the fear of *What the hell do you think you're doing?*

Justin. He was doing Justin, and screw everything else at the moment.

"Let's find somewhere to sit." He nudged Justin toward the sliding glass door and the crowd gathered there. "Walk in front of me." It took Justin a moment to obey—no doubt he was still zoned out. Eli's skin tingled and heart pounded from the taste of Justin's mouth and his own spunk.

Justin stepped forward, shoulders squared, head high. *Good.* That boded well for later.

Sam slid open the door. Pink-tinged cheeks, as likely from the nipple clamps he loved as from their little show. "Took you long enough," Sam said.

Justin shrugged. "Late bloomer."

"Bullshit." Sam met Eli's gaze. "I think you owe me a second dinner, E."

Sam's grin slipped into a shiver when Michael pressed

his hand to the flat of Sam's stomach. "Not the time, nor the place to make demands of Eli, Sam."

Eli coughed a laugh. "Thank you, Michael." He touched Justin's shoulder. "Back the way we came, if you please."

The warmth of the hallway and the press of people were cloying compared to the deck. Some of the looks Justin received—envy, astonishment, jealousy—ripped through Eli. *Yes, he's mine. No, you are not.*

This part of the Scene Eli disliked, the desires of others wrapping around him. He chose his own path, much to the dismay of many.

A man reached out to brush his fingers over Justin's arm —but Eli swung his cane up, knocking the offending hand away. "Don't even think it."

Justin faltered, turned.

"Fuck, that hurt!" The man clutched his hand.

"It was supposed to." This one he knew. Brandon or Brad. Something like that. One of the men who stood too close, flirted too hard, and always smelled faintly of cheap beer when he arrived. "You know the rules."

"Eli?" Probably too buzzed to have even noticed the other man's gesture.

"You're fine." Eli slid a hand up Justin's spine and savored the shiver. Everything he'd dreamed about...

B-something opened his mouth. "I was just—"

"Do I need to fetch Master Lyle?"

"You don't." Lyle cut through the crowd, opening a swath before him. "I'll handle this."

He'd owe Lyle later, even though it was the host's job to handle such disruptions.

"What... I missed something." Justin continued forward.

"Someone was about to touch something that didn't belong to him." The hallway opened up into the great room, and Eli moved next to Justin, his hand tightening around his waist. "I am not inclined to share tonight."

"Oh. I don't think I would have liked that. Not so soon after..." He glanced back down the hall. "Do you share?"

One of so many questions that needed to be asked and answered. Eli pointed farther into the room with his cane. "Couch."

With the warmth of Justin against his side, his shirt sliding against Eli's gloves, every step was a delight. Justin was an obedient, blue-eyed thrill. And Eli's, at least for the moment.

They reached an empty two-seater couch. "Sit, please, Justin."

He did, though his movements were jerky. Hesitant. Eli folded himself down next to Justin. "How are you feeling?"

Again, Justin looked back the way they'd come. "Did we really just—?" A warble in his voice. "Do you really want...?"

There was the panic Eli felt building in himself, too. One way to fix that. He set his cane on the ground, then stripped off his gloves, aware he had Justin's undivided attention. He placed the gloves on the armrest. "Every time you fail to finish one of your sentences, I'm going to add a stripe to your backside."

The lovely blush was back. Justin swallowed, his hands twisting around themselves in his lap.

"That's four, I believe."

Justin's eyes narrowed. "That's not fair. Two of those were from before you..."

Eli waited for Justin to continue. He didn't. "Five."

Justin shuddered. "Fuck." But he didn't look away. Didn't protest.

Perfect. Time to start negotiating. Eli leaned forward and caught Justin's collar again. So very handy that had been.

"Eli, I..."

A sharp tug and Justin's mouth was his. As before, every muscle in Justin relaxed when Eli forced his tongue past Justin's lips. One of them moaned. Justin still tasted of salt—intoxicating. However, they did need to talk. Eli relented and broke the kiss.

In between gasps for air, Justin said, "That better not be six."

That mouth never quit. "I won't punish you when I make you fail to finish, but I'll add another if you give me attitude." He kissed Justin's neck above the leather collar.

A tremble and a hiss. "You *like* when I give you attitude."

Eli nipped the skin. "Six."

Justin groaned. "See?"

"Seven." Eli laughed. "Such a masochist."

"Mmm-hmm."

Eli pulled Justin onto his lap and continued tasting and nipping the skin at his neck. Well, conversation could wait a *bit*.

"Can I—can I touch you?" Justin's question was half moan, half breath.

Finally. "Yes."

Magic word. Justin tangled his hand into Eli's hair and ran the other down Eli's back. "You are so hot." He arched and exposed more of his throat.

Eli licked down to Justin's collarbone and kissed the flesh there. "I want an honest answer this time, Justin." Eli drew back. "How are you feeling about this?" Maybe if he had Justin's answer, he could find his own.

The eyeliner around those bright eyes was still perfect. Waterproof, no doubt. "Better now." Justin placed his hand against Eli's chest. "This is a hell of a first date."

Laughter and joy rose in his chest. "*First* implies you want another."

"Oh God yes. Even when I hated you, you set my blood on fire."

Hated? Eli pulled back farther. "What reason did I ever give you to hate me?"

Justin played with one of the buttons on Eli's vest. "You didn't. You were... cold. Standoffish, compared to Sam. And this past week, we weren't exactly getting along."

Well, that was true. Eli cupped the back of Justin's head and pulled him down, shifting so that their limbs tangled and Justin's head rest on his shoulder. Justin melted into him, except for the bulge he rocked ever so slightly against Eli's thigh.

"Sam is a people person." Eli toyed with Justin's hair. "I'm not." This week had been evidence enough of *that*.

"I can't believe Sam's a sub," Justin murmured. "He's so... dominant in the office."

Sam was, enough that Eli deferred to him almost naturally. "Sam's a masochist. He's a submissive for Michael, but I don't know if he'd be so for any other man."

Justin's heart thudded against Eli's chest. "Wow." He pushed himself up, and there was the calculating man Eli glimpsed at work. "You know quite a bit about him."

"We've worked with each other practically every day for ten months, and I've known Michael since undergrad."

"So he knows a lot about you, too."

Very nice. "Part of the reason I came on board."

Justin settled back down. "Where does this leave us?"

Indeed. That was the point of this discussion. He stroked Justin's hair—soft despite being dyed. "I still intend to flog and fuck you tonight."

Justin's shudder was sensual and delicious. All that shifting and rubbing. Fire sank down into Eli. Coming twice in one night would not be an issue, and how long had it been since he'd been this aroused? "I'll take that as consent."

"Please." He thrust against Eli's thigh. "You have no idea how much I want you."

Eli twisted his fingers into Justin's hair and lifted. "I have every idea. And if you come before I tell you, you'll get far more than seven strikes with a cane and you will not like it. At all."

That produced a different but equally delightful shudder. "Yes, Eli." He settled back down. No more coy sliding.

Good. "Do you want more beyond this night?"

A long pause. "If you're willing."

Oh, Justin. "We wouldn't be lying here otherwise. I *scene* at parties, that's it. I don't do this." He gestured at them and the couch. "Not at parties. And not very often at all." Never, actually.

The sound that came from Justin was a squeak.

Here was the part where he needed to tell the truth. "I'm not an easy Dom. I'm exacting and demanding and I will punish you—not for failure when you put in the honest effort, but if you don't work for it."

Justin *giggled*. "So basically, the same as at work, but with a crop in your hand?"

"Yes." He paused. "And that's eight, Mr. White."

His breath caught. "I'm not going to be able to sit on Monday, am I?"

"Oh, you'll sit. You're just not going to like it." Eli fingered Justin's collar. "And you'll get no sympathy from Sam whatsoever."

"Fuck."

Soon. "Tell me about this." He tugged at Justin's collar.

"It's—I bought it. For when I'm not with anyone."

"Good." He hadn't realized how much that had been bothering him until Justin answered. That possessiveness should have frightened Eli. It didn't.

Nor did it seem to bother Justin. "You're going to replace it."

"How very astute." As soon as Justin set foot in Eli's home, that hunk of leather would come off. "Leave it for now. It'll make a fine handle when you're naked."

Justin sucked in a breath. "You're going to keep me on edge all night, aren't you?"

Oh, yes. Until Justin was pleading for release. Screaming for permission. "You're the one who claimed that you always come right on time."

"I am *never* going to live that down."

"No. Certainly not when I get to say when the right time is." Eli touched the top button of Justin's shirt and worked it free before sliding down to the next and unbuttoning that, too. "It's fun to use your own words against you."

He moaned. "Sadist."

Eli explored the warm flesh of the well-honed chest beneath the silk of Justin's shirt, plucking at Justin's dusting of golden-brown hair. "You say that as if it's a *bad* thing."

Justin's breath hitched.

Eli circled a nipple before pinching it gently. "Safeword?"

"Saturn." Justin squirmed. "And that wasn't me saying it."

"I should hope not." Eli pressed harder and twisted.

Justin about levitated off the couch. "Fuck!" But he didn't thrash, didn't try to escape. After the initial shock, he fell back and quivered, eyes closed, face a mask of pain and pleasure—but mostly pleasure.

Good. Eli increased the pressure until Justin was writhing on top of him. Wasn't that the best thing he'd felt in years? Justin bucking against Eli's body, hands locked on Eli's arms, nails biting into flesh even through the dress shirt. Justin. *His.* Finally.

White-hot need drove straight up to Eli's head and down into his balls. With his free hand, Eli caught Justin's head and took his mouth, breathing in the whimpers and moans like smoke—more intoxicating than any drug. If Justin kept moving like that, Eli would be just as on edge and out of control.

Part of Eli wanted that—to become as lost as Justin. Not here, though. Not with so many eyes and ears present—so he relented, releasing the nipple, but not Justin's mouth. Justin quieted and stilled.

Oh, Eli. You are so lost.

When he broke the kiss, Justin collapsed completely, his breathing harsh, heart beating so fast, Eli felt it against his own. "Oh, fuck."

Eli stroked Justin's hair. "Wait until I start on you with toys."

A little tremble. "Please tell me that'll be soon."

That forced a grunt from Eli, and he shifted beneath

Justin, his shaft hard and thick. "Not averse to public sceneing?"

"A tad late to ask that, don't you think?" Amusement laced those words.

It was a bit of an admonishment, but well deserved. "I should have asked. There aren't any private spaces here, but this is your first time, and you didn't know."

"Would have been hotter if I had."

Like lava up Eli's back. "I'll keep that in mind."

"You'd better," Justin muttered.

Such a mouth. "Nine."

"Flatterer."

"Ten, Mr. White." Eli pressed his cock into Justin's thigh. "I swing a cane quite hard and I have no qualms about laying strikes down *after* I've flogged your ass."

This time, Justin held his tongue, though his harsh breathing spoke volumes.

"Serious question time."

Justin stirred. "Yes?"

"Dislikes. Things you hate. Nonnegotiables?"

"Scat. Water play." Justin paused. "I'm not good at role-playing. Master/slave stuff. I had a bad experience with that. Just so you know." He propped himself up on one arm. Though his cheeks were flushed, the rest of his expression was hard and serious. "Please don't belittle me. It's one thing to call me on the carpet if I've screwed up. It's another to..." Justin's jaw worked, as if he were struggling to find the words.

"Verbally abuse you for the sake of it?"

"Yeah," Justin said. "That."

"I've never been that kind of Dom."

"Good." A pause. "Shouldn't that be eleven?"

So he was counting as well. Interesting. "I told you I wouldn't punish you for trying and failing."

"So you did."

Was that a hint of disappointment? "I can certainly make it eleven, if you'd like."

"Wouldn't want you to think I'm a brat."

"Eleven, because you are a brat." He stroked Justin's cheek. "Speaking of things you like..."

Justin's huff of laughter vibrated through Eli. "Everything you've done to me tonight."

That was obvious. "Want anything I haven't done to you yet?"

"I believe you mentioned flogging and fucking?" Those lovely lips pulled into a smirk.

"Are you begging, Mr. White?" Eli pushed himself up to sitting. The things he wanted to do to Justin... and could. His balls ached.

"No, not really."

Eli tightened a hand in the hair beneath his fingers and Justin's change from smiling to panting lit a fire in Eli's veins. "Well, you should be, don't you think?" Eli let go.

Justin slid from the couch to the floor and knelt between Eli's knees, his lips wet, his blue eyes wide. "Eli, will you please flog me until I've screamed myself hoarse? Please fuck me until I beg you to let me come. I want your whip on my back and your cock inside me."

Oh hell yes. Eli reached for his gloves and walking stick. "If you insist, Justin."

CHAPTER SEVEN

Justin's lungs ached and his blood was on fire. When had Eli morphed from cold to so hot all Justin wanted was to be touched by him? Fucked by him? Sometime between when he'd handed Sam his résumé and when he'd met Eli the morning of his interview. Crawling around in Eli's office might have cemented his lust, but that hadn't started it.

Here he was, being led by Eli to a room to be stripped, tied up, whipped, and fucked.

Finally.

He hadn't been flogged in ages and if he didn't feel Eli inside him soon, his brain might melt. Even better with people watching. When they'd lain on that couch, he'd caught a few of the looks—the stares, the whispers. As they moved down the hall, there were more. Evidently Eli was popular, but hard to get.

I don't do this. Not at parties. And not very often at all.

But for Justin, he had. He would. And fuck it all, if that alone didn't make Justin fly.

Down a set of stairs and another hallway and into a

sizable room and... *Holy shit*. He'd never seen a dungeon like this. Rack. Cross. Horse. A net. Bars. Too much to take in. Eli cupped Justin's ass and guided him farther into the room. "Cold feet?" he murmured in Justin's ear.

"Fuck no. I just don't know where to beg you to start."

Eli's teeth scraped Justin's earlobe. "Not something you need to worry about." He stepped into the center of the room and gestured for Justin to join him. Gloved fingers swept over temple and cheeks. Low words, meant for him alone. "Do you trust me, Justin?" Eli gripped his collar.

"Yes." He did. Right now he did.

Eli pulled him into a deep kiss that burned its way down to his toes, then spoke louder this time. "I want you to turn and see all the people who have come to watch us play."

So many pinpricks danced down his limbs it was a wonder he stood. Justin did as told, meeting all those smiles, frowns, and stares. The jealousy, the desire. He found Michael standing nearby, Sam at his feet. Somewhere along the line, Sam had lost his shirt and the nipple clamps and gained welts on his shoulders, but he was relaxed—and highly amused.

At least the boss approved. Michael was focused on Eli, his pride clear as day.

There was a story he wanted out of Eli. He shivered, a flicker of images playing through his head. He turned, taking in the rest of the room before meeting Eli's gaze.

"Did you see how many ached to be you?" Eli spoke low as he stroked the pit of Justin's throat.

"Yeah. Also saw how many wanted to be you."

"Shall we make them all envious?"

Yes. But that wasn't the reason Justin stood with Eli's

hand on his hips. "Whatever pleases you will please me, Eli."

Warm breath on his neck. "You are going to fly *so* high tonight."

No doubt of that. Hell, he was already halfway there. "Then let's make them all wish they were us."

Eli stepped back. "Lyle, if you'd be so kind." He held out his cane and Lyle took it.

"Shoes and socks off, Justin."

He obeyed, sliding them off to the side with his foot. Sam reached out to pull them completely out of the way.

"Toenails, too?"

He'd painted them black, like his fingernails. "I like when things match."

The devil's smile returned. "Well, that's good to know."

There was the shower of sparks down his limbs. Of *course* Eli would use that against him. And he'd likely love every second.

Eli stalked forward, his limp barely discernible but his desire clear in the flush of his skin, the hard line of cock in his pants. "Let's see what's under all this silk."

Justin groaned when Eli skimmed his belly before yanking the shirt out from where he'd tucked it into his jeans. Buttons next, until the ends fluttered open. The intensity in Eli's gray eyes poured through Justin, sparking every craving to kneel, to beg, to plead for whatever Eli deemed fit to give him.

The tips of Eli's gloved fingers barely touched his trembling abs, but Justin felt the heat from his head down to his pained toenails.

"What a treasure."

"Wait until you get to the pants."

Eli lifted an eyebrow. "Twelve, Mr. White. A full

dozen." He stepped forward and gripped Justin's shoulders under the shirt. "Actually, let's make it thirteen, a master's dozen, since you can't seem to help yourself." He shoved the shirt off Justin's shoulders and it slid down his arms to the floor.

Justin shuddered when Eli's hands followed the silk, leather gliding over arms before wrapping around each wrist. "No more lip, Justin. Or I'll gag you. I'd much rather hear you begging and screaming."

Oh, fuck. Eli's smile was slight, but full of lust. Every bit of Justin shook. "Yes, Eli." *Please.*

"Good." Eli let go of Justin's wrists, but caught his chin, his leather-clad thumb pressing against Justin's lips. He opened to Eli, sucking in the digit. Sparks in the back of his head. *Nothing* tasted like leather. Nothing. The strange tang, a hint of salt.

Maybe a gag wouldn't be so bad after all, to have leather biting into his mouth while Eli plowed into him. He licked and sucked at Eli's thumb the same way he'd taken his cock —with everything he had.

Eli's breath hitched, a sound no one else could have heard, and it just about made Justin come. Eli on edge, wanting this just as badly as Justin did. Never had that before, not with... Justin threw the name out of his mind. That man didn't belong here. Eli slid his thumb out slowly and their eyes met.

The knife's edge of desire twisted in Justin. "Eli?"

Eli stroked his throat, and worked his way down to Justin's chest. "Yes?"

He'd come here to forget Eli. Maybe Eli would make him forget the past. "Take everything I have tonight." A whisper of words.

Eli's smile was as bright as it was deadly. "Challenge accepted."

Fuck mashed against *yes*. Both won.

Eli's gloved fingers moved down over Justin's sternum. Lower still, moving over abs and belly until they met the top of his jeans. Justin couldn't move, couldn't breathe while Eli worked the button free and pulled down the zipper.

Eli stepped in so close his vest brushed Justin's bare chest with every matching breath they took. Gripping the edge of Justin's jeans and boxers, Eli pushed them down until they slipped free of Justin's cock and slid to the floor. If the room lacked heat, Justin couldn't tell. The heat of Eli's body seemed to radiate straight though Justin.

He tipped his head back when Eli's hot leather hands caressed his ass. He gasped when he pulled their bodies together, the cloth of Eli's pants rubbing against the crown of Justin's dick. As if his balls weren't burning enough. More. He needed so much more.

Eli nudged him backward, out of the pool of his pants and closer to pain and pleasure.

Now the coolness of the room flooded across Justin, raising goose bumps, but it was Eli's stare that set off every nerve. The quirk in his lips dissolved into something beyond lust. The slight furrow in his brow, the flush in his cheek as he looked down. He reached a hand forward but didn't touch Justin.

"'*Fortitudo e dolore.*'" Eli's strong voice rang out over the murmur of the crowd around them.

The tattoo. Right above his thigh, in simple script. He had no doubt Eli understood the Latin. He replied anyway. "Strength from pain."

Justin's heart sat in his mouth. Eli's expression was

unreadable—a complete mask. He stepped close, place his hands on Justin's hips, and looked Justin in the eyes.

Then Eli dropped to his knees and *kissed* the words.

Justin wasn't the only person to let out a sound—half gasp, half moan. What that must have cost Eli—but God, the heat from his mouth, so close to Justin's cock and so far away.

Justin fought against the fire in his balls. He didn't want to disappoint Eli, but on edge didn't even begin to describe the sensations in his body. He curled hands into Eli's hair, instinct overriding better sense.

Eli looked up. "Having issues, Mr. White?" Still in control, even on his knees with his curls clenched hard in Justin's fists.

Justin let go. "Just... sensitive there."

"So I see." Fingers traced over the letters, every stroke igniting a tremble in Justin. Eli chuckled and rose with grace. Seeing a twinge of pain fucked with the rhythm of Justin's heart. A Dom—Eli—*falling to his knees. For him.* I don't understand you. I want to understand you.

Eli took both wrists. "Everything?"

After seeing him on his knees? "Yes." And more.

"Cuffs, I think." Eli turned over his wrists. "And the frame."

Not the cross. More motion, less support. He shivered. *Perfect.* A few heartbeats later, Eli wrapped leather cuffs around Justin's wrists. Where they had come from, who the fuck knew. All that existed now was a frame of wood, the stretching of his arms and legs and the warmth of Eli's hand on his back.

"You are so beautiful."

Justin arched against his bonds when Eli traced a single finger down his back and into his crack and brushed his hole. Nothing to thrust against, no purchase in the air for his cock. He groaned.

Firm hands settled his hips and the leather-covered length of Eli's dick rocked against Justin's ass. "Eventually," Eli said. "And perhaps right here, like this." His hand closed around Justin's shaft.

The low moan that filled the room was his own. Eli didn't stroke, just held him there, fist so tight around Justin. "Not yet."

He knew that, but he was too far gone to argue. "Yes, Eli."

Eli's chuckle rattled Justin's bones and echoed in the rattle of chains above Justin's head, and then Eli was gone.

Justin opened his eyes—he hadn't realized he'd closed them—and saw his naked form in reflection. Flushed, limbs carefully stretched by chain and cuff—and Eli standing behind him, smiling. Same expression Eli always wore just before he made Justin pay in spades.

This would hurt. Just what he wanted, and from the very man that made him need it so badly, crave the stab and the spark.

Eli walked out of the reflection, only to return holding a flogger—a soft one. Didn't matter. Even something like that could induce pain in the right hands.

The first impact shook Justin and he caught his breath against the thud, the weight of impact. Then the same, on the opposite shoulder. Muscles heated and unknotted under the slow, gentle blows. Again and again, until his back and ass felt warm and pleasant.

Then a hard hit, quick and loud, spreading fire over heat. *Yes.* He arched onto his toes when the second landed and hissed when the third crossed his back. After five, he lost count—each time the tails met flesh, they bit harder, flew faster.

And that sound, so rhythmic, so beautiful. Someone moaned over and over and it wasn't until the words tumbled from his mouth that he realized it was him.

"Please, oh fuck, please, Eli. Please. Don't..."

Eli swung harder and light burst in Justin's vision. *Yes. God. That.* Bright pins of fire in his back, on his ass, glowing hotter with each *crack* and *thud*. His arms and legs ached and his cock—if he'd had any purchase whatsoever, if he could have reached down, but that, too, was at Eli's mercy.

Justin slitted his eyes and peered at the mirror, but couldn't see through the blur of his vision and the shaking of his body. Every strike drove a cry from his throat and took him up and up, toward that singular place where there was no difference between the fire in his back and the heat in his core.

Eli muttered something that Justin could not decipher. But a handful of blows later and— *FUCK*.

Icy cold raced through Justin and burst into burning sparks behind his eyes. Then the second blow landed and he arched up and away. Every point the flogger hit—and who the hell knew how many tails were on that thing—felt like a million stings. Eli didn't stop, laying blows down and then back up, taking Justin higher until all that existed in the world was the end of Eli's whip, the sound of leather flaying skin, and the light and heat and *pleasure* of living. Gold flowed through his veins and into his heart, the joy and brightness of being alive.

Justin rattled against his cuffs and grappled with the moment until it stretched and covered him, blanketing his skin with pins and needles and glass burning at every inch of his back. Every time he fell, Eli drove him up again with a rain of fire and ice.

How long it lasted, Justin couldn't tell—just that it ended, falling like a sheet of silence and darkness. *No. Not yet!* He cried and slipped down, only to be caught by the cuffs and chains that still held his arms outstretched to the heavens he'd just occupied.

"Justin."

He peeled his eyes open and Eli was there, holding his face, stroking his skin. Flushed face, sweat beading at his forehead, damp curls clinging to his face. He'd lost his vest at some point.

"Justin?"

"Here." His own voice was cracked and broken. He knew he'd not reached the top of agony, suffered to his fullest. Though Eli's touch radiated against the buzzing and thumping of Justin's veins, it didn't lessen the burning ache in his soul and skin. This couldn't be the end. A thought formed and he caught it, wet his lips, and spoke one word.

"Thirteen."

Eli's lips parted. "Are you *sure?*"

He pushed the words out with each breath. "Did—you hear—me safeword?"

Lips on his, nearly downing his need before Eli broke the kiss. "My beautiful Justin."

The pride in Eli's voice lifted Justin. "Yes." *Everything. I want you to have everything.* It had been taken once before. This time, he offered.

"Then thirteen it is, Mr. White."

Justin arched in his bonds. *Yes.*

Eli pressed his forehead against his shirt sleeve, partly to blot the sweat from his face, but mostly to give himself a moment to breathe, to think. *God.* He'd flogged Justin harder and longer than any sub he'd had, pushed him into screaming agony and wordless pleasure, taken him to the top—or so he'd thought.

Thirteen. A whisper, a plea for more.

A caning. Against the welts on Justin's backside? Agony. He walked to the table. And delight. Lyle lingered there and Eli met his gaze. Wonderment and a tiny slice of envy. But he nodded. He'd heard Justin, too. They all had, so silent the room had fallen.

A cane. Not the carbon fiber one—later. There would be time for that later. While Justin wanted pain and, fuck, Eli wanted to turn Justin inside out—he still had to be in control. Keep them both on this side of the edge.

No mistakes.

No matter how much he wanted to go tumbling over with Justin.

Heart beating in his throat and skin and muscle vibrating against bone, Eli drew one of the thinner rattan straight canes off the table. Still quite painful and it would leave beautiful stripes across Justin's ass.

Wouldn't that be a delight to see: Justin squirming in his chair at work from the welts Eli had laid there.

He stepped back, ignoring the ache in his leg, the burning in his arms. No idea how long the scene had gone. Didn't matter. He still had the strength and Justin needed him. He gave the cane a flick in the air, testing its flexibility.

Justin started, the chains rattling against the frame.

Electricity snapped through Eli, down to his cock and balls. He lined himself up and swung, cracking the cane across both buttocks, and Justin's cry vibrated down to his soul.

"One."

He let Justin inhale and manage the pain, his lithe form trembling until those slim hips rocked forward, looking for some purchase for Justin's hard cock.

Enough of that. Eli laid down the second cut, eliciting a longer cry. "Two."

He didn't let Justin rest nearly as long before the third or fourth, just enough to count the blow out loud. Justin's shouts and whimpers, his shudders as each blow landed only drove Eli to land the next stroke harder. "Five."

He caught himself, balls tight, shoulder aching, and took a breath.

The edge was right there, heady and wonderful. Eli flicked his arm—firmly but controlled.

"Six."

Justin thrashed in his bonds. "No, please!" Tears had finally ruined Justin's eyeliner. His face shone with sweat and ecstasy.

Shit. He couldn't want... Eli swung a bit harder, the *crack* of the cane against Justin's ass resounding like a shot.

There is was, reflected back in the mirror, Justin's pain slipping into pleasure, mouth open in a scream that made Eli groan. The dark head of Justin's cock bobbed, tip slick with fluid.

It took every ounce of Eli's willpower to steady his voice. "Seven."

He laid eight across one of the other stripes and the sounds Justin made, the twist of joy and hurt in that mirror nearly undid Eli. Nine and ten followed and Eli tightened his grip, grateful for the gloves... his palms were wet—hell every inch of him was drenched. And his cock—

That, he wanted to bury in Justin. Right now.

Eleven. The chains shook and Justin's voice cracked. A woman somewhere behind Eli moaned.

Twelve. Pause. Breathe.

Justin shook like a leaf. He opened his eyes and found Eli in the reflection and mouthed one word.

Thirteen.

Eli snapped the cane out, harder and faster than before, and the sharpness of Justin's cry shattered against the roof of the room. But it was the expression on Justin's face that nearly undid Eli—transcendence. Eyes closed, mouth open, face relaxed. Joy. Rapture.

"Thirteen, Mr. White."

Justin sagged in his bonds. Eli dropped the cane and strode forward to pull him back up. "I'm here."

"Eli."

Fuck, he needed inside Justin. "Yes."

"Want—"

Eli scraped his teeth against Justin's shoulder and gripped Justin's shaft. "I know what you want." He rocked his bulge against Justin's crack, driving another moan from him. "Say it."

"Please fuck me. Please. I need you."

Eli couldn't dig the condom out of his back pocket fast enough. Thank fuck he'd had the sense to slip that and a small container of lube into his pants before he'd started flogging Justin.

He held the foil between his teeth just long enough to undo his pants and free himself, before he ripped it open. Hard to roll it on with shaking hands and nearly impossible to think with Justin moaning, "Please, please, God, I need you," over and over. Lube next, over the condom, on his glove, then he was against Justin's entrance, pushing in as Justin shoved back.

Fuck. So tight and hot. He gripped those slender hips and thrust in deeper, savoring Justin's cry, the brilliance of joy in his blue eyes, the tears on his lashes, and all that smeared eyeliner.

Deep and hard strokes, forced breath from both their lungs. Justin arched and stretched up onto his toes, elegant neck exposed. Beautiful. All his. Eli thrust in and held Justin on his cock, delighting in the trembling around his shaft, the rattle of the chains holding Justin, and those lovely hoarse cries from deep in Justin's throat.

"This what you've been craving?" He licked the back of Justin's ear. "My cock inside you?"

"Yes." Almost a hiss. "Feels... so good."

He drew back and slammed in again. "I bet you want to come. Empty your balls in front of all these people for me."

Justin tightened and whimpered and Eli nearly spilled himself, desire wrapping sharp tendrils of need into his spine and balls. He pushed the rising tide of chaos and need back down.

He slammed into that tight hole again. "Not an answer, Mr. White."

Even tighter. *Fuck.* Eli pressed his hand against Justin's belly and wrapped the other around his dick.

"God, Eli." This time, the plea was edged in desperation. "I—yes. Here. With everyone. For you." The words tumbled out of Justin's mouth, one on top of the other. He shook and rocked and tried to find the movement Eli denied him.

Justin gasped and moaned. Chains rattled down into Eli's bones. "Please!"

The cry filled the room.

So much pleasure written in Justin's body. So much pain. The need and desire. Liquid heat in Eli's spine. Sparks raising the hairs on his skin. Eli's doing—and Justin's gift back to him.

Eli pulled out and pushed in with short, tight, hard strokes. A rough, fast fuck. Neither of them would last through anything more, but he would take Justin to the edge. Make him hang there. Beg. He loosened his grip on Justin's cock and stroked with the same tempo.

Justin's whole being shook, his breath turned into moans that put everyone else's to shame. Deep, powerful, and from the soul. So close—he must have been so close. "Don't you dare come yet, Justin. Not until I say."

"I can't. I can't." Justin's head lolled back against Eli, the rest of his body taut as a bowstring.

So tight. Eli barely moved inside Justin as the sparks of his own release shivered up to his brain. "You will because I want you to."

Groans and gasps and curses. Eli ground in, pulled out, rammed in. Someday, he would put Justin on the edge like this—and then say no. He kissed Justin's shoulder and whispered one word.

"Come."

Justin thrust between Eli's fingers and coated the glove and floor with spunk. Between the shout that ripped through Justin and the way he tightened around Eli's shaft, there was no holding back his own orgasm. He bit down on Justin's shoulder and plowed into him. Fire rose to Eli's skull and his vision blurred to white as he emptied himself inside Justin.

The rattling of chain kept Eli in the present and he blinked his vision clear.

Justin shook in his bonds, from exhaustion, not delight.

Eli steadied himself and kissed the nape of Justin's back. "I'll get you down."

"I—I'm fine." Justin's voice was all breath. "It's okay."

A little lie, but Eli let it go. Given how high he'd driven Justin, it was no wonder he didn't feel what his body showed.

"'Sides, I like you here. Like this."

Eli's heart twisted in a way it hadn't in far too long. "I like this, too." He pressed his lips to Justin's back once more. "But I'd also like you wrapped in my arms on a couch."

"Okay with that, too."

Good. Eli pulled out, making sure the condom came as well. He stripped off his gloves—the one coated in lube and semen was too slippery to grip much of anything. His dropped to his knees, his leg protesting the movement—he'd been on his feet quite a lot this night—but he needed Justin down. One ankle cuff free, and the other—he'd leave the leather bands around Justin for now. So nice to see him cuffed and collared.

When he rose, Lyle was nearby with a trash can. Eli stripped the condom and threw it away. He tucked himself back into his pants before reaching up to free the wrist cuffs. Justin half hung from the chains. "Can you stand?"

"Hmm?" Justin took a deep breath and placed his feet more firmly under him. "I think so."

Well, they'd find out. He unhooked one wrist. Justin swayed, but managed to stay upright, though the trembling didn't lessen. Eli unhooked the other and caught Justin as he sagged, stifling a hiss when his leg protested against the added weight.

Lyle cleared his throat.

No fucking way. If it took every ounce of his will to

manage the pain, he'd not let anyone else touch Justin. "Think you can walk?"

Justin's chest heaved. "Want to." He wavered in Eli's arms. "Not sure, though."

Well, okay. Thankfully, Justin wasn't *that* heavy. And Eli did have several inches on him.

"E." Lyle spoke softly.

Justin stiffened in Eli's arms.

"We're fine." Eli bent, and scooped Justin up. He ignored the stab of pain that flew up his leg, ignored Lyle's frown. "This is going to hurt a bit, Justin."

Justin wrapped his arms around Eli's neck. Lovely blue eyes, rimmed with smeared eyeliner and moisture, and a smile that wrapped itself around Eli's heart. "I like pain."

"So you do." Eli stole a kiss and carried Justin out of the room. And, *fuck*, did it hurt. The entire walk up the stairs and back into the great room was one halting mass of agony. But he wanted the space and distance from the other scenes, and the sofas were more comfortable upstairs.

One look cleared the couch he wanted. Much to his relief, Eli was able to sit and not collapse down onto the cushions.

Justin touched his face, brushed something away.

Moisture. Tears.

"Eli, you didn't—"

He pressed fingers to Justin's mouth. "Don't make me start counting again."

Justin's lips twitched under Eli's fingers. "Yes, Eli." Humor there.

Good. Because he would not take Justin's pity, not one bit of it. He wouldn't wipe his tears away, either. They weren't a weakness. Anyone *here* who thought *that*—didn't belong. Any reminder Eli needed of that was written on Justin's face and in the welts across his back.

Iron strength, once the snark and insecurity were stripped away. *What holds you back, Justin? How do I help you?*

A cough interrupted Eli's thoughts. This time it was Michael. He knelt and placed Eli's cane on the floor and handed him a blanket. "We have Justin's clothes and your vest, too. I've sent Sam for water." Soft, neutral words, but Eli had known Michael too long not to see what lay behind. Understanding. Pride.

That tumbled Eli's heart, nearly as much as the kiss Justin planted on his neck. "Thank you." He nudged Justin so that they both lay on the couch before draping the blanket over them.

Justin melted into Eli and at least for this moment and in this space, everything was perfect. Eli shut his eyes and clung to that, writing it into his memory as strongly as he could.

Justin White, in his arms. Pressing kiss after wordless kiss against his lips.

CHAPTER EIGHT

JUSTIN HAD NEVER BEEN SO TURNED ON BY A CAR RIDE, but then he'd never been tied up and placed in a car before, either. Complex bindings held his arms to his side and bound his hands and palms together in front of him. Rope crisscrossed his torso and back and the knots dug into the welts on his back as he sat in passenger seat of Eli's car. Leather creaked when he shifted, earning him a twist to a nipple through his shirt or a caress of his cock through his jeans, depending on Eli's mood.

He was belted in but without his hands free, he was acutely aware of how off balance he was every time the car turned—and how absolutely hard he'd become. Between the ache in his back, the restriction of his arms, and the occasional spike of pain from Eli's relentless torment of his nipple, the only thing keeping him from a mind-blowing orgasm was the tightness of his pants.

Oh, but did Eli try to bring him off. When the road emptied enough, Eli massaged Justin's length until Justin rocked his hips, pressed his head back against the seat, and moaned.

At the moment, they were driving through a busy stretch of road and both of Eli's hands were firmly on the steering wheel. Justin watched the lights swim by through the window. He'd half expected to go home with someone tonight, even brought a change of clothes. *This is every one of my erotic dreams come true.*

"Is it, now?"

A shiver slid straight down Justin, even as embarrassment rose like summer heat. "I... didn't mean to say that out loud."

Eli's chuckle was almost inaudible over the car noise. "Yet you did."

"Guess you're used to hearing that."

"No, actually. You're the first."

No way. "How is that even possible?"

Silence for a moment as Eli switched lanes. "I'm a bit much for most, really."

All those jealous looks at the party. "But everyone wants you."

"Everyone *thinks* they want me. Most subs I've scened with like the experience, but I'm a bit too—much—for long-term."

"Most?" There was the stab of jealousy. Not like Justin hadn't been with other men. Or been dominated by them. Or kept by them— *Francis.* He shivered.

Eli glanced over, brows furrowing. "Most. Some want that intensity, but my D/s relationships have been no more than that—Dominant and submissive. And always short-term."

No romance. Nothing long. *I don't do this.* Justin turned to Eli—as much as the ropes allowed. "Why me?"

"Because we already had more." Eli changed lanes then

slid his hand over Justin's jeans, so close to—but not touching—his cock. "And you thrive on the intensity."

He did. Would have loved it even more if Eli moved his hand up a bit.

"See?" Warmth and playfulness in Eli's voice. But he didn't shift his hand one inch.

Justin flexed, the ropes pressing against flesh and silk, and swallowed, trying to wet his throat. "I don't suppose you could drive a little faster?"

"No." Eli's fingers found Justin's shaft.

Justin grunted, but it sounded more like a whimper.

"I don't think the cops would quite understand your... predicament... if they pulled me over for speeding."

Eli didn't let up for what felt like miles. Lights blurred and the thudding of Justin's blood mixed with the rumble of the road. His balls ached—hell—every piece of him ached for the bliss of release. He never wanted it to end.

Which was par for the course with Eli, it seemed.

They were both breathless when Eli finally put both hands back on the steering wheel. Downtown Pittsburgh rose above the road like a glass and steel medieval fortress—all points and towers and lights. Justin's stomach tumbled as they curved over bridges, changed lanes, and zipped under more bridges. He swayed in his seat, completely at the mercy of physics and Eli's driving.

Exhilarating. Nerve-wracking.

When they neared the exit for Forbes Avenue and Oakland—the one that would take them near Justin's apartment—Eli cleared his throat. "Are you sure?"

He didn't even think about the answer. "Yes."

They passed the exit. Justin exhaled. "Are you?"

"You wouldn't be in my car if I weren't." This time,

when Eli reached over, he squeezed Justin's knee. "I know this is rather fast."

No, not really, but he wasn't ready to tell Eli how he'd jacked off in the coffee shop bathroom after his interview. "I'm fine. Honest."

They exited at Squirrel Hill, and in a matter of minutes, they were parked in Eli's driveway. Eli got out of the car and retrieved his cane. A moment later, the passenger door opened. "Up and out, if you please."

Harder to do than Justin expected, but he managed after the second try. The trip to the front door was a blur of kisses and stumbling, tugging and pushing. In between sucking in air and tangling with Eli's tongue, Justin stammered out two words. "My bag."

"Tomorrow." Eli pushed him against the door. Teeth scraped against Justin's chin. Keys jingled and the door against his back swung open. The only reason he didn't tumble back was Eli's grip on the ropes.

"In." Eli spoke against Justin's ear. "Before Lavi gets out."

"Lavi?" Justin stepped up and walked backward into the dark entryway.

Eli wrenched Justin around and pushed him against the door, shutting it behind them. "My cat."

Sure enough, an annoyed meow sounded from nearby, but was drowned out by the thudding of Justin's heart when Eli bit his shoulder. The sharp pain tightened his dick and he fought the ropes holding his arms. More than anything, he wanted to tangle his hands into Eli's hair. So frustrating. So fucking hot.

Eli ground his cock into Justin's. Fingers grazed his throat. "Time to get rid of this."

The collar. A moment later, it hit the floor. Eli pulled him off the door. "Upstairs. Now."

No argument there. "Which way?"

A groan. Eli rotated him and Justin faced a dimly lit set of stairs—with a pair of reflective eyes halfway up.

The cat meowed again. Eli placed his hand on the small of Justin's back and pushed, forcing Justin to the foot of the stairs.

Justin eyed the cat. "Will she move?"

"He. And he'd better, if he knows what's good for him." Another bite against Justin's shoulder, this one harder than the last. "You'd better as well, if you know what's good for you."

Justin knew exactly what he wanted: out of these pants and into Eli's bed. He took one step and another. The cat regarded him with disdain, but did move out of the way when Justin got within a step.

He trilled as they passed.

"Daddy's busy, Lavi," Eli murmured. "Besides, you've had your dinner."

"Talkative thing." Justin reached the second floor.

A sharp smack against Justin's ass made him jump forward and ignited all the welts on his backside. "He talks almost as much as you. To the left, please."

That had better be the bedroom. His jeans were too tight and Eli wasn't close enough. He walked through a doorway and—yes. Bedroom. Finally. A click of a switch and a floor lamp bathed the room in a soft glow. Not that Justin saw much before Eli yanked him around and kissed him hard, using the ropes as handles. There was the clatter of Eli's cane falling to the wood floor then Justin toppled over onto the bed. Eli followed him down onto the soft surface. White bedspread, white shirt, Eli's hair a dark frame around his face. He hovered above Justin, lips almost touching—as if waiting.

"Please." Justin arched up, seeking lips, skin, or any part of Eli at all.

What he got was a sweet and gentle kiss. "I should untie you."

"Don't have to."

Eli cradled Justin's face with his hands. "The sex doesn't have to be rough." Gravel in his voice and his hard cock rocked against Justin's thigh.

"I know." Justin caught his breath. "But tonight, it does. You want it. I want it. I can't... get enough of you."

There was a look of wonder in Eli that shifted to joy and lust, and then Justin couldn't breathe for the kiss. Eli massaged Justin's bulge and one of them moaned. Eli stripped Justin's pants and underwear off and hoisted him farther onto the bed before he closed a hand around Justin's shaft.

The ropes seemed tighter and sweeter and his orgasm so close.

The next groan wasn't Justin's. "Fuck. Condoms. Need..." Eli's kiss seared Justin's blood. "I'll be right back."

Then there was nothing but a white ceiling with an interesting plaster pattern. *Really?*

A door opened to a muttered curse and closed. Two objects landed on the bed and Eli crawled over him.

"Most people keep that shit in the nightstand." Justin peered into Eli's gray eyes.

Eli shrugged, a blush creeping up his neck. "Haven't had a lover in a while." He traced fingers over Justin's cheeks. "Now where were we?"

A languid kiss, then a deeper one, and another. Eli's hand closed around Justin's shaft and Justin twisted in the ropes, even as is mind whirled around Eli's words. Skin and blood flared when Eli shifted and pushed his knees wider. Eli's cloth-covered erection rocked against Justin's balls and then both moaned.

"Fuck, Eli, just..." Justin let out a breath. "Lovers?"

"Yes." Lips brushed lips before Eli pulled back reached for something. Foil. Lube. The clatter of a buckle and the whisper of a zipper.

Lovers? The weight of it pinned Justin to the bed more tightly than any rope could ever hope to. He didn't know if he could trust another Dom enough for *that*. "Submissive?"

That bright smile lit in Eli. "That, too, when you want." Another shift and the fullness of Eli's cock head pressed against his ass. Eli moved forward.

Justin couldn't help the cry that ripped from him. The pleasure of Eli filling him, the burn of being stretched and entered so quickly, so smoothly, trembled his whole body and forced the air from his lungs.

Eli curled fingers under the rope across Justin's upper arms and thrust in deeper until they couldn't be any closer, though they both tried. Justin wrapped his legs around Eli as he took him deep, over and over. Hard and unmerciful pounding.

But the way they kissed, lips and tongues teasing, the moans and gasps and mutters—this wasn't a Dom fucking his sub into oblivion. Despite the ropes, the clothing that still covered Eli, the pain from welts on Justin's back, they made love.

Justin's heart ached against his ribs. He'd gone to the party looking for a fuck, not a relationship, least of all with Eli, but here they were in his bed. Last time he'd done this, it had been a horrible mistake. But the torment of the ropes against his back mixed with the sweet friction of Eli's shirt against his cock. "Eli, I can't—" Eli kissed him hard, rocking in deep and hitting him right.

"Then don't." Slurred words.

Everything turned bright, the sharp blade of ecstasy slicing into Justin's balls and brain and he spilled himself against Eli's shirt, suspended between the pain of his back and the joy of Eli wrapped around him. Justin hadn't tumbled down from the high when Eli's rhythm broke with a sharp curse and a low cry until he slowed to a stop, his whole body shaking against Justin's.

Despite the all the aches, with Eli buried inside him and his breath rasping against Justin's cheek, this was the most peaceful Justin had felt in ages.

Eli shifted and pulled out. He trailed fingers across Justin's forehead. "You okay?"

Justin wet his lip. "God yes. Just need to lie here for a thousand years and I'll be fine." He closed his eyes, but a haze of light ringed his vision anyway. Every muscle weighed him down. Bones of lead.

A chuckle. "Give me a moment."

A gentle tugging forced Justin to open his eyes. Eli knelt next to him, unknotting rope. "Can you sit up?"

With Eli's help, yes. So very heavy, though. His head, his arms. "Sub drop."

"Hadn't noticed." Eli's dry reply spoke otherwise. "Let me get these ropes off, put some salve on your back, and you can crash."

That was fine. He leaned his forehead against Eli's shoulder. The tension against his arms and torso ebbed until all that remained were the ropes binding his hands. Warm lips brushed Justin's forehead.

"Stay with me a bit longer."

"Sure."

How he ended up on his stomach, face cradled by the softest pillow he'd ever felt, he wasn't sure.

Eli was applying something cool to his back, quenching the fire there. Justin relaxed into the quiet stillness of the room and Eli's touch and closed his eyes.

WHEN ELI RETURNED FROM WASHING HIS HANDS, Justin was asleep, sprawled on one side of the bed, his naked, welted back uncovered. Slow steps forward. He didn't want to wake Justin. He shouldn't have worried. Even when he draped the sheet and blanket over Justin, he didn't move, his breathing deep and even. Eli scrubbed his face. He should undress, crawl into bed, and let that same sleep consume him.

He couldn't. Too much buzz, too much energy, and a single question kicked around in his brain.

Are we doing the right thing?

He didn't know. He still didn't know. Eli pressed the heels of his hands against his forehead. *Fuck.*

Downstairs. Sleep was not an option and he needed not to look at Justin, not to want to kiss his skin or feel his heat. Eli stripped off his button-down—too much Justin on that. The t-shirt beneath was damp, but with sweat. His leg hurt like mad with every controlled step from the room. While the pain descending the stairs made him cling to the bannister, it did nothing to clear his head.

Eli stumbled into the living room and sank down on the couch. *What* was *he doing?* No clue. Absolutely none.

Through the dim light filtering in from outside, Eli picked out bits and pieces of his life. The photo of the Western Wall he'd taken in Jerusalem. Noah's Kiddush cup.

The sculpture of a cat he'd bought in Egypt. The tacky rainbow mug he'd picked up last year when Michael and Sam had dragged him to Pride in the Street. Plants. Candles. Items that meant something, but only to him because no one else knew the reasons they were in this room.

For the first time in ages, that *hurt*. He wanted Justin to know him—not the CFO, not the Dom, not the cold man with the cane and limp, but the guy who sat in the dark with his heart in his throat. The one who had a fuckload of issues and a therapist on speed dial and a patchwork heart.

He'd known Justin two months.

He didn't bring men home from parties. Didn't fuck them in his bed. Hell, when was the last time he'd dated? Eli pulled his aching leg up onto the couch.

That was easy. Michael, during undergrad. They'd salvaged a strong friendship from the debacle, but after that, he'd given up completely. Too many broken pieces, too many odd quirks he wasn't sure were him or the result of the fallout from the accident.

Eli leaned his head back against the couch and looked up at the lines of light and shadow on the ceiling. Justin's obvious pain had burned through Eli like a firebrand.

Even now, even after coming three times, the memory of Justin's cries, the shuddering way he sucked in air after each blow, the tracks of tears down his face warmed Eli. Justin had a body built for thrashing.

God, he was such a *monster*. Eli covered his eyes and grit his teeth.

Are you, Eli? Dr. Brohmer's voice rang in his head. Not like they hadn't had that conversation a few dozen times.

I love their pain, love making them feel it. How they

move, how they sound. I—how can I not be a monster? People aren't like this!

Her snort had been indelicate. *Many people are like this. These men crave what you offer. Are they monsters, too?*

A trilling meow shook Eli from the past and Lavi jumped up onto the couch, padded his way onto Eli's lap, and head-butted him in the chin. Eli wrapped his arms around Lavi. He was soft and warm and purring up a storm. "Daddy's not doing too well."

Lavi merely rubbed his chin against Eli's and snuggled his nose into Eli's ear, his purr pitching to a squeak. Adorable. Heart-melting. He pressed his face into Lavi. He'd leave a few tears behind, but Lavi never seemed to mind.

Eli was human. That was the conclusion he'd reached each time he had that conversation. No doubt he was a sadist, but playing without consent twisted his stomach. The few times he'd misjudged a sub's limits and he'd safeworded—those moments were burned into his brain. He'd dealt with the aftermath, talked it out, and made sure all was well. Then he'd come home and emptied the contents of his stomach into the nearest toilet.

You cared about those men, Eli.

He had. He hadn't loved any, but there'd been affection there, a desire to shepherd them to the next stage in their kink—usually to a more permanent relationship with a suitable partner.

Justin was different.

He couldn't pinpoint the moment when Justin had morphed from someone he wanted to fuck into the man he wanted to wake up next to. Make breakfast for. Share bits of his life with. It was insane. Or wonderful. Terrifying.

Exhaustion finally plowed into Eli's bones. Bed, next to

Justin: that's where he belonged, at least for this night. They'd figure out the rest a day at a time.

Eli scratched Lavi's head. "You always say the right things."

Lavi's bashed his head against Eli's nose before he hopped to the floor, tail in the air, purr still resounding. He headed for the kitchen.

"If you think you're getting food now, you're quite mistaken."

Lavi vanished into the darkness of the kitchen, then reappeared, rubbing his face against the edge of the doorframe.

Eli hobbled up from the couch. "Bedtime, sweetheart. Breakfast tomorrow."

The response was a long, pitiful meow.

"Oh, don't give me that." He limped toward the kitchen. "Fine. A few treats." *You are such a sucker.*

Once Lavi was placated, Eli took to the stairs, pulling himself up each step. Justin lay exactly where Eli had left him. Even when he flicked off the light, Justin didn't stir.

In the light from the street, Eli stripped and slid into bed next to Justin.

No, he wasn't a monster—just tired. Top drop.

He and Justin had given and taken what they needed, finally consummating the desire they'd been dancing around for two months. They'd make it work, somehow.

Because lying next to Justin was sublime. Sleep washed over Eli and pulled him under.

CHAPTER NINE

THE FIRST HINT JUSTIN WASN'T HOME WAS THE BED. Both too firm and too soft, it wasn't a lumpy mess. The room was light and airy and smelled of lavender, wood polish, and sex, not of damp mildew under awful air freshener.

Eli's house. Eli's bed. Justin stared out into the bedroom. His back and ass ached with a dull glow he knew would flare the moment he moved.

Last night he'd been stripped, flogged, and fucked by Eli. Now they were dating? Or in a Dom/sub thing? Justin's head swam. Rolling on his back would hurt, but he needed to see if Eli really slept next to him. He turned, gritting his teeth when his back connected with the mattress, and looked.

Mussed black curls and stubble that made Eli's jawline look so sharp by the end of the week. Relaxed and still, Eli looked younger, nearly Justin's age, if he had to guess. Beautiful.

Justin rotated to his side and Eli's eyes flickered and opened.

Eli cupped a hand against Justin's face and stroked his cheek with a thumb. "Justin. You're here."

Drenched in sleep, Eli's voice slipped through Justin, stirring desire and need. "Yeah. I am."

"Good." Eli closed his eyes, but the gentle swirling of his thumb didn't stop.

"I thought it might be a dream."

Those gray eyes opened again. "A good one, or a nightmare?"

He slid closer and kissed Eli's chin, running his tongue over the stubble there. "Dreams of you are always good."

"Even when you hated me?"

Justin flinched, but he deserved that. "Even then." Eli shifted his hand to the back of Justin's head, pulling his hair, the sharp tug thickening Justin's cock. "I don't hate you now."

Eli's laugh vibrated Justin's body. "I should hope not," he whispered in Justin's ear.

After that, time slipped away into touch and taste and bites and moans. Fingers and lips and tongues moved over flesh. Hard cocks rocked together until Justin realized the whimpers weren't all his and that the last "Fuck, please," hadn't come from his mouth.

They were equals, at least at the moment. It had never been that way with Francis. He kissed Eli's shoulder, breathing in the deep, rich scent of his skin. "I like this."

"Me too."

The spell broke. "What's going to happen, Eli?"

Nimble fingers brushed over one of Justin's nipples, and pinched—hard enough that Justin threw back his head and gasped.

"Well, first I'm going to fuck you until scream, then I'm going to make you pancakes."

Hell yes. "I'm more of a waffle guy."

"I've noticed you like to waffle." Teeth in Eli's smile.

Justin's witty reply died when Eli wrapped his hand around his cock and stroked. He nibbled his way up Justin's chin. "Sex and pancakes?"

Anything. "Please." It came out as begging. But—"I don't think my back can take it again."

Eli kissed him and took his breath and thoughts away by fisting his cock at the right pace to drive him wild. Justin moaned into Eli's mouth.

Eli grazed his lips down over Justin's chin and throat. "I don't need you on your back."

No, he didn't. They moved, Eli turning Justin around. "Hands on the headboard."

Justin complied, head already in the clouds, body burning. "Fuck. Please."

"Patience."

Soft touches over the welts and bruises on his back sent shivers down his length to settle in his balls. "Not good at that."

"I've noticed." Eli kissed the small of Justin's back. The familiar sound of foil being torn and the *snap* of a bottle of lube filled the room.

Anticipation burned like sparks across his body as he waited—and waited.

Eli's laugh was dark. "Someday, I'm going to make you hold yourself like that for hours."

Justin let his head fall. "Better not be today."

Eli pressed his cock head against Justin's hole. "That's four." He thrust inside, hard. And again and again, until Justin couldn't breathe for the pleasure of being taken so fast. A coarse cry ripped free from Justin's chest.

"You feel so... good." Eli's words were fully weighted with lust. Each stroke drove Justin off his knees.

Eli lit Justin's nerves and blood and flesh—he should have been ash from the friction, the hard ramming. His back burned anyway and Eli's thighs ground against the welts from his caning, the pain flaring at the back of his skull and blending with the absolute ecstasy of Eli ramming deep into his ass.

He managed one word. "Eli!" It was half a moan, half a gasp.

That only made Eli plow in harder and circle a hand around Justin's cock. "If you come, I'll fuck you straight through until I'm done with you."

Oh hell. Those words, Eli relentless pounding, and being jacked off pushed Justin right to the brink. Eli covered Justin's hands on the headboard with his own. Lips pressed against Justin's shoulder then Eli bit down, digging into muscle. Heat like hot coals coated with silk and wine flared down Justin's back and he tumbled into bliss and agony, screaming all the way down. Everything went white.

How long the orgasm lasted, he couldn't tell, but Eli held true to his promise and fucked him mercilessly the entire time until he, too, came, his shout long and loud.

Justin lost his grip on the headboard, landing against pillows and mattress and sheets, Eli heavy on top, breath shaken and hard.

"Holy fuck."

Not Justin's words. He tried to push up but couldn't manage to stop trembling long enough to get his arms under him.

Eli slid his cock free and they both groaned at the loss.

"Justin?"

Though his throat felt like sandpaper, he managed to speak. "Here." He paused. "I think."

A croaking laugh from Eli. He rolled off. "I'm not much better."

Justin finally lifted himself up on his elbow. Eli was a mess of sweat and curls and scruff and smile, and the most glorious thing Justin had seen in a long time. "You said something about pancakes?"

Eli's laughter shook the bed. "You know, that would be five, except the room's spinning. Since you caused that, I'll give you a break." He reached over the bed's edge and dropped the condom. Hopefully into a trash can.

"I'm at your mercy."

"Don't you forget it, either." Eli nudged him with his foot. "And yes, pancakes. As soon as I can move off this bed."

Justin sank back down onto the pillows. That had totally been worth it. "I can wait."

"Oh, *now* you can wait." Eli's grin lit his face. "What am I going to do with you, Justin?"

"Feed me breakfast, apparently."

Eli rose enough to grab hold of Justin's arm and pull him over into his arms. "And coffee." Eli dug his fingers into the welts in Justin's ass.

Justin twisted in his arms. *So deserved that.*

Eli relented and kissed Justin on the brow. "I am, after all, quite merciful."

"Very." Justin listened to Eli's heart and pushed away the doubt that kept creeping back into his mind. Right now was perfect.

Eli ran his hand through Justin's hair, smoothing out tangles and enjoying the slip of the silken locks against his fingers. *Justin* was in his bed. Abrasive, messy, Justin was all the things Eli should hate. But that content face, the brown scruff that didn't match the blue-black of his hair, those cheekbones as sharp as knives—he'd never wanted a man more. Even after the lust had been satisfied. This... closeness. He wanted more. Beyond work, beyond play.

Favorite flavor of ice cream. Best album. Comfort movie. Eli shifted. "I should make us coffee. Feed Lavi."

"Coffee would be good." Justin sat up and scrubbed his face. "Mind me catching a shower?"

"Not at all." The grin came naturally. "Do you some good."

"And whose fault is it that I'm covered in sweat?"

A little more than just sweat. Eli pulled him close. "Are you complaining?" His lips hovered over Justin's, heart tumbling when Justin smiled.

"Not at all." Justin brushed his mouth, and that was all Eli needed to deepen the kiss and steal Justin's breath the same way Justin stole Eli's. When Justin moaned, Eli relented. "Towels are in the hall closet."

Justin's shaky exhale was delightful. "Want to join me?"

So tempting, but they had time. No need to rush. "There are things I want to do to you later. Breakfast first."

Justin's eyes were so blue and so full of desire. "I can wait."

"Good." Eli climbed out of bed and headed for the closet to find a pair of shorts. "No jacking off."

"I'd rather you do that to me."

"Damn straight."

When Eli returned, Justin was sitting on the edge of the bed, and his gaze slipped down Eli's body—and stopped.

Shame and embarrassment tightened Eli's throat. This is why he hated being naked in front of anyone else.

Justin looked up and paled. "I'm sorry. I shouldn't have..."

Eli waved the words away, but didn't put anything in their place. Couldn't without giving away too much of his pain. He took a long breath and pushed that down deep, where it belonged. Finally words came. "Don't worry about it."

Justin gripped the edge of the bed. "Um, my backpack is still in your car."

So it was. "I can get it for you."

"If you wouldn't mind." Shyness there. Trepidation.

Stupid leg fucked everything up. Eli closed the distance, drew Justin off the bed and into his arms to chase away the ghosts and the worry. "I don't mind."

Justin relaxed. "Maybe I should make the coffee? I do know a thing or two about brewing a cup..." He pulled back. "Assuming you have decent coffee and not some store-bought shit."

Now there was the Justin he knew and lo—shit. Eli stepped away. "Brat."

"Barista, thank you very much."

Eli snorted to cover the sudden uptick in his heart. "Not anymore."

"Once a barista..." Justin's smirk was exactly the kind Eli loved to flog away.

Later, perhaps. "Whole beans from Commonplace Coffee. There's a drip maker, but I usually use a French press."

Justin nodded, seriousness wiping away the snark. "I can work with that."

"Let me grab a t-shirt and I'll get your backpack." After all the years of modest dress being pounded into his head, going outside shirtless was a bit too much. Shorts were hard, but he could manage that. He grabbed the top shirt off a pile in his closet and put it on. Might be cold, given the time of year, but he didn't feel as naked.

Justin was entirely naked and in Eli's hallway. "Hey, is this a chin-up bar?"

Eli stepped into the hall in time to see Justin grab the bar and execute a well-formed pull-up. The muscles of his back rippled and highlighted the bruises and welts there.

Justin hissed and dropped to the floor. "I forgot." He rolled his shoulders and stretched his neck.

"Your back will remind you."

Justin laughed. "And my ass. And whatever other part you beat."

Eli nodded to the stairs. "Coffee. I'll get your bag."

"No hints?" Disappointment there.

"If you want, open the door to your left."

He did and reddened, his dick twitching. "Holy shit!"

The playroom wasn't huge, but it did have quite the collection of floggers and whips and canes hanging on the wall. "If you're good, I'll let you do more than look."

Justin swallowed and shut the door. "I make very good coffee."

"You'd better." With that, Eli gripped the railing and headed downstairs. He was already falling for Justin; no need to *actually* do a header down the stairs.

Coffee did nothing to ease the apprehension rising in Justin. He sipped at the cup he'd brewed and stared at the photos above Eli's mantel. He recognized two from Jerusalem. One a long shot of the city with the Dome of the Rock prominent, while the other had to be of the Western Wall—a close-up of large stone blocks with tiny pieces of paper shoved in between the cracks. Prayers to God.

Had Eli left one of those slips? Was he even religious? How much had the trip cost?

Francis had been very well traveled.

Justin's back ached from the shower, but his limbs were languid from the marathon of sex he and Eli had been having.

Lovers. Eli wanted to be more than just a Dom. And that playroom? It promised even more pleasure and mind-blowing orgasms. He should have been ecstatic, but the prickling in the back of his brain had started. Didn't matter that Eli was amazing in bed and considerate out of it.

He scratched his neck. Doms lied to get what they wanted. And everything about this house screamed the differences between Eli and him, and it was the same gulf that had existed between Justin and Francis.

Money.

For fuck's sake, even the *coffee* was decadent. Justin knew what these beans cost per pound. Sure, it was an excellent cup, but not anything he would *ever* have as a daily brew. Eli? There wasn't any other coffee in the house. The kitchen was bigger than his apartment, and it sported shiny stainless steel appliances and granite countertops. The stove was restaurant-grade. Everything in the cupboards and fridge was top-shelf, from the crackers to the freaking organic, hand-pressed orange juice. Sparkling, too, like the bathroom had been. Which meant a cleaning service, since it wasn't Eli on his knees scrubbing the floor or the tiles in the bathroom.

Francis's apartment hadn't been this big, but it had been as spotless and as full of all the luxuries Justin could have wanted, save the one he needed.

Freedom.

He would not be drawn into that trap again. Schoolwork was as good an excuse as any to get the hell out of here. Last thing he wanted to be was the happy little submissive for another rich guy. Been there, done that. Didn't have the t-shirt because whores didn't get to own anything.

He liked being a sub. Loved the flogging and the sex and obeying, within *reason*. For guys like Eli and Francis, reason came down to gold watches and money in the billfold. Chains made from gifts and presents. He wouldn't be locked up again.

The creaking of the stairs signaled Eli's arrival. Justin took another sip of coffee to fortify him and faced Eli.

Eli wore *jeans* and a dark green sweater that clung to every inch of his tall, slender frame. Justin gripped his mug tighter. Entirely unfair that Eli was even hotter when dressed casually.

Uncertainty in Eli's expression. He stopped at the bottom of the stairs, hand on the banister. "Are you all right?"

No, he wasn't. How could he want someone so wrong for him this much? "Just... catching my breath."

A gentle smile, as if Eli had heard the lie. Limp apparent in each careful step, he entered the room. "It's okay. I understand."

No, you don't. Not when you buy coffee at thirty bucks a

pound. Justin studied the photos above the mantel. "Did you take those?"

Eli stood next to him. Too close. Not close enough. "Yes, a couple years ago. I needed to go and see." Eli stared at the photos. Pride and sadness marred his expression. "I don't have the easiest relationship with my heritage." He folded his hands behind his back.

So many things in this room spoke of Judaism. The photos. The menorah. A silver cup with obvious religious symbols on it. Sure, there were other objects that didn't. A small bear on a bookshelf, a cat sculpture, a rainbow mug, but everywhere Justin turned, there were hints of Eli's background. Hebrew lettering. A Star of David.

That set this house apart from Francis's. So different from Justin's stark, undecorated apartment, too. All his mementoes were gone, shoved into a storage locker by Francis. Even his diploma. Probably sold off as abandoned property by now. "I don't have much of a heritage at all."

Eli shifted with his whole body and Justin looked up into gray eyes. Not feigned interest, either.

"I'm a military brat from a long line of military brats. I was born in Louisiana, but we moved around so much..." Justin shrugged. "First kid not to go into the service."

"That's a heritage, too."

So much compassion. Unusual for a Dom, even more so for a wealthy one. Justin retreated to the kitchen because he couldn't take any more of Eli's understanding. "I guess." He finished his coffee and put the mug down on the expensive countertop. "It's nothing special." He paced to the breakfast bar and sat on one of the stools.

"Neither is mine. It just—shaped my past." Eli pulled a mug—another pride one—from a cabinet and poured coffee from the French press. "Would you still like breakfast? I was serious about making pancakes."

"I—" No. Yes. What *did* he want? With Eli so close, so different from the cold bastard of two months ago, it was hard to decide. "I don't know."

No count, no note of infraction, though there should have been, given the long pause. With another master, there would have been. Hell, Francis would have bent Justin over the nearest stool and spanked his ass until he cried.

Eli leaned against the kitchen counter and took a swallow of coffee. "Justin, would you like me to drive you home?"

"No." That came out without thought. "I'm not ready to leave yet."

"But you're not sure you should stay."

Was he so obvious? He didn't need to be played, least of all by Eli. "I guess the morning after is old hat to you."

"Hell no." Eli didn't move. "I've woken up next to three guys in my life." He paused. "You're number three."

Good thing Justin was sitting, because that would have taken his legs out. He grabbed on to the edge of the bar to steady himself. "What? How is that even possible?"

Eli set his cup down and hoisted himself up on the counter. "Simple. I either go home after we play, or he goes home after we play."

"I think I need more coffee." Justin retrieved the last of the coffee from the press. "Why? I mean, if you're dominating and fucking the guys, why not take them home?" That's what Francis had expected, for Justin to be available around the clock. That had meant living with the fucker, basically.

Eli picked his coffee up and sipped. "The whole

Dom/sub thing is easier when there are no complications. And I'm... a bit complicated."

No shit, Sherlock. Justin's brain spun trying to piece all the bits together. Everything Eli said—as odd as it was— made things safer. "But *why* me?"

Eli glanced away then refocused on Justin. "Because you remind me that I'm not alone in the world. That I don't want to be alone, despite what I tell myself."

Oh. "Definitely need more coffee." That made his heart full and heavy. Thrilling. Terrifying. A vulnerable Dom was kind of like a unicorn.

"My offer for pancakes still stands."

All things considered, that might be what he needed. "You make food. I'll make more coffee."

Eli slid off the counter, landing on his good foot. "Staying?"

"Yeah." Whatever the hell this was, it wasn't the path Justin's hookups usually took. That meant there was hope that it wouldn't end like Francis.

Complicated, indeed.

CHAPTER TEN

SUCH A STRANGE AND TENUOUS BEGINNING. ELI poured batter on the griddle and watched it bubble then solidify. He couldn't blame Justin for being hesitant—he was. But he couldn't run from his own house. Or his feelings. When the sheen on the batter turned matte, Eli flipped the pancakes.

I like this. Too much. Liked the normalcy of breakfast, though there was nothing normal about Justin standing in his kitchen on a Saturday. The fear that had caught him last night surfaced—then submerged. Monsters didn't make pancakes.

Somehow they would manage. Work. Play. A relationship.

He turned the cakes onto a serving plate and repeated the task. The coffee grinder ran and the scent of fresh grounds filtered through the aroma of cooking batter.

A typical morning, except it was anything but. "How did you end up as a barista?"

Justin tapped the grounds from the grinder into the French press. "I like coffee and I needed a change of pace.

When I got to Pittsburgh, I checked Craigslist for jobs, and Brian was hiring." He gave a small shrug. "I suppose I made a good impression."

"With the goth look?" It certainly was eye-catching, if messy. *You're starting to like messy.* Eli slid the last of the cooked pancakes onto the serving plate. There was charisma, nearly as much as Sam had, when Justin wanted to turn it on.

"Not a fan?" Justin set the electric kettle to heat the water and leaned against the counter, all smirk and black fringe. Still had the chipped nail polish, too, but the eyeliner was gone, washed away with tears, sweat, and a shower.

"I didn't say that." Eli carried the plate over to the breakfast bar. "You're in my kitchen, after all."

Justin laughed, but there was a catch to it. "There is that."

He'd hit a nerve. "I don't imagine you were sporting that look working at ErazaTech, though." He hobbled to the fridge and pulled out butter and maple syrup.

The kettle clicked off and Justin poured the water into the press. "No. I got tired of being told how I should look, what I should wear, who I should be. I wanted..." He shook his head and pressed the knob on the press down. "The change was a reaction, I know. But this"—he gestured at his face—"is more me than I was in LA. I'm glad Sam hasn't asked me to change."

"I won't, either." The thought of a neater, boring version of Justin rankled, and no one should be forced into a role they didn't want to play. He'd left home to be the man he wanted to be. Cut his hair. Shaved his beard. Loved men.

Eli placed the butter and syrup by the pancakes.

Coffee and mug in hand, Justin joined Eli at the

breakfast bar. "Good. I..." He laughed. "You aren't keeping count anymore, are you?"

Unfinished sentences. He actually *had* kept count. "I've noticed, but this is not the time for that game." As Justin poured the coffee, Eli added, "I'm not sure you want that full-time."

A shiver ran through Justin. "I don't."

"Good, because I'm not the Dom for that."

Every muscle in Justin loosened as he sat on the bar stool. "Thank God."

"Been there, done that?" Was there a story there?

Justin winced and took the butter. "I don't like being controlled all the time. Didn't work in LA, like I said. One of the reasons I like working for Sam."

Eli took the syrup. "Sam is rather accepting." Part of why he'd agreed to work for him when Michael had suggested it. Sam wouldn't blink at Eli's predilections. Not when Sam was dating Michael.

"So I've noticed." Justin pushed the butter over. "You keep syrup in the fridge?"

Eli shrugged. "Read the label. Besides, I don't go through it that fast."

"I guess pancakes for one *is* a lot of work." Justin's eyes were bright. "You really haven't done this for anyone else?"

"No."

"Not even the other two?"

The ones he'd spent the night with. "No. Noah was—well, we were teens and hiding the whole thing from our parents. With Michael, we were undergrads and—"

"Michael?" Justin's fork hung in the air. "Wait, Sam's Michael?"

Right. He hadn't said that before. "Yes."

"You dated *Sam's* Michael?" Justin set down the fork, a horrified look widening his eyes.

Eli cut his pancakes with his fork and tried not to smile. Probably failed. "As I said, we were undergrads. The relationship didn't last long, but the friendship did."

"But he's a Dom."

"That was the main reasons we split, yes. But I wouldn't have known I was as well without his help."

Justin reached for his coffee. "And now you work for his boyfriend."

"Yup." He ate around the grin that wanted to spread across his face. "And I don't have to worry about being fired for being gay *and* a sexual deviant."

"You were fired?" Justin took a gulp of coffee. "I guess from the outside, the whole BDSM thing seems a little weird."

A little? "I tie men up, whip them, and fuck them." Eli took another bite and watched Justin squirm in his seat. So very lovely when he moved like that. "Not exactly a normal hobby."

There was the understanding. "Certainly not in the same class as macramé."

Eli laughed. "No, not at all."

Justin smiled into his coffee. "Speaking of rope... ?" He raised his head and peered through the ragged locks in front of his eyes.

A rush of desire and the heat of joy wrapped itself around Eli, burning his blood. "Is that what you'd like for lunch?"

"Yes."

Oh, the turn of Justin's lips, the spark in his eyes, and flush in his cheeks. Delectable and a welcome change from the start of this conversation. "Finish your breakfast and help me with dishes, and we'll see whether you get what you want."

"Yes, Eli."

How he loved the sound of those two words together. Eli inhaled the dark scent of coffee. "Perhaps we can do something about the collar I stripped off you last night?"

Justin's shiver was visible. "I'd like that."

Eli took a sip of coffee and sent up a silent prayer that Justin was telling the truth. "Good."

FOR ONCE, JUSTIN WELCOMED WEALTH. THE LEATHER Eli wrapped tight around Justin's neck was soft and supple, like one of his gloves. A shower of sparks trickled over Justin's skin as Eli buckled the collar into place.

He hadn't expected Eli to pull leather and tools out of a drawer in his playroom and make a collar for him right there. So personal, so... exacting. *God.* His balls ached with the need to be naked and kneeling while Eli fitted the band of leather to his neck.

Bliss followed by terror. Francis had made him kneel like this once, and to receive a collar as well. But nothing else about this day and that one was similar, not the care Eli took with cutting the leather or his gentle questions of comfort and fit. Eli loosened the band, drew back, and picked up a hole punch. "It'll likely stretch over time. Let me know if it becomes too loose, and we can add some holes later."

Justin swallowed. That implied a long length of time, rather than a fling. Something he wanted, and didn't. He dug his fingers into his thighs to keep from balling them into fists.

Eli cupped Justin's chin and lifted it until their eyes met. "You can say no to this. You can always say no, Justin."

"I don't want to say no." This was Eli and not Francis. This was Pittsburgh and not LA. Eli wasn't asking him to pull his entire life apart to become a pet.

He set the collar aside. "You have to be sure of this."

That... wouldn't happen. Not yet. But fake it until you make it. "You said you weren't a full-time Dom."

"I'm not," Eli murmured, fingers skimming Justin's chin. "I don't expect you to wear my collar all the time. There's no lock. You're free to remove it when you wish."

"Then I'm sure."

Eli stroked Justin's skin and raised an eyebrow. "No lies." Gone were the casual clothes of the morning. Eli had changed back into leather pants and a crisp white shirt.

Justin let out a huff of air. "Okay. I'm nervous, but I want to try this with you. It helps that I can..." Leave. Be free. "Choose."

Eli's forehead furrowed for a moment before smoothing out. "I do expect it on during scenes."

Of course. "Not an issue." It was outside, in life, where the problem lay.

Eli ran his thumb over Justin's jawbone. "Then let's see how it fits." Eli picked up the collar and placed it around Justin's neck.

Smooth. Soft. Tight. A touch tighter while Eli buckled it into place, but then it fit perfectly. Constraining enough that there was no mistaking what it was, but not so tight as to block air, not even when Eli slipped a finger under the band. A cascade of pinpricks swept down Justin's back to the soles of his feet.

"Better?"

Justin swallowed, which only tightened the band and

sent another tumble of electricity to his toes. "Yeah." It was, too. Now that the leather was in place, the constriction was just right. Perfect. His body responded as it always did, cock hard, the need for pain and pleasure swirling in his head, blotting out stray thoughts and warning bells.

"Ready for more?"

Justin nodded.

Eli's smile had the sharp edge Justin associated with the sting of a whip and the crackle of command. "Stand up, please."

It was not a request, despite the wording, not with that depth of tone, nor with the tug against his collar. Justin rose and turned as Eli nudged him in the appropriate direction— toward a Saint Andrew's cross.

"Back against the cross."

He settled against the cool leather, flinching at the friction against the welts on his back. When Eli approached, he lifted his arms. "I think we'll save rope for later." With the same care he'd taken with the collar, Eli buckled Justin's wrists into the cuffs at either end of the cross and adjusted the straps to keep Justin's arms firmly in place.

Eli placed his hand against Justin's chest, the contact of flesh on flesh sending little shocks of up Justin's arms.

"How does that feel?" Eli's breath caressed Justin's skin and lips. So close. Too far.

"Like heaven." The stretch, the restraint had him not into subspace, but in that narrow band between anticipation and utter frustration.

Then Eli kissed him, taking his mouth not with force but with a demand of submission that had Justin moaning around Eli's tongue. The last vestiges of nervousness fled and he filled with the need to give whatever was desired. Eli trailed his hands down Justin's arms, brushing over the hair and tender flesh of the pits. Ice and fire up danced up Justin and he twitched and whimpered. Eli broke the kiss, but didn't move away. "Ticklish?" He stroked those same spots again.

Very ticklish. Justin danced in the restraints, nearly kicking out. "Please, no. I can't."

Eli flicked fingers over the sensitive skin once more. Justin fought against the cuffs, thrusting hard against Eli's body. It took all his control to suck in a breath of air. He wanted to get away, but he didn't want Eli to stop. This torment didn't have the bite of a whip, but a dazzling pain all of its own.

Eli moved his hands to Justin's hips, ground his cock against Justin's, and stole what little breath Justin had left with another quick kiss. "That will be fun later, but first let's deal with those twitchy legs of yours."

The heat of Eli's body vanished when Eli stepped back. The pull of his brow was one Justin recognized from the office—hard determination.

Eli knelt. First down on his good leg, then onto the bad one. If Justin hadn't been strapped to the cross, he would have joined Eli on the floor. The sight of Eli kneeling, even to fetter Justin, was stunning.

Eli peered up and Justin shivered. The devil resided in that turn of the lips. *So hot.*

"Hope you're flexible. I want you spread wide." Eli grasped Justin's leg and pulled it over to the cuff and buckled it around his ankle.

Holy shit. Justin hadn't considered just how far apart the arms of the cross were. "What if I can't..." That thought disappeared when Eli grasped his other ankle and dragged it over. Justin flattened his head against the cross. The pull in his thighs wasn't unbearable, and he'd been spread-eagle before, but Eli forcing his legs apart and buckling leather around his ankles flatlined his brain and made his balls draw up. Didn't help that Eli's breath warmed his calf. A caress of hands up his legs only poured more heat into every vein.

"Perfect," Eli murmured. He nipped at Justin's thigh.

This was far worse than the tickling. He shook against the cross as Eli worked up Justin's thigh. He sucked on his balls, one after the other. Justin's curses mixed with moans and poured out in a stream he couldn't stem.

Francis had never knelt, never touched him like this. Subs knelt, not Doms—that's what he'd said.

Eli might have been on his knees, but there was nothing submissive about the way he licked Justin's taint and balls.

Fuck, he wasn't going to—

The neighborhood probably heard his shout when Eli's mouth closed over the tip of Justin's cock. He banged his head against the back of the cross and stretched his bonds to the limit.

Eli took him deeper. Fucking Eli, who wasn't playing by the rules, who shouldn't have been on his knees. This was torment. Absolute, wonderful torment. Eli hit every sensitive spot with a tongue that should have been illegal.

When Justin tried to find purchase to thrust deeper, Eli pushed Justin's thighs back against the cross—and teased his cock head until Justin couldn't see straight.

"God, please..." A whisper because Justin could not catch enough breath.

Eli relented, pulling off Justin. "Not just yet, I think."

So close... He'd been so very close. "You learn cocksucking from Michael?"

Eli's laugh was deep. He pulled himself up and only a

flicker of discomfort marred his features. "Yes, actually. And so much more, too." No smile, but the crinkle around his eyes hinted at amusement and power.

Justin pulled against his bonds instinctively. He couldn't imagine Eli submitting to anyone, even after watching him kneel. "Like what?"

"Like how to torment a man without touching him." Eli smiled. "How to cause agony with only a gentle touch. How to make a man beg for everything I want to do to him."

Holy fuck. Just those words made his skin tighten from his fingers to toes, and his heart tick faster.

Eli's gloves lay on a table nearby, as did one of his canes, this one with a simple brass knob top. He stepped back, picked up one glove, and slid his long fingers into the leather.

Justin squirmed. Would Eli touch him? With what? One of the toys hanging from hooks behind him?

Eli picked up the other glove and donned it, all the while studying Justin. He might as well have been sucking Justin's dick, the way his balls ached. He rocked his hips forward, thrusting his cock against nothing at all.

A click of the tongue. "You know better, Justin."

He did, but watching Eli watch him, want him—it was torture. Just as Eli had said it would be.

Eli chuckled and turned away, providing a respite from that intense inspection. Justin's relief was short-lived. Eli's leather-clad fingers closed around the shaft of his cane and his gray eyes focused on Justin again. That smile—

Shit. The grin only widened. As if Justin's heart wasn't beating fast enough. What the hell would Eli do?

"I think it's time I got to know you a bit better, don't you?" Eli stepped closer, not using the cane for support but holding it by the shaft.

"I... don't know, Eli." Dry mouth. Sticky throat. This was not a game he knew or understood. He'd expected pain. Nipple clamps, a flogger. *That* cane wasn't the type used for punishment.

"All I want you to do is answer my questions. They'll be simple ones. Small things. No right or wrong answers. You can even refuse to answer, but you will respond. Is that understood?"

Easy enough. But with Eli so close Justin couldn't help tense against the cross. "Understood."

"Good." Eli stroked Justin's collarbone with his fingers and ran the palm of his gloved hand over Justin's pec.

The sensation of body-warmed leather sliding over Justin's skin and against his nipple curled Justin's toes. Goose bumps rose everywhere and he groaned.

"... color?" He barely caught the end of Eli's question.

"What?"

"Five," Eli said. "Pay attention, please. I have a wicked little carbon fiber cane I'd *love* to use on you."

Shit. He'd seen subs caned with those. Yet the prospect of experiencing that much pain tightened Justin's balls. "I'm sorry. I'll do better."

This time, Eli touched his thigh and drew his fingers up the front. "I'm sure you will. Let's try again." This time Eli smoothed his hand over Justin's abdomen, drifting perilously close to his cock.

He caught Eli's smirk. "What's your favorite color?"

A simple question. If only Eli weren't caressing his balls, maybe he could have remembered the answer.

"Don't make me say *six* so soon, Justin."

Right. He turned his focus away from the touch of warm, smooth leather cupping his ass. "Yellow." A gasp of breath.

"Such a bright color for someone who wears black so often." Eli ran a finger between Justin's ass cheeks before stepping back. "Why?"

Thank God. Justin relaxed—as much as the fetters and the cross allowed. "It's... sunshine. Lemons. Happi—" The last word dissolved into a gasp. The brass handle of Eli's cane—the *cold* brass handle—touched the inside of Justin's left thigh.

"You were saying?"

Justin screwed his eyes shut as Eli drew the handle up until it hovered close to his balls. "Happiness. Summer. Yellow is"—he opened his eyes—"the color of joy."

Eli nodded. "Very good." The cane didn't move. "Favorite vacation spot?"

Pretty sure he knew where the brass knob was heading next. He sucked in a breath when the cold metal lifted his balls. "Fuck!" He squirmed against the cross and cuffs—and Eli's cane.

"Six." Eli rubbed the knob back and forth, sounding far too pleased. "You're disappointing me, Justin. Focus."

How could he when his brain wanted to crawl out of his ears? Justin tried not to thrust in time to the slow motion of cool brass between his legs. "Beach. I like... the beach."

The cane didn't move away. Eli added a little pressure. Justin closed his eyes and moaned.

"Which one, Justin?"

"Any. All." The knob moved farther back. No way it could enter him from that angle, but the thought had him rocking his hips forward.

Eli tutted, but kept the cane in motion. "Words, Justin."

He couldn't form sounds let alone piece them into syllables, not with the end of Eli's cane sliding so close to his hole. But if he didn't say something, he knew a number would be the next thing from Eli. "Love the ocean. Sounds of waves. Gulls. Sun." The smell of sunscreen. The shirtless skin. "Doesn't matter where."

Finally Eli pulled the cane away. The absence was as painful as the presence had been. Every inch of skin tingled and the welts on his back throbbed. Probably because he kept dancing against the leather of the cross, fighting his bonds. His vision swam and sharpened. "That was intense."

Not a chuckle or a laugh, but an inhale of breath. "Did you think we were done?"

Oh fuck. Justin's blood boiled into a fury of daggers and pins. A whipping would be relief—a known pain, a familiar agony. This had him on every edge, and the high he chased was so unlike subspace. Still, he surrendered to it, crying out when cool metal touched his side.

"Now"—Eli rolled the cane upward—"favorite ice cream flavor?"

So, so unfair, this game. He fought to get his brain to work. "Mint chocolate chip."

"Nicely done." Eli stepped in a bit. "Very nicely done." As the cane hit his ticklish spot on one side, Eli caressed the opposite side.

Sparks danced in Justin's vision, a wordless cry falling from his lips. He tried to find some friction for his cock, but there was nothing. Eli was everywhere except where Justin most wanted.

On and on the questions came. He answered as best he could, in between begging Eli to stop, to continue, to fuck him. At long last—or maybe just minutes later—Eli stepped back. Justin sagged against the cross, heart hammering in his chest, lungs burning for air, and let the cuffs hold him up. A thin thread of pride wound through Justin's ache for release—Eli was breathing as rapidly and a flush had drifted up his neck from underneath his nice white shirt.

Eli closed in, but this time the brass knob touched Justin's cheek. "Very well done." Eli's words were soft as velvet and as rich. Combined with the cool touch of the cane, Justin couldn't help the tremble of delight.

Pain and pleasure. Both giving and taking. This—this he loved. Flustering Eli and giving him what he needed. Justin met those gray eyes and smiled.

The cane's knob touched Justin's lips and he opened, kissing it as if it were tip of Eli's cock.

Same effect, too. Eli's breath hitched and the moan that sounded between them wasn't Justin's.

Only one response to that—he went down on the head of the cane. Hard, metallic, warmed with his own heat, wet with saliva, sucking on the cane was oddly exciting. But it was Eli's wide eyes and hungry look that sent pinpricks of heat and ice through Justin.

Got you.

WATCHING JUSTIN FELLATE THE HEAD OF HIS CANE while bound to his a cross was something out of a dream. A very filthy dream. It flipped Eli's head inside out—itching his skull and stealing his breath. He nearly dropped the damned thing.

Instead, he worked it in and out of Justin's mouth, same way he would a dildo or plug. Justin's lips around brass were hotter than hell. Might as well have been Eli's cock, the way it made his balls draw up and his heart hammer. The knob was no larger than any of the toys. He had several that were thicker—but this was his *cane*. All of his canes were personal. Needed. A part of who he was every day. He'd never used one for play before, but it had seemed so perfect a tool. He'd kept his other partners at arm's length, away from the man he was outside of the leather and the whips. Using his walking canes for play was out of the question. It crossed a line.

Not with Justin, though. Heart racing, head pounding. Everything was personal. And here they were. Eli drew the cane away from Justin's mouth.

Swollen lips, flushed skin. Justin ran a tongue over his upper lip. "Gonna fuck me with it, too?"

Slide the head of his cane inside Justin? *Holy* fuck. He felt the heady trip of losing control, same as he had at the party—was it only *last night?*

He stepped back and turned away from Justin, more to compose himself than anything else. "Perhaps, perhaps not. I haven't decided." He studied the wall of toys with unfocused eyes. A condom and lube—yes. It could be done safely. Didn't mean he should. "So many lovely *options.*"

The creak of skin shifting on leather floated through the room. Justin squirming against the cross. At this point, it wouldn't take much to get Justin off given his arousal—hell, a few strokes and Eli would come. He studied his cane. When would he find such a perfectly deviant partner again?

Partner. There was the tumbling in his head, the sense of utter rightness. Yes, he'd fallen. Hard. He set the cane aside and turned back to Justin. "You're just going to have to wait and see what I've chosen."

Beautiful, flushed body, trembling in need. Want. Pain. Eli's pulse thudded in his ears. He'd brought Justin to this. Now it was time to take him higher—all the way. Wring as much pleasure from Justin as he could.

He had to kneel to release Justin's ankle, but as aroused as he was, the pain of his leg paled to the ache in his balls, cock, and head. He rose and freed Justin's arms, half holding, half guiding him to the sawhorse and bending him over its leather-padded length leaving enough room that he could take Justin's cock in hand, should he desire.

Which he did, but not yet. Justin in a torment of need drove Eli to his own high. How long could he keep Justin on edge, keep him in agony?

Well, he'd find that out, wouldn't he? He fetched the cane, a condom, and lube.

Ripping the foil open caused Justin to slide against the leather, probably seeking relief for his aching cock. Eli snapped the back of his hand against both ass cheeks. "Behave if you want to be fucked. I'd be more than happy to add stripes instead."

Justin settled. "Anything... just..." The words dissolved into an exhale that was mostly moan.

Warmth tingled up Eli, straight to the back of his head. Yes. This control. He cupped his palm over Justin's ass and skimmed a finger over his hole.

Tense, trembling legs. Hitched breathing, but Justin didn't rock, didn't move against the horse. *Good.*

"Look at you, so hungry, so eager. A finger? My cock? A toy?" He leaned closer and touched the brass head against Justin's side. "My cane?"

A flinch, but Justin stilled himself. "Cane, please, Eli."

Dirty, filthy Justin. So *perfect*. Eli finished opening the foil and rolled the condom over the head of the cane. Lube next.

Justin hissed when the liquid hit his ass and gasped when Eli worked it into his hole. Eli wasn't sure who was breathing harder, him or Justin. The leather of his gloved fingers stood out in sharp contrast to the pale and ruddy striped flesh and the heat—even through the gloves—was incredible. Slow strokes, enough to loosen, excite, and frustrate.

Beneath him, Justin moved ever so slightly, trying to impale himself deeper, hissing when Eli pulled out.

He clicked his tongue, and that was enough. He could have taken the count to seven, but he felt Justin's desire and agony as surely as if it was his own.

Probably because it was.

More lube, both in Justin and over the cane. Eli drew the head down Justin's crack.

Justin's intake of breath was sharp. "Oh... fuck." His whole body shook.

"Something wrong?" Eli smoothed his free hand over Justin's ass before placing it on the small of Justin's back—both for comfort and control.

"No. Just—cold." Justin held still.

Good. Eli would be the one to set the rhythm, the motion. Justin wanted to be fucked and—Eli pushed the brass knob against Justin's entrance—he would be. Soundly, too. The head slipped in—slowly and easily as Justin bowed his head and pressed back. Brass vanished into flesh, stretching Justin wide.

"Fuck." Eli's voice was a whisper—but yes. He'd been the one to speak.

Tension left Justin and he crumpled against the sawhorse. "Oh God—that feels..."

Whatever Justin had to say devolved into a moan as Eli slid the cane farther in and pulled it out before plunging it back in, more quickly this time.

Justin shook beneath Eli's hand. Part tremble, part moan, all lust.

"You should see yourself. So desperate."

No reply, though Justin rocked back, taking the head deeper.

Well, then. A few more slow strokes—smooth and deep enough to elicit a grunt from Justin—and then he increased the tempo and shifted the angle.

Justin arched, gaping—and thrust back. "Oh God! Don't stop. Don't..."

Eli's cock might spill just from the sight. Taut muscles, flushed skin still bruised and red from whipping, midnight-black hair. Eli grabbed a handful and yanked back. "This what you wanted?"

Justin's mouth opened in wordless pleasure, his fingers indenting the leather padding of the sawhorse. So beautiful. This moment was *theirs*. He'd not do this to another.

Justin whimpered. Plunging the cane forward became much more difficult.

Close. Very close. "Not yet."

"Please," Justin whispered.

"No." He loved seeing Justin like this, struggling to obey and entirely in Eli's control. He fucked Justin with short, sharp thrusts, until Justin gasped with each one, until moisture formed at the corners of Justin's eyes.

There—the knife's edge. Pleasure and pain. "Come."

Justin's cry sent a shock of lightning through Eli and he moaned, too. Trembled as Justin shuddered on the horse and spilled onto the floor. Every bit of Eli burned and the only way to quench the fire would be in Justin. But—

Eli loosened his grip on Justin's hair and slowly drew the cane out, careful not to lose the condom.

Utterly spent, Justin sagged against the horse. "Holy fuck, Eli."

He ran his hand over Justin's shaking body. "I'll be right

back." He dropped the cane back onto the table and hurried back, pulled Justin up and into his arms.

Clear blue eyes. Huge pupils. "That was—that..." Justin slurred his words. "Need to do that again."

"Mmm-hmm. Let's get you into bed."

Justin didn't object. Eli helped him down the hall and poured him into bed and kissed him. Justin responded, curling fingers around Eli's shirt. It took several tries to break the kiss—not that Eli wanted to. "I need"—he claimed another taste of Justin—"to clean things up."

A soft moan before Justin let go.

So hard to leave Justin curled in the bed. Eli limped back to the playroom and tidied up all the things that couldn't wait—the floor and the used condom—and left everything else. The gloves came off in the hall, his shirt by the bedroom door, and everything else by the foot of the bed. Then he was on the sheets and tangled into Justin's arms.

"You haven't—" Justin pressed his hip against Eli's hard shaft, a slur in his words.

"I can wait. Rest." Sex with Justin now would be all take. Not his thing.

Justin nestled in close, tucking under Eli's chin. "You immune to blue balls?"

"No." He smoothed his hand over Justin's hair. "I just have a lot of patience and control."

Justin's short laugh shook them both. "Lucky me."

"Lucky me, too." He pressed a kiss to Justin's forehead. "You can thank Michael."

Justin opened a bit of space. "You were actually his *sub*?"

"No, not really." He traced the edge of Justin's face, those sharp cheekbones. "That was the problem. The more

he exerted control, the more I found ways to circumvent it."
Eli shrugged. "Michael loves orgasm denial."

Justin let out a breath. "Wow."

"I loved frustrating Michael—pretty much how I figured
out I was a Dom."

"So you learned patience and control to out-Dom a
Dom?"

His turn to laugh. "Exactly." He paused. "And I always
won."

Silence. Then Justin spoke. "Monday's gonna be
weird."

No doubt about that. Eli slid his hand against Justin's
neck and pulled him close. "We'll manage." They still had
some time to kill before they had to worry about that. And
while Eli had patience, he also knew exactly what he
wanted.

Every bit of Justin's pleasure, again and again. His
moans and screams and pleas. Every inch of Justin alive
with need. That was well worth the wait.

CHAPTER ELEVEN

As walks of shame went, this one was a bit different. It wasn't *shame* that filled Justin but a rolling ball of exhilaration mixed with a hefty dose of fear and apprehension. He peered up into the gray October sky—the same color as Eli's eyes—and blew out a foggy breath as he walked beside Eli. The air had chilled since Saturday and cold seeped into Justin's already aching bones. On Friday he and Eli had cemented a friendship. By this morning they had fucked so many times it was a wonder they both could move.

It had been like this with Francis, too—a weekend of carnal pleasure—only Francis didn't work and had been furious when Justin had left on Monday. *I can give you everything you need. Quit that shit job.* He was wearing one of Eli's t-shirts because he hadn't intended two nights away. Eli had offered a sweater, but they all smelled too much of Eli—felt like him.

Right now, Justin needed to be himself. He shivered and pulled his jacket tighter around his neck.

The movement must have caught Eli's attention. "Are you okay?"

Long wool coat. Tailored suit. Silk tie. Rolex watch, and that cane. The same one that had been inside Justin. A little electric shock zipped up to his brain. Money. Power. Dominance. Just like Francis.

"I don't know. I'm..." He shrugged. The leather collar was tucked away in his backpack. True to his word, Eli hadn't stopped Justin from removing it, as if Justin casting off submission was a normal, everyday thing. He didn't trust that. "...thinking, I guess."

Hard to read Eli's expression. "I understand that."

No idea what churned in Eli's head. Maybe that was part of the attraction—the unknown and surprising. Like the tender way Eli had made love in the morning, raining kisses on Justin's body and moving slowly inside Justin until all he knew was Eli's touch and taste and a pleasure he hadn't thought could come from such gentleness. Too used to fast and furious fucking, to the pain of whip and cane.

He shivered again. Which was Eli's true face? Justin didn't know.

Again, Eli glanced over but didn't speak.

They came to the dual doors that lead to Grounds N'at and S. R. Anderson Consulting. All that was left was to climb those stairs together. Except... they never arrived at the same time. Sam would *know*. The party was one thing. Spending the rest of the weekend at Eli's had been something else.

"I'm gonna grab a coffee."

Eli paused by the door. "Okay. I'll see you upstairs." His smile was faint, tinged with tension that could have been worry or anger. No way to know.

Justin pulled open the door to Grounds N'at and

breathed in a lungful of brewing coffee. Brian stood behind the counter. "Dude! How's it going?"

He answered Brian's smile with one of his own. "It's Monday and it's cold. Figured I'd grab a cup before..." He nodded upward.

"Pittsburgh for you. One minute warm, the next freezing." Brian gestured at the machines. "Mind making your own? I gotta catch up on dishes."

All the invitation Justin needed. He set his backpack down and got to work. The perfect antidote to Eli—or so he thought until he ground his favorite blend. The sound and smell took him back to Eli's kitchen. *Fuck.* Wasn't anything his anymore?

He'd offered to make Eli coffee. Demanded it, actually. Why was he angry?

Justin shook his head and set about finishing his cappuccino. Gave it an extra shot just to clear his head of Eli. Or maybe of Francis—who shouldn't even *be* there. He was about to ring himself up when Brian came out of the back.

"Hey, get away from that. It's on the house."

He wasn't about to argue, so he saluted Brian with the cup. "I owe you, man."

Brian waved the comment away. "Nah, you don't."

He would have argued, but the bell on the door sounded. More customers. Justin grabbed his backpack, gave Brian another wave, and headed upstairs. He took a sip on his way, savoring the taste. Not the same as Eli's, but still deep and rich, even with the milk.

Francis hadn't liked coffee.

Maybe—just maybe—he needed to let that past go. Trust that Eli wasn't a rich dude looking for a toy, that there were true emotions behind the sex, a friendship to underlay the lust. That it wasn't some dumb hope of Justin's that there was more than endorphins and orgasms and doing exactly as told for the pleasure of another.

He entered the office and glanced into Eli's office—and met Eli's smile and the warm crinkle around his eyes. Justin's heart skipped.

Yeah, maybe this time it would work. He returned the smile and sat at his desk. Maybe. Hopefully.

Please.

IT WOULD HAVE BEEN EASIER TO WORK IF ELI COULD have focused on something other than the way Justin's hair had felt against his skin or how Justin's breath had caught every time Eli had ground into him. Or the way his heart dipped whenever those blue eyes met his.

He pinched the bridge of his nose and closed his eyes. Of course that was the moment Sam chose to close Eli's door.

Except when Eli turned and looked, it wasn't Sam lounging against the wood—it was Michael. The reproach Eli had formed died in his throat.

Michael smiled with the same twist of lips he always had when he'd beaten Eli at his own game. That had never stopped—the tiny power games they played. Most of the time, Eli welcomed them. "Oh, fuck you." He turned back to his computer.

A snort from Michael. "Nice to see you, too, Eli."

Hearing his full name made Eli swing back around. Michael had folded himself into one of the chairs at the guest table. "Why are you here?"

Michael wore his usual five-o'clock best, though the

tropical shirt had long sleeves and socks had sprouted between his feet and Dockers. Winter wear. "I wanted to see how you were." Quiet words, and personal. No masks, no games.

"I'm..." He never *had* managed to be able to lie to Michael. He stole a glance at the door, wishing for a moment he could see Justin and glad he could not. He returned his focus to Michael. "No, *why are you here?*"

Michael sat forward, elbows on knees, and leveled a long, measured stare at Eli, as if trying to peer inside. Eli knew there were cracks in his façade and Michael was one of the few who could see every single one.

"Justin White."

Like the shock from static or the first lash of a whip. Eli tightened his hands around the armrests of his chair. "What about him?"

Michael tilted his head. "I've watched you scene before and fuck men afterward. Never with that kind of intensity, with that much passion."

The floor might have fallen away, because Eli tumbled fast enough to gasp. He held on to the chair as the room shuddered. Only it was him shivering in his warm office. Passion. Yes. That, too. "He's... different from the others."

"No shit," Michael said. "You took him on as a sub, didn't you?"

Now it was too warm in the room. "No." The words were thick in his throat. "I took him on as a boyfriend."

Both of Michael's eyebrows hit his hairline. "Have you dated anyone since... ?"

"Since you? No." He was on his feet in a heartbeat, despite the protest in his leg. But he needed to move.

"E..." Michael didn't even need to finish the sentence.

"I don't know, Michael. I have no idea what I'm doing.

You know I'm shit at these sorts of things." He paced to the door, turned, and paced back. There, against the wall, was the cane he'd used to fuck Justin. And there was the spike of desire and elation at having done so. He faced Michael and waited.

And waited. Michael straightened but didn't rise. "I honestly came by to see if you were okay. Taking on a sub for more than an evening is unusual for you. But this..." He huffed a laugh. "This is a *good* thing, E."

"Is it?" He sat against his desk, not willing to give up the inches he had on Michael. Not in *his* office.

Another chuckle.

It was a strange, wonderful predicament. He relaxed and let go of the walls. "I haven't felt like this with anyone. Not since... Noah. And that was puppy love. This is richer, more expansive. I can't even describe..." His gaze strayed to the door again. "I can't get him out of my mind. He's infuriating. Brilliant. Amusing."

"Hotter than sin?"

"I don't believe in sin." Eli focused on Michael. "But yes. That, too." He paused. "I suppose people noticed."

Michael laughed. Loudly, too. "Noticed? Jesus, Eli! You *knelt* and kissed his tattoo. You *cuddled* with him on a couch, and then *you took him home*. Yes, people noticed."

Eli's cheeks burned. "We spent the rest of the weekend together."

"Good."

Good? "That's it? No comment, no quip?"

A grin—one that always warmed Eli even in friendship —graced Michael's lips. "If it makes you happy, E, it's good."

It did make him happy—giddy, even. But... "I'm not sure Justin feels the same way."

Michael's expression slipped. "What do you mean?"

"He nearly left Saturday morning. I don't know why."

Michael shrugged. "Nerves? You *are* a bit intense. Give it time."

"I know. It's just—what if it doesn't work?" Even thinking the words drilled a pit into the depth of his soul. Had he gotten attached to Justin's snark and smile so soon?

Michael studied his hands. "You've been there before."

He had, with the man who sat before him. It had *hurt*, that breakup, because there were so many things *right* about Michael. They'd settled into a good friendship, and that had allowed Eli to be there to help when Michael's world—personal and work—had fallen apart.

"I don't want to go there again." It had been bad enough with Michael. With Justin? He rubbed his eyes. "There are so many unknowns."

Michael shook his head, but the smile had returned. "Oh, Eli. That's part of the thrill."

And the terror. "I'm not in love."

Michael stood. "You've always been such a horrible liar." It took three steps for Michael to cross to the door on his long legs. "One of your best qualities." His smile was heartwarming, then he was out the door and crossing the hall to Sam's office.

In Michael's wake sat Justin. Meeting his gaze only made Eli's heart race faster. The world wobbled and tilted. Michael had been right, as usual. He really couldn't lie for shit.

CHAPTER TWELVE

Justin shut his apartment door and threw his keys onto his kitchen table. A night at home—such as it was. That had become a bit rare over the past five weeks. He'd spent quite a few nights at Eli's—it was closer to work and school. But he needed to do some laundry, balance his pitiful excuse for a bank account, and call his parents.

None of those he wanted to do in Eli's pristine house.

As usual, his mom answered the phone. "Hey, honey, how are you?" Relief colored his mother's words.

Justin winced. She always worried when he didn't call regularly. "It's only been a week, Mom." He'd even called on Thanksgiving from the party at Sam's house.

She chuckled, but it lacked humor. "I just like hearing your voice."

For so many months, not too long ago, she'd heard nothing from him at all. His fault for becoming trapped by Francis. "I know. I'm fine. School is going really well."

"Your advisor likes your work?"

"Yup. I met with Don a few days ago." He filled her in on the highlights of his classwork and the capstone... as far as he could without boring her to pieces with talk of finance and business psychology. "And working with Sam Anderson is still fantastic. I'm learning so much."

"He's not worried about your schooling, right? Or pressuring you too much? I know you enjoy the job, but…" There was the hint of mom worry. "You've done so much toward your degree. Don't leave it behind."

He'd left his last, very good job for the high of being fucked and beaten into submission. For a moment, he felt Eli's lips on his neck and Eli's voice in his ear. *This what you've been craving?* Like Francis had said.

Justin stood to shake off the memory. "Sam knew about the MBA when he hired me. There's no pressure, Mom." Not from Sam, anyway. "Don says it's great experience. I'm getting credit for it." Something *clang*ed on the other end and Justin glanced at the clock. It was just past seven… so six there. "Did I call during dinner?"

"I'm getting things ready. Mercy had a support meeting tonight. Also your father's picking up some extra hours at the shop."

Time and a half. Justin kicked at his bag. If he hadn't screwed up so royally in California, his dad wouldn't be working so hard right before retirement. "I'm sorry I'm not helping out more."

This time, the sound of running water slid behind his mother's voice. "Justin," she said in a sweet and gentle tone he didn't deserve, "you help out more than enough as it is. Moving to Pittsburgh, getting your MBA… That's quite enough. Sounds like things have turned around for you."

"They have."

"Focus on that. Mercy wouldn't want you killing yourself over her, and neither do we."

"I know." But he owed them so much. They'd saved him.

"You still having issues with that man at work? The one with the cane?"

Oh shit. Eli. He hadn't mentioned him during the last three calls. "No!" He coughed. "No. He's..." Beautiful. Demanding. Wanton. Justin glanced at his apartment. It could fit in Eli's living room and half of his kitchen. "He's been fine."

Silence on the other end. Even the clanking of dishes had stopped. He pictured his mother, her long silver hair pulled back, hand on her hip, while the other held the phone. Her lips pulled thin. He'd never been able to discuss a man he liked without tripping over himself. He knew exactly what was coming next. Dreaded it. Maybe if he talked about Eli, he could figure his head out.

"Is there something between you two?"

Justin bit his tongue and answered. "Yeah. We started talking more. We're..." How hard was it to admit? "We've been dating." God, how would his mother react? Hell, he couldn't believe he was dating Eli.

She started speaking a few times, the sounds staccato in his ear. Finally, the question formed. "You're not... in one of *those* relationships again? With the collars and whips and..." She trailed off.

Justin wrapped an arm around his middle. She'd seen him after he'd left Francis, the bruises, the cuts on his wrists from hanging in rope too long. "It's not like it was with—"

"Justin, please please please don't do this to us again." Her voice cracked and broke his heart.

She'd read between the words and tone. His back bore Eli's marks and his ass was still sore from the last glorious caning scene. His memory of that crumbled to ash. "Mom, it's not..." The words stuck in his throat.

It's not the same. Was it? He was wrapped up in another rich, domineering man's life.

"You're not living with him, are you?"

"No!" Sure, he spent a lot of time at Eli's, but he still had this place. Still had his own life. Mostly. Except on weekends and some evenings. "I'm in my apartment, Mom."

A sigh of relief. "Good."

"We just see each other at work. Sometimes on the weekends." Most of them. Hell, he'd even taken to doing his homework in Eli's kitchen. It was quiet, and Eli rewarded him with sex and pain. Justin shivered.

"It's not like it was before." *Lie.* Even his mother heard it.

"Oh, *honey*."

"I'm being careful, Mom. I'm not going to vanish again." Justin glanced over at the suit that hung from his bathroom door, perfect its plastic bag. Finely tailored to his measurements, bought with Eli's money for him to wear this weekend so Eli could take him to dinner and a show in the Cultural District without being embarrassed.

His gut felt full of rocks and pins. Bile rose.

"I know you need to live your life," his mother said into his ear. Justin closed his eyes when his stomach tumbled. "But please be careful? And call. Or e-mail. Mercy loves hearing from you."

Keep in touch. Don't become trapped again. Don't become a *thing* again. Justin swallowed. "I will, I promise. He's not like the other guy, Mom. I swear." Dusty words. He barely heard them over the pounding of his heart.

"I hope so." The sounds of pots and pans resumed. "I

should go. Your sister will be home soon, and I need to get this in the oven."

Justin opened his eyes. The suit was still there. "I love you, Mom. Thank you."

"Love you, too, honey. And we're here for you, you know that. Anytime."

For anything. He shivered again. Was the apartment cold, or was it the ice in his blood? As much as he wanted to, he couldn't turn away from the suit. "I know."

"Bye, sweetheart."

"Bye, Mom." He didn't turn off the phone until he heard the *click* on the other end. Even after, he stared at Eli's suit. A gift, Eli had said. Justin had trusted that.

Fuck. He was doing it again, wasn't he? Justin set down the phone and dropped his head to his hands. Hook, line, sinker. He'd been caught.

CONFERENCE CALLS MUST HAVE BEEN CREATED BY A bastard who actually got off on people being truly miserable. Eli rubbed his temple to abate the growing headache and stared across his guest table at Sam, whose creased brow gave away his annoyance.

At least he wasn't the only one.

"Mind if we take a bit of a break? Say five minutes?" The smooth voice of Gerald Cunningham slithered from the speaker like a snake over rocks.

"Not at all." Sam's cheerful tone didn't match his haggard expression.

"We'll start again at ten 'til."

"Great." Sam hit the mute button on the Polycom. The false joviality fell away. "They're toying with us."

Sanhex still hadn't signed the deal. They'd been working on their shit anyway, in good faith. "You think?"

"Eli," Sam snapped. He rubbed his forehead. "Sorry. I shouldn't..."

He waved it away. "No, I'm being a prick. I thought we had this all worked out." They even had an unofficial e-mail from Sanhex's CEO saying they planned to sign today. Now this hellish call to explain *everything* again. When Sanhex did commit, the money—and the references—would be more lucrative than gold. It was a gamble, but one Eli had agreed with.

"One of us is going to have to go out there." Sam leaned back in his chair and blew air, puffing out his cheeks. "Or both of us. Jen and Fazil weren't enough."

"If I go, I'm taking a crop and using it on Gerald's ass."

Sam gave him a look that could peel paint from walls. "Not funny, Eli."

It wasn't. But the quirk that had always gotten him into trouble at every other company, very much wanted to rail at the executives of Sanhex until they submitted to him and listened. "I wouldn't do that. I'm just—"

"Frustrated." Sam glanced at his watch.

Only a couple more hours and he'd be off to dinner and a show with Justin. "At least it's Friday."

"Amen to that."

The speaker crackled back to life. "We're back!"

Sam rolled his eyes. "Here we go." He unmuted. "And we're here."

About ten minutes into explaining, yet again, their plan to pull Sanhex out of its tailspin, Gerald asked for a face-to-face 'to smooth things over with the board.' Just as Sam had predicted.

Eli stabbed the mute button. "You do not want me going."

Sam chuckled. "I'm tempted to send you. They need their asses handed to them." Eli opened his mouth, but Sam held up his hand. "I said *tempted*. I'll go. I may hand them their backsides in a bucket, but..."

"You'll get the deal." Sam could negotiate anything with the right amount of force, a friendly smile, and knowing *exactly* when to bend.

The latter talent had never come to Eli. Ever.

Sam unmuted the line. "Of course. When?"

It took another couple of minutes to work out the general schedule before they were finally able to hang up. Eli ran a hand through his hair. "Are you sure we need this?" There were other companies, other opportunities. Not so lucrative, but not every decision revolved around money.

"We knew they'd be a hard nut to crack." Sam stood and stretched. "But this is their last chance. If I don't come back with a signed contract, they can fuck themselves."

There was the CEO he knew and liked. "Good."

Sam grinned. "So, which show?"

Not any question he'd been expecting. He stretched out his leg. "Hmm?"

"Justin's got a suit hanging on the back of the door."

That would be a giveaway, more than Justin's snapping. He'd been a bit more moody lately, but with the weather, everyone was temperamental. "You're not going to believe me."

"Oh?"

"*The Nutcracker*." Eli attempted to keep a straight face as he watched Sam's expression morph into confusion then stay there.

"But you're..." He waved a hand and leaned on the chair.

"Jewish?"

Sam had the decency to blush. "Well, it is very Christmasy."

He couldn't hold back the grin any longer. "I know. I snuck out of the house to go when I was seventeen—just to piss off my parents. Friday night. Missed temple and everything." He shrugged. "It's tradition now."

"You... are very weird, Eli." Sam pushed off the chair. "Can't see it as Justin's thing, though."

He rose, ignoring the twinge in his bad leg. Too much sitting. "He's never seen it." Justin had been as confused as Sam when Eli had suggested going, but there had also been a spark in his eyes and that sexy little quirk to his lips. *You're taking me to watch guys in tights? I'm in.* "And he does enjoy theater."

"There's theater," Sam said. He crossed the room and opened the door. "Then there's *The Nutcracker.*"

And there was Justin, across the hall, all spiky hair and eyeliner. He was going to look stunning in his suit. And even better when Eli peeled it off at the end of the night.

"What's wrong with *The Nutcracker?*" Justin's smile was just as cocky as his clothing.

That threw Sam. "It's very..."

"... Christmasy," Eli said, deadpanning the word. He leaned against the doorframe.

Justin shrugged. "I can do Christmas if it involves watching fit men in tight clothing move in ways that should be illegal."

Sam raised his hands in surrender and stalked into his office.

Fazil walked down the hall, toward the front of the

office. "I'm going to pretend I didn't hear that last bit," he said. "Coffee, anyone?"

"Always." Justin rose from his desk.

"I'll even buy." Why not? It was Friday. He had a hot date and the offer to pay halted Fazil in his tracks. *Excellent.*

Fazil rotated around. "Did you just say what I think you said?"

"Yes."

That he'd raised a blush on Fazil and caused Justin to snort? Made up for conference call hell.

"For everyone?" Fazil held up a sticky note that had three orders on it.

Eli shrugged. "Yes."

"Medium cappuccino," Sam called from his office.

Eli gestured to the door. "You heard Sam."

As Justin passed, he brushed Eli's hand with his. "Can't wait for tonight."

"I didn't just hear that, either," Fazil said. "What would the boss man think?"

"The boss man thinks they're cute. And he wants his coffee," Sam said.

Cute? The heat in Eli's face probably matched the shade on Justin's. Well, if the rest of the office hadn't figured it out by now... He gestured toward the front with his cane. "Go. Both of you."

They filed out in front of him. "Remind me to mark this day down on my calendar," Fazil said. "Eli's buying, and apparently he's capable of *cute* as well as scary."

"Scary cute." Justin looked back over his shoulder. "It's a thing."

"It most certainly is." As Justin would discover as soon as he had him in private.

CHAPTER THIRTEEN

The suit fit Justin perfectly, which wasn't surprising since it had been tailored to do so. He brushed his fingers over the sleeve. Fine dark gray wool. Italian. He'd never worn something so expensive in his life. The thought of how much this had set Eli back threatened to bring out a cold sweat in Justin.

Eli had the money. Justin didn't. No way in heaven he could pay Eli back for this. With cash, anyway.

There are other ways for you to earn your keep, Justin. The voice in the back of his mind sounded like Francis's had, right before he'd bent Justin over the dining room table.

He rubbed at his ears. Eli wasn't like that... was he? No. Besides, Justin did want to see *The Nutcracker*. A childhood memory he'd never had. Justin straightened his tie and brushed his hair back into place and left the bathroom.

No one remained in the office other than him, Eli, and Sam. The faint sound of Sam's voice and the resonant deep rumble of Eli's laugh filtered up the hall. Justin paused, a line of fear wrapping itself around his heart. What was he doing? *Oh honey.* His mother's voice took Francis's place.

It's not the same. He's different. He's— Justin shook his head and marched to the front of the office.

Sam whistled. "Nice. You'd stop a boardroom in their tracks."

Eli didn't say a word, just leaned on his cane and smiled his devilish best. Appreciation—and lust—shone there and ignited Justin's desire.

To have Eli want him was always a trip. *Please don't let it be a bad one.*

After a moment, Eli cocked a finger for Justin to come close. Already ordering him around, and with predictable results. Justin's cock filled with every step he took and his heart skipped beat when Eli handed his cane to Sam. "Hold this, will you?"

Sam complied and Eli fixed some imperfection with Justin's tie and smoothed down his collar, all the while staring into Justin's eyes. "You look stunning." A low murmur of words.

His reply was a whisper. "Thanks."

Eli slipped his hand around Justin's neck, his fingers finding the sensitive skin right below Justin's hairline—then Eli pulled Justin in for a kiss.

He shouldn't have been embarrassed to have Sam standing there. He'd seen more—far more—at the party weeks before. Heat rose, as did his dick. There was something sexy about being watched. And kissed. Eli teased open Justin's lips, drawing him closer until their hips met, cocks pushing against each other through fabric that was worth a fortune.

Or at least a couple grand.

Eli broke the kiss. "Hungry?"

Yes. In every way. "Would be a shame to waste that reservation."

Sam cleared his throat. "Please go before you set my office on fire."

Eli's chuckle was rich and dark. He took his cane back. "Shall we?"

"Sure."

Justin followed Eli out of the office, but not to his Audi. Instead, there was a black Cadillac with a driver at the curb. "You hired a car?" How much did *that* run?

Eli looked a bit sheepish when he opened the passenger door. "I'm not fond of driving downtown, to be honest."

Justin slid onto the leather seat, Eli close behind. "I could have driven." The interior was plush, like a mini-limo, which was what this was, come to think of it.

"I know you could have, but I wanted this to be a gift. From me to you." His grin was large and endearing. "Having you drive kind of defeats the purpose, eh?"

And there was the money word: *purpose.* Justin looked away. "I guess it would."

"Hey." Eli slid his hand over Justin's. "If it bothers you, we can—"

"It's fine." He turned back and smiled as best he could. At least Eli noticed his discomfort. "I'm just not used to"— he waved his free hand to encompass the car—"this kind of thing." At least not while dressed in a suit.

"It'll be fine." Eli leaned forward and tapped on the partition and the car moved forward.

Easy for him to say. Justin doubted Eli had ever knelt on the floor of a moving car while giving a blow job. Those weren't memories Justin wanted to relive, even if it had been exciting at the time. Everything afterward hadn't been.

Still, Justin had said yes to this night and had looked

forward to it for weeks. What had changed? He studied Eli, who smiled back.

"Thank you for coming with me. First time I've ever had company for my odd winter habit."

"Not even Sam or Michael?"

"No. This is... very personal. But I wanted to share it with you."

Justin's back unknotted. Good—that was good to hear. "I'm glad I can." Maybe he was being too wary. This was *Eli*. Justin sat back. *Enjoy the ride.*

But he'd said that to himself last time, too.

WHEN THEY PULLED UP TO THE CAPITAL GRILLE, Justin's heart dropped into his stomach. *This place?* They didn't let people like Justin into restaurants like this. He glanced at his black nails. But the maître d' greeted Eli by name and they were shown to a table without fuss. No one commented on Justin's hair or his nail polish. Then again, Eli cut a figure that spoke of money and power.

The delectable aroma of good beef cooked to perfection overcame Justin's trepidation. If Eli wanted to wine and dine him, who was he to argue?

After two steaks, several sides, and a bottle of wine that had to have cost half Justin's rent, they were well and truly fed. Worry evaporated into a food coma sent from heaven.

"We still have a show to see," Eli said, stifling a yawn.

They opted for coffee, no dessert, to finish the meal.

Justin picked up his cup and breathed in the aroma. "Kick me if I fall asleep."

Eli chuckled. "You'd better not."

Mild words, but the raised eyebrow and smile were anything but innocent. Justin's heart thumped higher and his cock shifted. He was just about healed from the last scene they'd done, and he hadn't spent much time at Eli's since he'd called home. Maybe a good fuck would straighten his head out. "I'll keep that in mind."

Their waiter brought the bill. Eli examined it before sliding a credit card into the folder. He pushed back from the table and grabbed his cane. "I'll be right back."

Bathroom. Justin nodded.

When Eli was out of sight, he grabbed the folder and flipped it open. An American Express Gold Card. Not too extravagant for someone at Eli's level. The bill for their meal, though—Justin had expected three figures, but not quite this number. The wine alone had cost one hundred thirty bucks. From the corner of his eye, he spotted the waiter returning. He closed the folder and handed it over without a word.

This *was* a nice evening. Eli *did* have the money. The sharp stab of doubt joined with whispers of Francis's lies and his mother's warnings. What price would Justin pay? There was always a cost, be it pain or sex.

Or love? He glanced in the direction Eli had gone. Did a Dom like Eli love, or did he possess?

He's never harmed you in any way. Justin had wanted the pain, had asked for it, and the sex, too. Begged. Everything had been going fine. Justin tried to shake off the worry. If he'd said no to this date, Eli would have taken a limo downtown to the show anyway. *You're jumping at shadows again.*

Ghosts and shadows. They seemed more real every day.

Eli leaned against the shower wall and let the hot water beat against his left leg. If he'd known ballet turned Justin on so much, he'd have taken him to a show *weeks* ago. They'd made love pretty much upon falling into bed, slow and delicious, and fallen asleep in a tangle. In the morning, Justin had begged Eli to fuck him mercilessly and hard—and he had. Each moan and cry pushing Eli higher until they'd both spent themselves senseless.

A sore leg was a small price to pay. Eli pushed off the wall and set about cleaning himself.

Justin had been quieter during breakfast, almost as ponderous as after his first night here. But coffee, bagels, and a few quips had teased out his beautiful smile.

The rest of the day? They'd play that by ear.

He shut the water off just as it started to cool and stepped out, grabbing a towel as he went. He'd just finished drying his hair when Justin appeared in the doorway, a blush tingeing his cheeks.

"I brought something up from downstairs." He held out a finger. His collar dangled there. Justin's lips curved into a grin that nearly made Eli lose his balance.

He beckoned with a finger, and Justin closed the distance, still holding the band of leather out.

Eli slipped it off Justin's finger and set it on the bed. "I should dress." He slid his hands under Justin's shirt, caressing his trembling stomach. "And you should get naked."

He kissed Justin while working his shirt up, breaking only to pull the fabric over Justin's head. The shirt landed somewhere near the side of the bed.

"Leather pants," Justin said against Eli's lips. "The ones you wore..."

An order? Eli bit Justin's neck. Not hard, but enough to

turn words into a moan. Perfect. He stepped back. "Lose the jeans."

Justin did, as well as his underwear. Good, very good. Already flushed from his chest to his neck, and hard, too. Probably had been since coming upstairs.

Justin knew what he wanted. Eli was more than willing to give it to him. He beckoned Justin forward again and picked up the collar. "Shall I put this on?"

A shiver quaked through Justin. "Please." Such a wanton whisper.

Eli buckled the leather around Justin's neck. "Stand there, like that, while I change."

"Yes, Eli."

His turn to shudder. He didn't hurry, enjoying the lust in Justin's body, the way his thighs flexed and cock rocked. His own dick ached, especially when he trapped it into the slick leather of the pants Justin had requested. He picked out a crisp white shirt. That was enough.

He wanted what Justin offered. Badly. He closed in and towered over him. "Ready?"

A smile like the sun. "More than."

"Good." Eli cupped a hand behind Justin's head and devoured Justin's mouth. A gentle nudge sent Justin moving toward the door.

THEY MOVED IN A SLOW DANCE OF SKIN AND LEATHER, fingers and tongues from the bedroom to the playroom, Eli hot against Justin's naked body even through his clothes. Whenever they touched, world narrowed down to Eli and only Eli, and Justin forgot everything else.

A nip of teeth from Eli. "What do you want today?"

Something different. "Rope. Tight. I want... not to move." Justin's breath caught. Was he asking for this?

"You want to be bound tight against the cross when I whip you?"

"Yes." His breathing stuttered.

Eli, once more in his gloves, cupped Justin's balls and he couldn't help thrusting. Bound to the cross by rope and not the cuffs Eli usually used. He shivered. Francis had done that. Once. Then left Justin there all night.

Two days later, Justin had left with only the clothes on his back and a one-way ticket to Louisiana.

Left? Escaped.

He shuddered again.

Eli ran feather touches over Justin's cock, leather soft as silk against his length. He tipped his head back to give Eli more of his neck. Kisses. Bites. He'd probably have a nice collection of bruises tomorrow.

Another sign to show how much Eli owns you.

They bumped against the cross. Eli pulled back, his face flushed and lips wet. "Do you want this?"

"Yes." No. Maybe. There were differences and similarities. He'd never told Francis no—not been allowed. He'd not tried with Eli. Would he stop? Did he want Eli to stop?

"Turn around, please." If he did as Eli asked, he would get what *he* wanted—pain, pleasure, release, oblivion. He pressed his body and his hard cock against the leather of the cross and stretched arms and legs wide, like he had so many times before. *You deserve this. Need this. You're mine.* Francis's voice echoed in his brain. Justin closed his eyes. Eli was not Francis.

Eli's touch was gentle and soothing. That hated voice in his head subsided. He could do this.

"So much skin to mark."

To mark Justin as his own. He squirmed against the cross, cock aching, and sought subspace. It usually came so easily with Eli.

No calm. No peace. He remembered the number at the bottom of their dinner bill, the price of the bottle of wine. The expensive seats at the Benedum Center. The limo ride.

Rope crossed over the back of Justin's wrist. Swiveling his head, he watched Eli wrap red rope across flesh again, binding him down to the cross. The more rope Eli wound around Justin's wrists and arms, the more Justin's mind swirled—but not with pleasure. The lust was there, the physical desire to be restrained, to be hurt—but his stomach flipped and the creep of a headache and nausea replaced the high he'd had when they'd been kissing in the bedroom.

Eli moved to the other wrist, planting a kiss on the nape of Justin's neck. "You're so beautiful."

The murmur of those words against sensitive flesh sent a shiver through him—but also curdled his stomach. He'd always been beautiful to Francis when bound. Kept. Tied up and fucked.

Francis was not as tall as Eli but much broader. Brown hair rather than black. But he'd had cold eyes and a huge wallet. Eli could be as cold, and his wallet was certainly as large.

Eli caressed Justin's shin, and murmured something Justin couldn't make out over the thumping of blood in his ears.

Rope around his left ankle. Up his leg.

He shouldn't be thinking of Francis. But this weekend had been similar to when he'd told Francis he needed to fly back to Louisiana to see Mercy. She'd come back from Iraq and was critical in the hospital.

Francis hadn't been happy, but he'd said he understood. Lied so hard and treated Justin to an elegant evening out in clothes Justin hadn't bought, a night of carnal sex and a flogging the next day.

Bliss. A perfect send-off.

But the words that came after that—when Justin had been spent and exhausted? *I don't give a shit about your sister. You are not leaving me, Justin. I own you. I've fed you, I've clothed you, I've paid for you. You're mine now.*

Francis had left him on the cross all night. *Cold and alone. Like you'll be if you step one foot outside this house.*

He moaned against the sinking in his chest and the ice that spread to each limb. The hairs on his arms and legs stood on end. Eli was not Francis. He could leave—had left —this house.

Rope around his right ankle.

Hell, he had his own place—that he never slept in on weekends. A job—where Eli worked. Eli had gone to CMU. Had the same advisor. Was best friends with Sam and Michael.

There was no leaving Eli.

Not after the dinners and the clothing and the gifts. All to buy Justin. To keep him.

Bile rose to Justin's throat, along with a whimper. Not again. He could not do this again. "Saturn."

Eli sucked in a breath. "Justin?"

"Saturn." He yanked at the bindings, twisting his wrists. "Did you hear me? Saturn!"

"Shit. Shit. I'm sorry. Hang on." A scramble of movement and cold metal met Justin's leg right before the rope fell away, ripping and rending suddenly.

Shears. Eli had shears. "Get me off this thing."

A pained cry, but not from him. Eli snipped the rope on

the other leg. Eli brushed Justin's wrist. "I don't want to cut you."

Justin forced himself to stop fighting the ropes, but it was hard. The second one hand was free, he started working on the rope around the other wrist. "Fuck."

"Wait!" Eli's eyes were huge, his face the color of bone. "Just let me—" A flash of silver, the sound of shears, and Justin was free.

He pushed Eli away. "Don't touch me!"

The sheers hit the floor, clattering against the wood. The open horror carved into Eli, the way his hands shook as he held them up and backed away... tore into Justin. It didn't matter that Eli wasn't Francis. Not anymore. This was over.

"I can't do this. I need to go."

His clothes were somewhere in the bedroom. The hardwood floor of the hallway cooled his bare feet and creaked against his weight.

"What happened? I don't... Please wait!" Eli's voice cracked. Anguish? No, no. Just a Dom suddenly losing what he thought was his.

Eli is not Francis. Only he might as well have been. "We're done."

When the scent of lavender engulfed Justin, his vision blurred and throat tightened. Why that scent? He'd have to avoid it now. And good coffee—though neither would be hard. He didn't have the money for fine things. Wouldn't have any money soon, once Sam heard of this.

He found his jeans and the rest of his clothes scatted underneath the suit Eli had bought him. He kicked it out of the way and pulled his clothes on. Backpack would be by the door. Justin turned—

Eli stood in the doorway. Gaunt and drawn, sweat

beaded at his forehead. Everything about his stance, his expression, was at odds with the leather pants and gloves he wore—a scared man in the clothes of a Dom.

Don't do this. He had to. Too late to stop. Too late to explain. "Get the fuck out of my way."

The fury in his voice pushed Eli back as if he'd been slapped.

Wide eyes, and such sadness.

Justin rushed past and ran down the stairs. Eli couldn't follow with his leg, not fast at any rate. Justin scooped up his backpack and helmet and threw the lock on the door.

"What did I do wrong?" That cracked voice followed him down the stairs. "Justin, please! I'm sorry. Just tell me—"

He opened the door and hurried out, slamming it behind him. He had only a bit of time before Eli made it down. It took a second to unlock his bike and another to get it off the porch. He had another bike lock at home, so he left this one tangled around the railing. When tires met concrete, he was on the bike and pedaling as fast as he could down Wightman.

Gone.

Free. He'd made it.

He'd had to sneak out in the middle of the night with Francis. Eli had let him go.

The ramming of his heart wasn't due to the bike ride. This is what he'd wanted. He couldn't date another rich Dom who took over his life.

Eli had let Justin go. Stopped. Heeded the safeword.

The screech of tires and the long honk of a horn focused Justin. *Shit.* He'd run a light. *Holy fuck.* He was never that careless. After swinging down a side street, he slowed. Paid attention to his surroundings.

Had he really just walked out on Eli?

Yeah, he had. *Oh God.* No undoing that. Not that he wanted to.

He peddled back up to speed on his bike, mostly to ignore the wrenching shakes that were threatening. He didn't have time for self-pity or for rich bastards. A few more blocks found him at his apartment. He dragged his bike down the steps and inside his hovel and collapsed on his bed.

He didn't know whether to cry, scream, or throw up. What, exactly, had happened? Justin pulled the rumpled throw from the corner of the bed and hugged it close. Eli had happened, another rich man expecting Justin to bend over and take whatever was offered. Dinner, fucking, beating. He'd been a fool to think this time would be any different. Justin unbuckled the collar around his neck and threw it across the room. Should have walked away when Eli first ordered him to suck his dick.

Justin scrubbed his face. Sam would fire him once he got wind of this. There was always the coffee shop, or maybe finding a job on campus until he graduated. Something. Anything.

Anything but Eli.

Tears pricked at the corner of his eyes. A tiny voice, his own, whispered about mistakes and trust. Eli wasn't Francis. He almost— *almost*—believed that voice.

He'd seen the bill. Knew his price.

Across the room, his backpack buzzed—a text on his phone. Justin pushed himself off the bed and dug it out.

Just tell me you're safe, please!

He deleted the message and turned the phone off

completely, then grabbed his laptop and sat down at the kitchen table.

Time to write a resignation letter.

CHAPTER FOURTEEN

As soon as Sam entered on Monday morning, Justin closed the outer door and followed him into the inner office. Now or never, the same way he'd gotten into this mess. His resignation letter shook in his hands.

Sam's expression went from wary to a mask. Poker-faced, except for a tiny twitch of the eye. Justin had seen him like this before, but with customers. Never with any of them.

No, Sam, you're not going to like this. He wanted to be packed and gone before Eli came to work. Once Sam sat, Justin handed him the letter. Sam studied it, set it down on his desk, and turned his gaze on Justin.

This man was so not a submissive. Not here, anyway. Justin resisted the urge to fidget under the weight of Sam's stare. Sam didn't even look at the paper as he pushed the page back across the desk.

"No."

No anger, not a demand, but such finality in that single word, more so than any order Justin had ever received from any Dom—or anyone else, for that matter.

"No?" He should be furious, but Sam had spoken so *factually*. That broke Justin's anger into tiny pieces of confusion.

"This is the result of something between you and Eli, yes?"

He nodded.

"Then no."

A spark of fury ignited finally. "It's a *resignation* letter, Sam. You can't say no to it."

"Yes, I can." Sam sat back in his chair. "I didn't make a mistake when I hired you and I'm not about to let you walk away from a job you're brilliant at because you've had a falling-out with your lover."

Everyone making decisions for him. Even Sam. "You can find another assistant."

"Yes, but I can't find another *you*." Sam steepled his fingers and touched them to his lips. "I haven't been grooming you to be my *assistant*, Justin."

That stopped Justin dead. He sank down into the guest chair. "Grooming?"

Sam lowered his hands. Tired and harried lines replaced the smooth expressionless demeanor. "Business is growing pretty fast. I'm going to need someone to... well... be me. Do what I do." He paused. "I'm going to eventually need a partner in the company."

"What are you... I don't even have my MBA yet!"

He waved that away. "You will, in a few months. What I'm offering is this—mentor with me. Learn what I do, how I do it. See what we can do together and we'll decide on the next steps. It won't happen right away. You're still ramping up on the office and the business, and yes, finishing your MBA. But if you walk away..."

The unspoken words hung in the air. If he left, there would be no chance. None at all.

God, his heart. Pain, hope, anguish. He wasn't sure which twisted his soul into knots and made it hard to breathe. "Are you serious? I mean..." He gestured to himself. "Not exactly corporate."

"Have you seen yourself in a suit?"

That made his face burn. Even Brian's head had whipped around.

"You might have to lose the nail polish from time to time."

He could handle that. But... "I thought Eli was your right-hand man." It came out as a whisper.

"He's my CFO and my friend, but he'd be the first to tell you he can't do what I do." Sam drew invisible circles on the surface of his desk with a finger. "Nor does he want to. My job is to be the friendly side of the company. Eli revels a little too much in making clients uncomfortable."

The sadist at work. Justin tried to hide the shiver—tried to convince himself it wasn't partly out of pleasure.

"Justin, what happened with Eli?" Worry there. Concern. It softened Sam's tone and drew different lines on his face.

"I... don't want to talk about it." Hell, he didn't want to think about it. The more he did, the worse he felt. Eli had trapped Justin—only he hadn't because he'd let Justin go. Eli had tried to buy Justin with dinners and clothes, hadn't he? Another poor guy for the wealthy Dom to play with, except if Sam had his way, that wouldn't be a concern.

Too much to think about right now. Sam's offer. Eli. The hammering in his chest, the hollow feeling in his brain, the tingling in his fingertips. Justin shook his head.

"Can you work with him?"

Could he? "I did before." But now he knew the taste of Eli's skin, the timber of his moans, the soft touches that came after the sharp and sensuous sting of Eli's whip. How his smile lit a room. "I'll make it work." He picked at a piece of lint on his black jeans. "If he doesn't ask you to fire me."

Sam exhaled. "If you believe Eli would ever ask me to do that, you don't know him at all."

Justin snapped his head up and looked at Sam. Sadness there, but a hint of understanding as well.

Maybe Sam was right. Maybe he didn't know Eli. Probably for the best that they were done. He couldn't imagine being Sam's business partner while being Eli's submissive. "I can be civil."

"That's all I ask." Sam gave the forgotten letter a nudge.

Justin picked it up and stood. "I guess I have some shredding to do."

Sam coughed a laugh.

After he slipped the letter into the shredder, he opened the door again and studied the office across the hall. Still no Eli.

Justin didn't know whether the tumble in his heart was relief or sorrow.

Despite the drastic dip in temperature, Eli walked to work on Monday. His lungs hurt by the time he entered the office, but that had nothing to do with the cold weather and everything to do with still not being able to breathe.

The image of Justin's back as he ran out the front door

replayed itself in Eli's mind. The echo of that one word sounded in his ears.

Saturn.

What had he done? Every time he ran through the scene in his head, there was nothing. No unsafe practices, no warnings. *Nothing.* Justin had been begging to be bound and whipped, moaning while Eli tightened ropes around his wrists, his cock hard, hips thrusting.

He hadn't even picked up a flogger yet, had just been looking at the beauty that was Justin wrapped in desire, and then Justin safeworded.

Dressed. Left.

No explanation. Not when he'd thrown apology after apology and begged to understand what he'd done wrong. No answer to the texts he'd sent to make sure Justin had made it safely home.

Now work loomed and he couldn't think, hadn't slept, and dreaded climbing the stairs to the office. He did anyway, leg throbbing the entire way, keycarded himself in, and headed to his office. He didn't look into the other room, but he'd caught enough out of his peripheral vision to see that Justin was at his desk.

Well, at least he was alive.

Eli swallowed and tried to move his heart back into the proper place. The weight of Justin's gaze on his back bore down, pressing between his shoulders. He stripped off his gloves and nearly dropped them onto the desk, next to the ruler.

No.

If Justin was going to safeword, walk away, and then not *talk* to him, there would be no games, no flirting, no anything. No more. He'd been a fool from day one.

Eli stuffed the gloves into the pocket of his overcoat and

yanked open the drawer beneath the ruler. The contents—pens, the stapler, paperclips, scissors—rattled in protest of the violent movement. He pushed the ruler in and slammed the drawer shut.

The sound echoed in his office. Probably outside of it, too. Then silence descended, but for the catch of his own breath. Blinking back the sting in his eyes, he shrugged off his coat and hung it on the back of his door. Scarf, too.

He'd been in worse shape than this, through worse confusion and pain, and survived. Thrived. He took a breath, steeled himself, and finally looked across the hall.

Justin stared back, more goth than he'd been in months. His stunning blue eyes peeked out from behind a thick mask of eyeliner and a hacked black fringe of hair. He'd dyed his hair red on the ends, cut it, and spiked it into a chaotic mess. Black clothes. No jewelry. Pale lips drawn into a thin line. Unreadable.

What did I do? The words almost slipped from Eli's lips. They tumbled in his head, the way they'd fallen from his mouth all the way down the stairs and onto the porch. The panic, the worry. *Justin, wait! What happened? I'm sorry! What did I do?*

Love. Yes, that was there. The reason he couldn't think or breathe or... Eli turned and paced back to his desk. Obviously Justin felt differently.

Somewhere, Eli had fucked up so horribly that Justin didn't even trust him enough to let him know why. A voice, one that sounded too much like his father, whispered in the back of his brain. *You're a monster. Lawless. Deviant.*

That hurt. More than it had in some time. It wasn't true, but the little voice still lurked back there, despite all the conversations with Dr. Brohmer. Even though he knew better. Always that voice.

Rote movements forced him to sit down, wake the laptop up, and wait for the monitors to catch up.

They say what I do is abuse.

They? Who, Eli?

He'd never had an answer to that.

What do you think?

The screens flicked to life with a log-in prompt, but he studied his own hands rather than touch the keyboard. *They want what I give. Get as much pleasure from the pain as I do. More maybe. I... No. I don't think so. Not from me.*

The dominance and sadism could become abuse. He'd seen instances of that, Doms who went too far, the trauma they left behind. He was not—would not be—that man. Ever.

Only now, it seemed he was.

No. Everything had been consensual. *You stopped and let him go, as you're supposed to, as you said you would.* He'd done exactly the right thing.

Justin had walked away, which he had every right to do. That he didn't want to tell Eli why burned and turned his guts inside out. Yet that was Justin's right, too.

He didn't own Justin. Didn't *want* to—just wanted—

The screens turned black again.

Eli cursed and nudged the mouse. This time, when the log-in box appeared, he typed his password.

The pain in his throat matched the ever-present sting in his eyes and the ache in his heart. He wanted to love Justin —did love him. But he also wanted Justin to return that love, and that was a dream. If Justin didn't trust Eli enough to tell him what had gone wrong... that didn't just kill the D/s relationship, it tore apart every other connection they had.

Which might be an issue in the office. Like it or not, they still needed to work together, at least until Eli figured out other options. He clicked open his e-mail and scrolled through the list. Nothing from Justin, but one mail from Sam.

Are you okay?

No. He wasn't. But that had never stopped him from functioning before. He deleted Sam's e-mail.

He rubbed the back of his neck, the tension rising up his spine. Sam needed him—that's why he'd taken the job as CFO. But Sam *required* Justin—the man was bright and worked in lock-step with Sam. In a few years, they would be a formidable team, even with Justin's penchant to wear eyeliner.

If Sam had to choose between Eli and Justin, he knew the decision Sam would make—and he didn't agree. The better option would be to eliminate the need for Sam to choose.

He picked through the rest of the e-mails from the weekend, marking the ones he needed to handle first, and looked through his to-do list. He had a plate of work to empty before he could talk to Sam about finding another CFO.

At one o'clock, Sam walked into Eli's office and closed the door, right on schedule. Eli rotated in his desk chair.

As he'd done so often, Sam leaned against Eli's door, back pressed against the hard, wooden surface. "You didn't answer my e-mail."

It took effort to hold his temper in check and not lash

out. He'd been like this all day, teetering wildly from wanting to punch the shit out of everything to wanting to walk home, curl up on the couch with Lavi, bury his face in that soft bundle of fur, and never see this office again.

Eli blinked a few times to clear the haze that marred his vision. "I thought the answer was blindly obvious."

Sam pushed off the door. "E, please."

Another breath, this one to clear the growing tightness in his throat. "I'm well enough, Sam. Leave me be."

Sam took two steps forward and stopped, brows furrowed, tension written in his body.

Eli gripped the armrests of his chair. *Please don't ask.* A silent plea.

Unheeded. "What happened between you and Justin?"

"Have you asked Justin?" Quiet words, because if Eli didn't whisper them, he'd use them like a whip, and Sam was the last person he should be yelling at.

Sam straightened. "I did."

"And?"

"He didn't want to talk about it."

Of course not. "Well, at least he's consistent."

"E, what the hell happened? On Friday, I thought you were going to set fire to the office. Now you two can't even look at each other."

Eli rubbed at his forehead. "I don't know."

"E—"

"I don't know!" Eli's voice cracked and it took all his effort to draw in a breath without releasing the sob that wanted to trail along. He would not fall apart in front of Sam and certainly not with Justin on the other side of that thin door.

Worry and something deeper passed over Sam's face.

"Can you— I mean, is this—" He shook his head. "You two work so well."

There was the stake, the one that kept being driven through his heart. "Apparently, we don't. And no, I don't think it's fixable, whatever the fuck it is." His voice wavered because he was having trouble breathing.

Sam wilted. "Shit."

Every wall in Eli crumpled in a sudden flood of pain. "You should find another CFO." He hadn't meant to say that, not yet, not until he had a plan in place, but he was done. Just... done. There weren't any other options left. Time to crawl back home and lick his wounds.

"No," Sam said. "You are not leaving."

"Neither is Justin," Eli said. "You'll need him far more than me in the long run." Brilliant, lovely, messy Justin. Should have left temptation alone all those months ago. Saved them all this trouble. His own pain he could handle— but Sam's? *Justin's?* He folded his arms and leveled a long look at Sam.

Sam didn't flinch, didn't turn away at all, turning into the stone-faced CEO he was so well known for being. "If he's hurt you this much, I don't need him at all."

"Other way around. I... hurt him. I don't know how, only that I did." He tried to shrug, but ended up wincing. "You don't need me."

The CEO look cracked and Sam threw up his hands. "Look, Michael and I sometimes fight and—"

"He safeworded out of a scene we'd hardly begun—one he asked for—then walked out of my house. That's what happened."

Sam stepped sideways, grabbed one of the chairs from the table in the center of the room, and sank down on it. "Oh."

Of all people, Sam would understand the ramifications. He uncurled himself a bit and ran a hand through his hair. "I don't know what I did. He hasn't said a word to me since I cut him off the cross."

"You... cut him down?"

"He'd asked to be bound tightly. So I used lots of rope." Hadn't that turned Justin on? Or had he completely misread the signals? "Shears were the fastest way."

"You're too good to screw up rope," Sam said, his expression far away. "It must have been something else."

"I know." A past trauma. A trigger point. Something inside Justin. "I know."

He wished Sam's eyes weren't so blue. They were different from Justin's but enough of a reminder.

"Yet you think you can't resolve this." A statement, not a question.

"He doesn't trust me." There was the yawning hole again, the one filled with pain. Noah. His parents. Justin. Noah hadn't turned from the monster, but there hadn't been enough time. "If he can't trust me..." He let the words die. Trust and love. One didn't happen without the other.

Sam folded his hands and looked down at the carpet for a few moments before looking up. "Yet you want him to stay here."

Of course he did. "He's exactly what you've been looking for. Young, smart, clever." He shook his head, stomach still a mass of knots. Last thing Justin—or Sam— needed was for Justin to lose this job. "It's an issue between me and him. It doesn't affect his work."

"Bullshit it doesn't." The words were spoken with a vehemence that pinned Eli to his chair. Sam stood in one motion and covered the distance between them in three steps. "He's as much of a wreck as you. And he handed me a resignation letter this morning."

No way in hell he was going to let Justin quit because of him. Eli rose up from his chair—and met Sam's hand on his shoulder, pushing him back down.

"Get the fuck out of my way, Sam."

"No." Sam spoke that single word with such force, it reverberated through Eli's body to his toes. This wasn't his friend, but S. Randall Anderson, the man who had been CEO of more companies than Eli had fingers.

Silence was the only answer he could offer.

"Do *not* forget whose name is on the front door of this office."

Eli exhaled. "You can't let him quit."

"I *didn't*." Sam paused. "And I'm not letting you, either."

"Sam—"

"You are exactly what this company needs, as well. Young, bright, intelligent—"

"Fucked in the head..."

Sam didn't even flinch. "And I'm not?"

Anger finally ebbed from Eli as pain took over. He slumped back in the chair and rubbed his forehead. He couldn't deny that Sam had his own demons. *Except you're weak. Broken.* Sam wasn't.

"Don't make the mistake I made, E."

Oh, he knew what Sam meant. Before Sam had met Michael, he'd run from his past by moving from company to company, never settling in one place. He'd nearly left Michael behind, too.

Eli had never had the luxury of leaving the past behind. His pain was carved into flesh and bone and always with him. "I've haven't ever run."

"Not the way I did, no." Sam backed off and flopped into the guest chair. "You'll retreat into that house of yours and either get wrapped up in your ennui or spend all your weekends at Lyle's, topping the shit out of men until you can't tell one from the other."

That added another stab to the growing collection of aches in his body. This one, though, made his cheeks hot and his blood boil. He sat up straighter.

Sam folded his arms and stared back. "Tell me I'm wrong."

He couldn't. That only twisted the knife in deeper. "There are days I hate how well you know me." How close Sam had become to Michael. How much he wanted that kind of connection with Justin...

There was another crack in the failing dam he'd erected around that particular tumult of emotions. He closed his eyes because it was the only way to keep the moisture in. Even then, he wasn't sure it would help.

Sam's voice softened. "Give him time, E. He's just as shattered—and that should tell you something."

That I've destroyed everything. He shook his head and opened his eyes—and the tears fell. Not many, but enough. "Three months." His voice sounded like sandpaper, even in his ears.

Sam's lips parted slightly, but then he nodded. "All right. Three months. After that, if you need to leave, I won't stop you."

He could endure, lock away what he needed to and deal with it later once he'd given Sam the time needed. There was hope in Sam, a wish that things would change, that this rift between him and Justin would heal.

Sam was a romantic at heart.

Eli knew better than to hope. It hadn't brought Noah

back to life. Or Rachel. Or Milka. Hope hadn't caused his parents not to despise and scorn him. Hope would never heal his leg.

The only thing hope ever did was carve a bigger hole into his life. "I'll do the best I can, Sam."

Sam's smile was small, but present. "You always do."

CHAPTER FIFTEEN

Justin woke for the umpteenth time, heart pounding and chest tight. Darkness surrounded him, and the ever-present smell of damp. His humid, basement apartment then, and not Eli's house. As it should be. As it had been for two weeks. Tears threatened. Leaving Eli shouldn't still hurt. He'd done the right thing.

He'd even called home that Sunday. *We broke it off, Mom.*

She'd worried about the job, but he'd explained the opportunity Sam had presented. And Eli? He'd been withdrawn, but professional.

Better you focus on your job and your schooling, and not be distracted. Someday, you'll find someone who really cares about you.

His mom's code words for "someone who doesn't beat you." Except he liked that part, but doubted he'd ever be able to explain it to her or his father.

Justin pretended not to notice how Eli's fingers trembled when they stood near each other or how tired and pale Eli looked, tried not to let his heart twist.

Everyone in the office was somber. Less laughter, fewer jokes, and the weekly office lunch had been him and engineering. Sam had been on a call with Sanhex and Eli had politely declined.

Thank God none of the engineers had asked him about Eli. He wouldn't have known what to say. *I ran from him because...*

Because he shouldn't be screwing around with rich dudes when Mercy had no legs. He shouldn't have ever gotten involved with the Scene, shouldn't have let Francis touch him. And he shouldn't have fallen for Eli Ovadia, his suits, his canes, his brilliant smile, or his surprising laugh.

Justin groaned and sat up. A stretch, a piss, and cold water would chase away the regrets. He threw his legs over the edge and his feet touched water.

What the *fuck*?

He reached for the lamp. When the light came on, Justin stared in horror at the sheen of yellowish liquid covering the floor. It had soaked through the rug by his bed. And through the book next to it. And everything else on the floor. "No. Fuck! No, no, no, no!"

He pulled the bedding up, lest it become drenched in the foul water, and surveyed the room, a fist of despair clenching his heart and lungs. Ruined books. His backpack.

Shit, the laptop. He was off the bed before he contemplated what was in the water and a moment later he had the bag in hand. The bottom was leather, the outside water-resistant to withstand rain. Hopefully... When his fingers touched the dry bottom and he pulled out the laptop, his knees nearly gave out. At least he had this—his schoolwork. The capstone project. The majority of his textbooks were piled on the kitchen table.

Justin hobbled over and set the laptop down next to his

books and the backpack on a chair. The water at his feet was faintly warm, but everything felt like ice—numbing him.

He was so very fucked. He didn't have the money to replace anything. Or move out. Or...

A faint hiss floated from the corner of the room. His radiator, probably. His footsteps made a series of wet smacks against the wet linoleum. And yes, there was the source of the leak: water dripping from the underside of the radiator. It took a few tries to close the valve, but he screwed it tight. Hopefully, that would staunch the dripping. Wouldn't know until he could get rid of all the water.

Justin stood, legs shaking. Water soaked the bottom of his sweatpants. Where did he even start? The top of his head and throat itched. Breathing wanted to turn into something that involved tears and snot, but he was not going to give in to that. Justin wiped his hand over his eyes and glanced at the clock on the stove. Three thirty-seven.

It wasn't like a call to the "emergency maintenance" number his landlord had given him would do anything. Never had before. Well, he had a bucket and a mop in the closet and several hours before he needed to get to work. That was as good a place to begin as any.

JUSTIN'S SOFT, BUT ANGUISHED "OH, FUCK" BROKE ELI out of his focus. The numbers on VentShaft's spreadsheet blurred for a second as his heart thudded up into his throat. The report he'd been writing might as well have been in Greek.

This was why he desperately wanted his door closed.

But Sam was off at Sanhex and Eli was in charge of the office until Monday.

Ten more weeks. He only needed to survive ten more weeks. Eli pushed back from his desk.

Justin stood in his office, staring into Sam's, jaw working. He was remarkably free of makeup—and wearing jeans, a t-shirt, and a too-thin coat.

Eli's fingertips tingled. The temperature had been in the twenties this morning. And Justin held his bike helmet. That jacket—

Justin turned and started. His red-rimmed eyes and worn face stole Eli's breath.

What happened? Eli chewed back the question. "He's at Sanhex this week."

"I forgot." Justin put his back to Eli but gestured at the office with his helmet. "I wanted to..." Something close to a sob came then.

Shit. "I have his number, if you need it. I know he wouldn't mind."

The helmet hit the floor and wobbled. Justin set his backpack down, his back still to Eli. So much tension in his frame. "It's not important."

The fuck it isn't. That stayed firmly behind Eli's lips. He gripped the arms of his chair to keep himself from standing up and marching across the hall. *What do you need? What can I do? I love you.*

Eli released his breath. Ten weeks. The chasm grew wider every minute.

Justin finally glanced back and words poured out of him fast. "I need some days off this week. I know I haven't accrued enough, but my apartment flooded and I—"

"Are you okay?" Eli couldn't help it.

"Yeah. It's just stuff." Too much anguish in Justin for Eli to believe that, even for second.

He wanted to take Justin into his arms and hold him until he stopped shaking. Until they both stopped hurting. "Justin, I know things between us went wrong. But if you need a place to stay—"

Justin's whole body stiffened as if Eli had hit him. "What, so you can fuck me again?" Justin kicked his helmet into the corner. "No, thank you."

The accusation embedded in those words punched Eli in the gut. "I never..." The violence in his own voice stopped him. A breath, followed by another, and he tried again. This time it came out cool and composed. "I never did anything you didn't consent to. Ever."

"If it makes you feel better to think that, fine. You still got everything you wanted out of me."

Monster. *Monster, monster, monster.* Eli turned away and struggled to breathe. There were techniques, tricks the psychiatrist from his childhood had taught him to combat the darkness when it welled up, when it ate him alive, when he wanted to change places with Noah because the world would have been better if he'd been the one to die.

Strange how some things never quite leave, and how easily they come back. By the time he finished reciting the Twenty-seventh Psalm in his head, the darkness had crept away. Justin stood across the hall, ghostly white.

"I don't know who you think I am, Justin. Who you thought I was." The weight was there, the heaviness, but he'd not let it take him down. "But I am not that person." Eli nudged his mouse and the monitor woke back up. "Take the time you need to get your life in order. It's what Sam would want."

He didn't bother to see what Justin did next. It didn't

matter. Moisture pricked at the corner of his eyes. *Eli, you are such a horrible, horrible liar.*

IN THE AFTERNOON, THE PROPERTY MANAGEMENT company finally called Justin back. They'd come over first thing the following morning to take a look at the situation.

Justin swallowed a string of curses. "You realize I have no heat and there's water damage everywhere?"

Yes, they did, but there were other emergencies that took precedence. When Justin finally hung up, he looked ruefully at his smartphone and longed for the past, when he could physically slam something down to end the call. He shoved the phone into his backpack.

He had a space heater, but those tripped the breaker. So it would be bundles of blankets and layers of sweats tonight after a run to the Laundromat to finish washing the clothing that he'd carelessly left on the floor. A bunch of books were lost and he'd need to replace all the furniture eventually. But... he'd survive.

Without Eli's "help." A part of Justin cringed at the memory of how Eli had looked that morning—so lost, so *young*. Then he'd woken his computer and ignored the rest of the office for hours.

After lunch, Justin had found a note with two phone numbers written in Eli's elegant hand. The first was labeled "Sam's cell." The second said "Sam and Michael Home" and underneath there was a note.

If you need anything, let Michael know. He can provide.

No signature.

A kind gesture. He nearly crumpled the note and tossed it, but having Sam's cell was useful, as was a contact number for another person that wasn't Kelly or Don.

He wouldn't be calling Eli for anything.

Everything they'd done together had been with consent. But hadn't that been the way with Francis? Until the day where it hadn't been and the day after that, and the weeks and months. Justin slipped the note into his backpack. He sent a quick e-mail to everyone in the office.

I'll be out tomorrow. Hope to be back Wednesday.

Out of the corner of his eye, he saw Eli shift and go still. A few heartbeats later, he went back to his spreadsheet.

Justin hefted the backpack and his helmet and walked out of the office. He didn't bother to say good-bye to Eli. The man didn't care.

If Justin repeated that enough times, he might believe it.

CHAPTER SIXTEEN

IF THIS HAD BEEN ANY COMPANY OTHER THAN SAM'S, Eli would have skipped the so-called holiday party. He loathed them, down to every shiny green and red ball. Sure, there were the requisite blue and silver decorations to be *inclusive*, but they were over in the corner, tucked away. They'd stuck a menorah out, even though Chanukah had passed.

Sam's trying. Stop it. He sighed and took a sip of water. *Nine weeks.*

No one came anywhere near him, which was good, because he wasn't in the mood. Too many couples, too much happiness, and too much goddamned Christmas cheer.

"Eli."

His heart skipped a beat and he nearly dropped the water. He knew the voice, but how someone so big could walk silently, he'd never known.

"Michael." He turned and forgot his anger. Michael looked resplendent in a way Eli rarely saw. His tux was a silvery gray, matched with a ruby red tie and cummerbund.

The only thing marring the perfection was a missing cuff link.

A hint of pain in his gut at what couldn't ever have been, but that faded. "Sam's a lucky man."

Michael chuckled. "Other way around, but I do appreciate the compliment." His smile vanished. "Are you okay?"

"I'm fine," he replied.

"Funny, because it looked like you were contemplating where to pour the gasoline before you threw the match."

Ouch. "That bad?"

"You're a bit of an open book, E."

Well, fuck. He tried schooling his expression. "I'm not into the holiday spirit this year." He took another sip of water and caught sight of Sam. His tux was darker than Michael's, and the accents a deep green. A matched set. Another pang. This one lingered, settling into the lump in his throat. He wanted that. Thought maybe he'd found it with—

There he was. Justin. In the same suit he'd worn to his interview all those months ago. Crisp white shirt. Gold tie. No makeup, which made his messy haircut and wide blue eyes all the more lovely with the sharp cut of his clothes.

Overwhelming guilt slammed into Eli, almost physically. He braced himself against his cane and let the grief wash through him, blur his vision, and dissipate to a quiet roar in his ears. *I'm sorry. Justin.*

A hand on his shoulder. "Eli?"

"I won't embarrass Sam, if that's your concern."

"I know that." Eli let Michael turn him, let Justin vanish from his view. "I'm worried about *you.*"

"Don't be. I'm hard to kill." He stared down at the cane in his hand.

The corner of Michael's eye twitched. "I hate it when you get like this."

"That makes two of us," Eli murmured. He sought out Justin again. There, over with Fazil and his girlfriend. Justin looked up, straight at Eli, before looking away. He couldn't help the sigh. "Did he ever contact you about his flooded apartment?"

Michael shook his head. "He did explain the situation to Sam, and Sam offered our spare room, but no dice." Michael sipped his drink, which was either Sprite with a lime or something not at all Sprite with a lime. Eli guessed the latter, given the quality of gin he'd seen stocked at the bar.

"Justin has a fierce independent streak," Michael said.

"Tell me about it."

"E—"

He waved Michael's concern away with his glass. "I'll be fine." Once he could move on. *What did I do?* He looked into his water.

"You love him."

The heart of the problem, straight from Michael's mouth. "I did. I do." Eli shook his head. "I'll get over it. I got over you." He looked up, because he *had to* with Michael. That would never cease to disconcert him, being the shorter man.

Michael wore his exasperated look. "You know we're here for you, too. If you need anything."

"I know." And he did. "I do appreciate it. Truly." Sam and Michael were the closest he had to a family. He caught Sam glancing over, the wavering expression. "You should get back to him. Tell him I'm fine."

"I'll tell him we talked." Michael gripped Eli's shoulder again. "But I'm not going to lie to him."

Eli nodded and watched Michael return to Sam's side and the joy that radiated between them. Eli set his water down then made his way to the balcony that had been left open for smokers.

It was completely empty. No one in the company smoked, but that made it the perfect place to hide. He slid the door open and slipped out into the cold night. Snow danced in the air. Already, the cars and street were covered in a thin shimmer of white.

The air cooled his lungs and blew about his face. It wasn't supposed to storm tonight. Eli glanced up, but the sky was a uniform gray reflecting the lights below. Old fear settled into the back of his head, sending an ache to his spine and down to his shattered leg. He ignored it as best he could. This was Regent Square, not the North Hills. He was only a few miles from home. Even in the worst of weather, he could crawl back safely.

Except that was exactly what Noah had said, all those years ago.

Eli turned away from the snowfall—and came face-to-face with Justin on the other side of the glass door. Suddenly the air around him didn't seem nearly as cold as the blood in his veins.

Justin opened the door and stepped out onto the balcony. "This seems familiar."

Eli would have stepped back, if he could have moved. "Not at all." Because he had no power—didn't want power here. Just wanted to... run.

The snow fell harder.

"Sam was looking for you."

"Michael already found me."

Justin didn't move. "I'm surprised you don't want me on my knees."

He did step back then. *Why are you doing this to me?* "No, I don't. You don't want to be there."

Justin's snort was an ugly thing. "You're a Dom."

Fuck that. "And a sadist. And a Jew. And a cripple." He threw the last word like a cudgel. "And much more, besides."

Justin said nothing, but his chest heaved.

"You say *Dom* like anyone with dominant tendencies is the same. I know you're not stupid enough to believe that, Justin." His name felt like ash in Eli's throat.

Ash was about the color of Justin's skin, too. "Funny, I'm pretty sure you think me a flaming idiot, the way you treated me."

"The way I—?" His voice broke when the anger took over. "When did I *ever* mistreat you? I don't do that shit." Because it was horrible and hideous.

Justin stepped forward and Eli's back hit the edge of the balcony. "You expected everything from me. Expected me to be your whore."

Where the hell was this coming from? "No, I... never." He didn't take. He never took, not without a signal. Approval. "You're mistaking me for someone else again."

"Am I?"

"Yes." Most certainly. "If you'd paid *any* attention at all, you'd know that!"

"I paid plenty attention. Paid in so many ways, too." They were inches apart now. Eli's heart slammed against his chest. Fury and something else blazed in Justin. "The *worst* bit is that I still want you. After all you've done, I can't get you out of my head."

All that he'd done? His spine hurt from the cold and the press of the balcony edge. "Please get out of my way,

Justin." He didn't smell any alcohol, but he was willing to bet Justin was a few sheets to the wind.

Rather than move, Justin reached up and touched Eli's cheek. Tentative and gentle. It did not at all match the expression on Justin's face. "I want to kiss you."

No, don't. But that's not what slipped out of Eli's heart. "I won't stop you."

Justin did, and Eli didn't. Like the touch, the kiss was sweet and light and broke every bone in Eli's body. He caught himself on the balcony edge and his cane clattered to the frosted floor.

Justin pulled back, his eyes too wide and too wet. "Leave me alone." He turned and left the balcony.

No taste of alcohol. None.

It's me. I'm the problem. Only one solution. Eli found his footing and picked up his cane. He'd endure the rest of the party, like he'd promised Sam. It was the least he could do, since he was about to renege on their other agreement. Monday would be his last day at S. R. Anderson Consulting, even if it meant losing Sam and Michael, too.

Because Justin needed to be whole, and that required Eli to be gone.

You love him.

More than you can possibly imagine, Michael.

By the end of the night, snow coated the roadways, enough that biking from Regent Square to Oakland would be suicidal. Justin shouldn't have stayed so late, should have left when the first flakes fell. Shouldn't have kissed Eli.

No matter how much time passed, he still tasted Eli, felt

the heat of his body, the press of his cock. Nothing had changed.

He wasn't going to apologize for what he'd said. And Eli wasn't going to forgive him for having said it. This would have been easier had they just been fuckbuddies, if things hadn't been so *complicated*. He shoved his hands into his pockets. Walking wasn't going to be fun, but what choice did he have? He started up Braddock.

"Wait, Justin!" Eli's voice caught him and he looked back to see Eli limping quickly after him, cane in hand. "Where are you going?"

"Home."

"You can't..." He caught up, took a breath. "You can't walk home in this!" Long wool coat. Ever-present gloves. No hat, though. Snowflakes dotted his hair, white against the black curls.

All Justin had was his suit jacket. "I really don't have a choice." He put his back to Eli and marched up the street—and slipped and fell.

Shit. Way to prove Eli's point. He struggled to his feet.

"Just." Anguish in his name. *"Please."*

He stopped, eyes stinging, heart pounding. Eli cared. That was the worst of it. Nothing Justin did made Eli stop caring. He pressed his lips together.

A hand on his shoulder. Fingers under his chin lifting his face until he peered into Eli's gray eyes. "Please stop."

"I can't." His heart would burst from the pressure squeezing it. If he stopped, he'd never be able to resist Eli. Never not want to be with him. He couldn't be the submissive whore again, not even for Eli.

"You can stop." Quiet words, made even more silent by the snowfall and the empty street. "For a little bit. Let me drive you home. After that, hate me all you like, I don't care. But let me see you safe tonight." Eli let go.

Like every other time, Justin missed Eli's touch once it was gone. Seconds stretched out as snow fell all around them. Eli was right, of course. The man was so infuriatingly *right* that Justin couldn't keep away.

Eli's shoulders fell and he stepped back. "I just want to see you safe."

Under Eli's thumb, no doubt. Because safe to a Dom meant something entirely different to everyone else. But in this case it *was* a little ridiculous to think he could walk several miles in this weather. If Eli wanted to offer him a no-strings lift? "Fine."

The relief in Eli was palpable. "My car's just up the street."

They walked in silence to the Audi. Eli let him into the car, started, it and dusted off all the windows. When he settled into the driver's seat, he was frosted in snow, ruddy-cheeked, and beautiful.

Fuck. Justin stared at the car in front of them. This was a bad idea. He'd walked away once. But a second time? Wasn't sure he had enough willpower.

At least Eli was a man of his word. If he said he'd take Justin home, he would. If it had been Francis, all bets would have been off.

Eli eased the car out onto Braddock Avenue. The car slipped a bit, even with the all-wheel drive, but they moved up the road. They even managed the turn onto Forbes without sliding much. The roads were shit, though, and getting worse. They never plowed in the city when they should, and while the streets were fairly flat here by Pittsburgh standards... they weren't entirely. Getting to and from Oakland in this weather, where there *were* hills? Justin bit his lip and glanced at Eli.

Pale and strained. Wide-eyed. In control, but behind that was a hint of wild panic and terror.

Shit. Shit. Justin knew that look. He'd seen it in Mercy when she fought against the memories of war.

The car accident. He didn't know a thing about it, just that it had killed Eli's high school boyfriend and crushed Eli's leg. But if he had to guess—he'd lay odds it had happened on a snowy night like this one.

Oh hell.

Of course Eli wanted to see him safely home, especially if what Justin suspected was true. But who would make sure Eli made it home? Because after this drive... He stole another glance at Eli. Fraying edges. White knuckles.

This was a horrible idea. No way they were making it to Oakland, unless the streets miraculously cleared up.

No such luck. The snow fell harder.

They crept down Forbes Avenue, the car occasionally wavering in what should have been a lane had there been anything but white in front of them. At least there was no one else on the road. Eli hissed a few times when the car slipped—he was as pale as the scene in front of them, every muscle bunched, his face pulled sharp into fear. Justin nearly asked if Eli wanted him to drive, but he doubted Eli would let anyone take control now. If they stopped the car, they might not get it moving again, anyway.

They made it to the edge of Squirrel Hill and thankfully, the lights were green straight through the business district, up until Murray Avenue. A red light halted them there and Eli slumped in the seat, chest heaving.

"Halfway there."

"I know." Tight words. Breathless. No anger, just unfathomable weariness. And terror—oh God, the terror in Eli. What Justin wouldn't do to lift that weight from Eli's shoulders, tell him it would be okay, that they would make it. Justin's eyes stung. Wouldn't work. He'd never been able to do anything for Mercy, couldn't make her demons vanish. Just... support her. That's what he'd done when he'd finally escaped Francis.

The light turned green and they moved forward again. Wightman was next—Eli's street. Another light... this one red as well. They slowed, but not enough.

Shit. Cross traffic. A lone car inching its way across Wightman and they weren't slowing enough. *Oh my God.*

The car shook—the antilock breaks kicking in. A thin cry from Eli. The Audi kept moving.

They were so fucked. Justin tensed against the door, the seat, everything. Eli let out a sharp curse that wasn't English and swung the wheel.

The car spun, crossing the intersection. A flash of the terrified face of the other driver as the cars slipped past each other. So close. Bright red lips and nails. Dark hair. Ashen skin.

She moved away... and they continued to spin... snow-covered trees, houses, parked cars all moving past in a pantomime of slow motion. Horrible. Beautiful. They banged up against the curb on the opposite side of Forbes and lurched to a stop. The Audi's engine stuttered and died.

Holy fuck. They were alive. In one piece. Pointed in the opposite direction. Justin took several gulps of air and tried to calm the pounding of his heart and throbbing of his head. Eli was...

Eli trembled in his seat. Eyes wide and unseeing. So

pale he looked gray. Lips pulled away in half a cry. Shallow breaths.

Lost. Totally lost. Still spinning. Still stuck in that horrible moment. Like Mercy.

"Eli?"

A shudder. Nothing else.

"Eli, we're okay."

Still nothing.

"Eli," he barked. "Look at me."

Eyes flickered and focused. Eli turned his head, still haunted—but present. "Justin?"

"Yeah. It's Justin. I'm safe. You're safe. We didn't hit anything—just the curb."

Eli turned back to the road, but didn't speak. Didn't relax. Still trembled.

"We're kind of pointing the wrong way." Justin paused. "But maybe that's better." Because there was no way in hell they were making it to Oakland tonight. Not in this weather. Not down the hill that Forbes turned into, and absolutely not with Eli caught up in a flashback. They needed to get him home. Now.

"Let's go to your place. We're close." Hell, Wightman was right there. Three blocks and they'd be in Eli's driveway.

"Yes." Only that from Eli and no more. Distant. Hard. Eli examined the car for a moment in an almost clinical way, put it into park, turned it over, and shifted back into drive. They crept forward—a green light for them this time —and turned. Three blocks and another turn put them in Eli's driveway.

Justin had never been so glad to see the house he swore he'd never return to.

Eli put the car into park, set the emergency brake, and

dropped his face into his hands. The trembling turned to shaking, with a thin wail that tore Justin's heart in half.

Shit. He hit the ignition button and popped the key from its slot. Thankfully, the house keys were attached. "Eli, let's go inside."

Eli's chest heaved, his breath came in stutters and short fits. Silence now.

That wasn't good. None of this was good. Justin undid his belt and reached over and released Eli's, too, before crawling out of the car.

No reaction when he opened the driver's door, even though the wind blew flakes all around. Eli still held his head in his hands.

"Eli?"

"Leave me alone." Thin words. A whisper that sounded nothing like the man he knew.

"I will, once you're in the house. But I need you to come into the house."

He lifted his head. "I don't want the house. I don't want any of this. It's all... blood and ash."

This wasn't working. At all. "Eli, do you want me to be safe?"

Eli started and looked over. "Justin?" Confusion—mixed with relief.

"Yeah. It's me." He offered his hand. "Do you want me to be safe?"

The answer was a half a sob that stabbed into Justin's soul. "Always. It's the only thing I want."

Justin throat tightened. "Then come inside."

Eli grasped Justin's hand and he pulled Eli up out of the car and into his arms. Unsteady, shaking Eli.

"I'm sorry." Eli's breathless words in Justin's ear. "I can't stop seeing them."

Justin pushed the car door shut and half walked, half carried Eli to the house. "I know." He unlocked the door, got them both inside, and peeled off Eli's coat and tuxedo jacket. Dropped them on the bench. His own suit coat followed. "You're all right. I'm fine. No one was hurt." Justin toed off his shoes. "How about we go sit down on the couch?"

Eli didn't argue, didn't protest when Justin led him to the living room sectional. Lavi took off when Eli sank down in the middle of the L, eyes still wide and distant. "It won't go away. It usually goes away by now." He peered up at Justin. "I'm so sorry—whatever I did." He whispered, "Are you even here?"

Words like fists to his chest. Justin ignored the pain. Instead, he tugged Eli's shoes off and swung his legs up onto the couch. "I'm here. You're not alone." Blanket—that always helped Mercy: the security of being wrapped up in something. He pulled a throw from the back of the couch and laid it over Eli.

Eli clutched at the blanket and rolled away from Justin. "I can't... I know you don't want to be here."

That wasn't entirely true. "It's fine."

Eli tugged the blanket over his head. Cut off from the world.

Justin slumped on the floor, his back against the couch, mirroring Eli. He did want to be here. Desperately. Wanted to be Eli's, but that meant not being his own. Mercy needed him. So did his family. And yet... He stared at Eli's blanket-covered back. Eli needed him, too.

Eli as the wealthy, sadistic, controlling Dom didn't mesh with the man huddled under the blanket on the couch. Or the one who had been at the office the past few weeks. Or any version of Eli. Justin's stomach felt like stone. How hard had he been shoving Eli into a box that didn't fit him? "Can I get you anything? Water? Tea? Booze?"

Eli rolled back, his head framed by the blanket. Rainbow colors. Crochet. "Tea. There's—" Eli took a breath, sat up, and peered down at Justin, eyes more clear than they'd been since the start of the drive. "There's valerian root tea in the cabinet above the coffeemaker."

"I can do that." Justin climbed to his feet and headed into the kitchen.

"Use the electric kettle for the water, not the microwave."

So very Eli. The tightness in Justin's chest eased a bit. He found the tea, a mug, and set the kettle. A few minutes later, he handed a brimming mug to Eli. "Careful, it's hot."

Eli raised an eyebrow. "I hope so." He took a sip and leaned back against the cushions.

The couch seemed a better idea than the floor. There was plenty of room on the L-shaped sectional. He wouldn't be crowding Eli. Or getting too close. "How are you feeling?"

He shrugged. "Better. More present." Another sip of tea. "It hasn't been this bad in a very long time."

"Well, considering what almost happened..."

A chuckle. Eli sounded more and more like... Eli. "To be honest, I don't remember. Not... clearly." He studied the cup before he drank more. "I know the car wasn't stopping and there was another in the intersection and we were going to hit... and then I was here." He shook his head. "That's the worst part. I can't even remember the present."

"We one-eightied, and somehow missed the other car. Ended up against the curb."

"And I drove us here?"

Justin nodded.

"God." More tea. "Thank you for all of this. I know you're not fond of me, but I'm not sure..." He got that distant look. "I don't think I'd have made it home if you hadn't been with me."

"It's not that, Eli, it's..." His turn to shrug. This wasn't the time or the place for that conversation. "Anyway. I'm glad I was here." *Glad I could help you. I'm sorry I hurt you so much.* "Is there anything else you need?"

Eli took a final drink of the tea and set the mug on the coffee table. He looked up, face drawn and weary. "Yes. You."

So much pain in those two words. Justin couldn't breathe for a moment. When he spoke, it was harsh and strangled. "Eli..."

Eli opened his arms in invitation. He made no movement toward Justin. But the agony and fear in Eli and the tremor in his hands spoke volumes.

How could he say no? Hell, he didn't *want* to. Justin slid across the couch and into Eli's arms, head against his chest. A hand on his back. One against his hair. Beneath Justin's ear, Eli's heart beat so fast, despite the slow rise and fall of his chest. Justin's heart beat as quickly—he'd missed this so very much. The warmth, the sense of belonging, of everything clicking into place.

Fingers grazed Justin's cheek. "Just for a little while. I know you don't want this. But—" Eli's voice cracked. Something warm and wet fell on Justin's cheek. "I need you."

Even if Justin had known what to say in response, he couldn't have spoken through his tight throat. The ache in his chest was unbearable. Had he read Eli so wrong?

Eli took a deep breath. "I'd known Noah pretty much all my life. We weren't friends to start with. I've never been good with people. Too sharp, too cold. Too much of a know-it-all."

Justin shifted, peered up. Tears in Eli's eyes. "You don't have to tell me this," he whispered.

Eli brushed his thumb against Justin's jaw. "I'd like to. May I?"

There was the search for consent. Always that question —always giving Justin a choice. Stay or go. Listen... or not. Maybe if he heard this—the heart of who Eli was—he'd understand. Nothing about Eli made sense. Justin nodded.

"I guess we first noticed each other about the time I was preparing for my bar mitzvah. My Hebrew was crap despite years of schooling—his was good, so he started tutoring me. I'm not sure why, but he put up with me. He wasn't afraid. Shot back at all my quips." He laughed. "Apparently, I was a scary little shit, even at twelve."

So much self-awareness. Justin shivered.

"Wait. Give me a second." Eli tugged at the blanket, pulling it out from between them.

It was natural—so natural to slide up against Eli, fully into his arms and soak up that warmth.

Eli drew the blanket around them. "You have to understand, both Noah and I, we were raised Orthodox Jewish. Well, I'm Sephardi, but... for all intents, Orthodox. You've seen the kids in the suits and hats with the tassels in the neighborhood?"

"Yeah." More synagogues than churches in Squirrel Hill.

"That was me, more or less. And Noah. He was two years older than me, almost exactly. Our birthdays were five days apart in January. The year after I turned fourteen, we both realized that we weren't just interested in each other as friends. We'd both heard the word *gay*, knew what it meant.

Understood that we were supposed to get married, likely to one of the girls in the neighborhood, and have kids. But we wanted each other. Desperately." His laugh was soft. "Hormones. Boys."

Justin couldn't help his own chuckle. "Yeah. Made high school interesting." He shifted. "I always thought of homosexuality as more of a Christian sin—but Leviticus—"

"—Is in the Tanakh—the Torah—yes. Short form for most modern Orthodox is that same-sex attraction isn't a choice, but gay men and women are supposed to get married to the opposite sex and have kids." Eli shrugged. "Reform Judaism doesn't give a shit."

"We'd been fooling around for a while. For our birthdays when we turned sixteen and eighteen, we decided to try anal. His birthday came first, but he thought it would be unfair for him to top me since he was older, so..."

"You topped him." Justin looked up. Color touched Eli's cheeks. That was unexpected.

Eli coughed and smiled. "Let's just say that I learned a lot about myself that night." The amusement faded. "Two days later, we went out with friends. Noah drove."

Eli shuddered once beneath Justin.

"Wasn't supposed to snow. Or maybe just a dusting. Something like that. It was Noah and me and Rachel and Milka. We'd gone out to celebrate our birthdays—someplace nice and not in Squirrel Hill. They had a vegetarian menu, so we didn't have to worry about kashrut. I was in the back, with Rachel."

Another tremble ran through Eli and his voice dropped. "Up in the North Hills, some of the roads are pretty twisty."

"It's okay."

"No. It wasn't. Noah was so careful. Driving slowly. Blinkers on and everything. But the truck in the other lane

—it came straight at us. I—don't remember exactly what happened. Just the lights and the sound and the heat and..."

Eli stopped. Exhaled. "They say Noah turned and that's pretty much the only reason I survived. The truck—it was one of those boxy delivery types—hit us, spun us, hit us again. And the car behind us hit us. There was an SUV behind the truck, too. Pushed the truck forward. We were crushed between them all."

Oh God. He'd seen the aftermath of a few bad accidents, the twisted remains of the cars, had nightmares about what it might be like... and Eli had lived it.

"I heard them die. All of them." The trembling started again.

The only thing Justin could do was hold Eli. "I'm sorry." Insufficient words. So meaningless.

"I couldn't move. Couldn't help them. There was blood and metal and people yelling." Another deep breath. "They had to cut me out."

More drops on Justin's face.

"I never lost consciousness. Not until the hospital. One moment, they were all alive. The next, all dead, but me. I had a couple of cracked ribs, abrasions, and a mangled leg. Lost some bone and muscle. A bunch of crap in my ankle will never be right, but I survived. I have no idea why I did and they didn't."

There was nothing Justin could say.

"I turned sixteen in a hospital bed. Noah was dead. Rachel. Milka. They were buried on my birthday. I couldn't go to the funeral, couldn't visit shiva. My friends—my *lover*—they were all gone, and I had no way to mourn them." He laughed, but there was no joy in it. "Then I made the mistake of telling my rabbi I loved Noah. That we'd had sex on his birthday."

"Like... a confession?"

"No, nothing like that. I—just needed someone to talk to. He was supposed to be trained in psychology or something. So I told him. Figured he'd keep it to himself." Another hollow laugh. "He told my parents."

Holy shit. "*That's* how your parents found out you were gay?"

"Yup. So next thing I knew, my parents were yelling at me. In my hospital room."

No wonder Eli reacted like he had at the Silk Elephant. "That's—wow."

A dark laugh. "It gets worse."

"How? How the hell can it get any worse than that?"

"Because my parents did the math. On Noah's birthday, he was eighteen and I was fifteen.

Legally..."

Justin sat up. Stared at Eli. "No."

"Yes." Lines of anger cut so deep into Eli's expression. "Of course, Noah was *dead*, so they couldn't charge him with rape. Or corruption of a minor. Or whatever they would have nailed him with... so my loving parents sued Noah's family. For *my benefit*, of course."

"That's..." *Unconscionable. Horrifying.* "Holy hell, Eli."

The anger shattered, leaving behind something so raw, so broken, it didn't belong on Eli. Tears ran down Eli's cheeks. "This house? All the things you see?" he whispered. "The car? My education? They were all bought with *Noah's blood.*"

Justin swallowed bile. Swallowed a second time. Kept it together because all he wanted to do was double over in shame, but he didn't have that right, not after this. He'd been so very wrong about Eli.

"On my eighteenth birthday, I received a trust fund that

contained all the money that would have been Noah's—and then some. I tried to give it back to Noah's parents, but they knew I had no part in what happened—hell, they knew I'd walked out of my parents' house that morning and I wasn't ever going back." He wiped away the tears. "They had no other children. The least—they said—they could do was see that I was cared for. Especially since Noah had loved me. They asked me to keep the money. Get a good education. A good job. Do all the things that Noah couldn't, in his memory." Eli closed his eyes and leaned against the couch pillows. "That's the entire story."

To live through that, to be constantly reminded by an injury that would never heal, an inheritance that belonged to someone else... "Eli, I don't know what to say. 'I'm sorry' seems—wrong."

"You don't have to say anything." Eli cupped his hand around the back of Justin's neck and Justin couldn't help the shiver that ran through him, nor the instinct that drew him back into Eli's arms.

"Just... be here. Please. For a little while."

Justin whispered into Eli's shirt. "As long as you need."

A hollow laugh. "No lies, Justin. Not tonight."

Now the tears were in Justin's eyes. He spoke around the hole in his heart, the tightness in his brain. "As long as I can be, then."

Eli didn't speak, just stroked his thumb against Justin's neck.

There was nothing Justin could do. No way to fix the mistake he'd made, the words he'd flung at Eli, the wounds he'd opened in both of them. The tears wouldn't stop, so he closed his eyes, listened to Eli's heartbeat, and tried not to think about how they'd both have to be apart for the rest of their lives.

CHAPTER SEVENTEEN

Eli let Justin weep. Hell, his own tears fell, though he'd shed more than enough in the eighteen years since that night. But Justin's tears, his shaking frame, weren't entirely about Eli's story, and for the first time in a while, the despair that engulfed Eli whenever he saw Justin or heard his voice shifted away.

Justin might have been crying, but he was in Eli's arms and world felt *right* again, despite all the shit between them, the unanswered questions, and the words thrown at each other.

He loved Justin. Desperately. Perhaps it was stupidity, but he couldn't help it. There wasn't much left in him but love. All the fear, the anger, the sadness had been poured out. Love and hope. That's what remained.

He stroked Justin's neck, drifted his hand down to Justin's waist, and asked the question he'd wanted to ask so many times before. "What did I do?"

A hitch of breath and Justin's body slid along his, deliciously so. "Nothing."

Fuck. A creeping sensation wormed through Eli. "That wasn't a reaction to nothing."

Slow breathing. Justin didn't move away. Quite the opposite, he relaxed into Eli, which was odd. Gratifying, but very odd given the conversation they were having. He stroked Justin's hair. This had to come from Justin in his own time, not be forced out with a command or hurried along with annoyance.

When he finally spoke, it was a whisper. "You didn't do anything wrong. I couldn't stay."

Still not the right time to speak, even if he itched to do so. He pressed a kiss to Justin's forehead.

A tremble. "You... bought me things. Fed me. Clothed me. Offered me a place to stay when I was in trouble."

The bottom dropped from Eli's stomach. This was... not his fault. But not good.

"The only thing I had to give you in return was my body. To fuck. To play with. To—" Justin's voice cracked. "Use."

That word punched a hole into Eli's heart and his calm shattered. He sucked in a breath and looked up at the ceiling, tears returning. *Oh damn.*

Justin had been paying him back with sex and pain. Didn't matter that Eli's gifts had come with no strings as far as Eli was concerned. Eli gazed around his living room, suddenly seeing it as Justin might—elegant. Full of expensive things. He wore a Rolex. Dressed in fine suits.

Justin struggled to make ends meet. Shitty apartment. Drowning in debt to support his family.

Eli let out the breath. He'd offered what he had out of love and respect and caring, and hadn't expected anything at all in return.

Justin stirred. "I—I felt trapped. So I ran."

Of course he had. All the conversations, all that had happened clicked into place. Every limb went numb. He should have seen this. Hadn't because he hated acknowledging the wealth. Noah's money. *Time to grow up, Eli.*

"You let me go." Justin pulled away again and sat up. He wiped his eyes. "Let me walk out. Didn't force me back."

"I don't own you, Justin." Such thick words. He'd thought he'd been emptied of pain. He'd been so very wrong. His heart twisted and knotted into new and agonizing shapes. "I never meant to trap you. I thought you liked—" The bondage. The sex. The pain.

"I do. I did. There wasn't anything you ever did to me that I didn't like."

But Justin had walked out. Felt unsafe and left. "The problem is me. Who I am." The wealth. The status. Things he couldn't change.

"You're not who I thought you were. To you, I'm not... a toy. Not a plaything."

"No. Never that." Flesh and blood. Messy, lovely, tempting, but a person. Never, ever a *thing*. That idea tore his soul out.

"You'd let me go again, after tonight. When the snow clears. Anytime. Every time. Again and again." Justin hugged himself, shaking. "Wouldn't you?"

"Yes. Always."

"Why?"

"Because I love you."

All air seemed to leave Justin. "You—" He shook his head, eyes too wide. "You shouldn't—"

Wasn't a matter of should or not, it just was. "I love you, Justin. Have loved. Will love." Eli shifted and sat up as well.

"I only want your happiness, to see you healthy and safe. If not with me, then... not with me. How could I love you and trap you?"

Those wet, bright eyes, the shock parting those lips.

"I don't need half of this." Eli waved his hand to encompass the house. "And I deserve *none* of it, but if there's anything I can do to make your life better—ask. Anything." He was going to break again. Felt the pressure in his head, all the signs of falling into a billion pieces. At least he understood why he'd lost Justin.

"If I asked for your forgiveness?" All tremble, those words.

Oh hell.

He had to hold it together. For Justin. For himself. Eli opened his arms. Justin hesitated only a moment before falling into him.

"There's nothing to forgive. Nothing." Agony in his chest. He pressed lips to Justin's hair and closed his eyes against the pain.

Muffled words. "I made your life hell."

Yes, he had. But reactions like that didn't come out of a vacuum. "What was his name?"

A laugh that was half a sob. "Am I so easy to read?"

"I've been in therapy more than half my life. You learn some things after all those years."

Justin tightened his hold. "His name was Francis. He... Well, I guess you can figure it out."

Enough, anyway. "Yeah." He rubbed Justin's back. "When you're ready, tell me. Don't if you're not."

"Not... not tonight." He sucked down a breath. "Too much."

That he understood. He was pretty overloaded himself. Eli leaned back against the couch, pulling Justin with him.

It was going to be all right. "We can just... be here. Now. For a while."

Somehow, they ended up lying on the couch, Justin above him. "Good." Justin leaned down and brushed his lips against Eli's "Because I want now. And here. And you."

There was only one answer to that. Eli tangled his hands into Justin's hair and kissed him like there was no other man in the world.

THE WAY ELI KISSED JUSTIN LEFT NO DOUBT TO HIS desire. Nor did the press of Eli's cock against Justin's thigh. He grasped the front of Eli's shirt and pulled him closer.

Fingers at Justin's throat, working his tie loose. How was he still wearing it? Why were there clothes between him and Eli? He wanted Eli against his flesh without linen and cotton in between.

Grappling at Eli's shirt seemed futile.

"Tie first." Eli spoke against his lips, all heat and husk. "And if you tear the buttons off this shirt, I swear I'll make you sew them back on while nude."

The things that came out of Eli's mouth. Eli had Justin's necktie free and the top button of his shirt open. He pressed lips against Justin's throat and Justin rocked his dick against Eli's hip in response.

He needed Eli undressed. Wanted both of them naked. He tugged at the silky fabric around Eli's neck. A real bow tie, not one of those premade clip things, so it unraveled. A quick flip and it was somewhere past the coffee table and out of their way.

"Bedroom?" It came out as a gasp, because Eli had

worked enough of Justin's shirt open to nip at the skin over his clavicle.

"Yes." Depth to that word. Heat and lust. Eli rose, even as Justin stood, both still working at each other's clothing. It took time to cross the living room, what with Eli's mouth on his, hands pulling shirts from pants. Along the way, Justin took off Eli's cummerbund. He pulled hard at either side of Eli's shirt and sent silver-rimmed buttons clattering against the wood floor. A white-and-black puff of fur chased one, thumping back into the living room.

Eli moaned. "Hope you can sew."

Yeah, he could. "Naked, even." Justin pushed Eli's shirt over his shoulders, sending it to the floor before he found himself up against a wall with Eli's knee between his legs, pressing against his balls. "Fuck."

Between kisses, Eli spoke. "Can't—take clothes off—on the stairs." He unbuttoned the rest of Justin's shirt and they both stripped it off Justin's body. Between nips and kisses, hands touching everywhere, they worked pants and underwear off. Eli gripped Justin's shaft and drew his teeth down Justin's neck.

Sparks in his vision and pinpricks to his fingertips. How he'd missed this—the way their bodies fit. How they moved, touched, ground, and pressed, each knowing what the other needed. Justin moaned. "Upsta—"

Eli swallowed the end of the word with a kiss.

When he relented, he grinned in the way that always made Justin want to drop to his knees. "After you."

He would have run up the stairs, but for the gentle touch of Eli's hand on his back. Though Justin led, Eli set the pace his leg would allow.

When they reached the hallway, they were back in each

other's arms. A seductive dance of touch, taste, and sound had them at the bed, then on top of it.

The scent of lavender slipped around them. That would always mean Eli.

"Still have condoms and lube in the drawer?"

Eli scraped his nails against Justin's scalp and pulled at his hair through another long kiss. They both moaned. "Yes. Get them."

Never so happy to obey Eli's command. So right to do so. He crawled only as much as he needed to find the bottle and the box and settled back, straddling Eli's legs.

Eli's skin was flushed—hot to the touch. The telltale traces of stress and tears still blotted Eli's face, but desire sparked in his eyes and rippled the muscles of his stomach. Eli stroked himself, his gaze claiming Justin as sure as cuffs and a collar would.

"Put one on."

Gladly. Hell, he'd ride Eli's dick all night. He needed skin against skin, the tangle of arms, the sound of Eli's moans and the release only Eli had ever given him. He reached for Eli's cock.

"No." Dark and delicious words followed. "On yours. I want you inside me tonight."

"You—what?" The foil packet dangled from Justin's fingers. He'd heard Eli, but wrapping his brain around those words? Wasn't happening.

"Have you topped before?" Concern. Gentleness—and that was so utterly Eli, too.

"Yeah." Not recently, not since he'd discovered how much he liked to submit.

Eli raised an eyebrow. "Do I need to start counting?" The devil's smile sent a shiver down Justin's spine. Proof Eli was still a Dom.

"No." Somehow, he managed to rip open the package, get his fingers to work long enough to roll the latex over his painfully hard cock. He was supposed to fuck Eli? Still couldn't grasp the concept, but there Eli was, beneath him. Waiting.

God, he'd missed this. The tumble of nerves, the coil of need that Eli built and stroked and commanded from him. Justin reached for the lube. "Prep?" He barely pushed the word out of his dry throat.

Eli nodded, his smile wavering slightly. "It's been a while."

That didn't help in many ways, given how spun up he was. But knowing Eli was nervous? The tension in Justin's shoulders eased. "Hands and knees might be easier."

"Not on my leg." Eli stretched his arms and folded his hands behind his head, the picture of relaxation. "Besides, I want to watch you while you fuck me."

Jesus. Those words moved like molten heat down Justin. He opened the lube with trembling hands. He wanted to watch Eli too. Wanted to see what happened when he pressed a finger into Eli just like—that.

Hard to tell who gasped louder. Seeing Eli's eyes widen and his head tip back? Beautiful. He pressed in harder the second time, twisting as he went. God, he was tight. Relaxed, but so firm around his finger. Couldn't imagine how it would feel to have Eli around his cock.

That grunt came from the back of *his* throat, not Eli's.

It *was* followed by a huff of laughter from Eli. "You're a bit bigger than that, you know."

Of course Eli knew his girth. Justin's cock had been in Eli's hand and in his mouth. He pulled his finger out, added lube, and thrust two in, pistoning Eli until he groaned and twisted the bedsheets in his fists. Justin leaned over and took the head of Eli's cock into his mouth, savoring the salty fluid pooled at the tip.

"That's more like it." Eli's fingers scraped Justin's scalp, urging him farther down. Justin complied and heard the heavenly sound of Eli gasping for breath. He added a third finger, stretching Eli, teasing his sweet spot.

Eli pulled Justin off his cock. "Fuck." Half a moan to that. "I want you inside me when I come, not the other way around."

That was an order he was more than willing to obey, and Eli was as prepped as he was going to get. Justin pulled his fingers out and slicked his cock, then pressed the crown against Eli's entrance and slid in.

They both gasped and groaned as he stretched Eli open. Justin paused to let Eli adjust and so he could catch his breath. Still hard to comprehend that it was *Eli* beneath him and around him.

Eli rocked his hips. "Don't you stop."

"Don't intend to." Not until Eli said, not until they both came. Justin pulled back and pushed in deeper this time. Eli met his stroke with a pleased grunt. Another stroke, quicker this time, then another and another, until he was lost in the rhythm and motion of their bodies grinding against each other.

Each time Justin moved forward, Eli met his thrusts in a way that drove Justin higher. "You feel so—" Justin lost the word when Eli's nails bit into his arms. Amazing, the sharp flick of pain on top of Eli's tight heat. He didn't want it to stop, this connection, the light in Eli's eyes when they met again and again.

Justin couldn't tell if he was fucking or being fucked. So not in control. Didn't matter. Never mattered, not here in Eli's bed, where their bodies met and the world vanished.

Justin leaned down as Eli reached up. The sharp pull of Justin's hair only fueled the fire already tangled in his blood, his soul. Eli's mouth met his and their tongues twined. Moans blended. Heaven. Hell. Both.

He'd been a complete fool to run from Eli. Submission was a gift, but so was this—the control, the pain.

"More." A command between bites and kisses and the delectable agony of Eli's grip on Justin's hair.

As if he *needed* a command to fuck Eli harder. Wouldn't last long at this rate anyway, not after all that had happened tonight. Might as well give Eli what he asked for. Justin shifted angles and drove deep into Eli, thrusting as hard and as fast as he could manage, shaking the both of them.

Eli's grip in his hair slacked and his head fell back on the pillow. "Oh fuck, Justin!"

The profound ecstasy on Eli's face—he hadn't come, but fuck, something had unlocked in Eli and made him surrender to Justin. For a moment, Justin couldn't breathe. He closed his eyes and gave everything he had and took all that Eli offered.

All those years, and he hadn't understood how love was supposed to work.

Fingers brushed Justin's cheek and he blinked to find Eli focused on him. They met, lips, mouths, fingers, bodies. Neither had the upper hand, or they both did. That thought was too much to take in.

Eli shuddered underneath him, and broke their kiss. "Just." A plea, a request, and an order.

He wrapped his hand around Eli's cock and stroked in time with the rhythm they'd found. Begging spilled from both their mouths, blended together, and pushed Justin closer to release. Eli kissed Justin's shoulder, breath hot against Justin's skin, staccato in his ear. "I'm close. I'm—"

Teeth scraped against Justin's flesh, then a blaze of pain rocked though him when Eli bit his shoulder and came.

Justin's shout probably woke the neighbors. Eli tightened around him and pressed teeth harder into his muscle. Agony blended with euphoria as he spilled into Eli, burying as deep as he could over and over until the white heat in his body faded into exhaustion and awe. They both collapsed against the bed and each other.

For a long time, they just held each other. Justin trembled. Or maybe Eli did. Hard to tell. Breathing took effort. Movement and speech were out of the question.

Eli brushed his lips against Justin's shoulder, over the spot he'd bitten, and dragged out a spike of pain Justin felt in his toes.

He finally found the ability to form words. "Can't wait to see the bruise."

Eli's chuckle rocked both their bodies. "Sorry about that."

"No, you're not."

Another laugh. This one moved Justin's soul. He forced the lump in his throat down. He didn't deserve this moment —these emotions—or Eli's happiness.

"Justin." Eli stroked his back. "It's all right."

He couldn't stop shaking, couldn't breathe right. "I don't want this to end."

"It doesn't have to."

He pushed up to peer into Eli's face. "But—"

Fingers against his lips. "It doesn't have to end. No, it won't be easy, and yes, we're going to have to—to start all over in some places. But I'm willing. I've never been more willing."

"Why?" He knew the answer; Eli had said it before.

Still, it came like the sweet fall of leather on his skin, shocking him to his bones.

"Because I love you."

And he loved Eli. Just couldn't say that yet. The whole concept was too new, too raw. "Give me time."

Eli kissed his cheek. "Always."

Nothing Justin could say would convey the tumult in his head. He pulled his softening cock from Eli, careful not to lose the condom. "I need to..."

Eli let him go. He climbed off the bed, tossed the condom, and washed his hands. He paused in the master bath doorway. Eli lay on the bed, eyes closed, but a smile across his face. Semen glistened on his stomach. "Do you want tissues or a towel or something?"

"Either." He placed his hands behind his head, same as he had when they started. "Or your tongue." He opened his eyes and grinned. "Whichever."

If he hadn't just come, he'd have been hard again from the glint in Eli's eyes and the turn of his lips. Justin crossed the space and crawled back into bed with Eli.

There wasn't anywhere else in the world he wanted to be.

CHAPTER EIGHTEEN

The ringing of the telephone had Eli stumbling out of bed and falling into the chair by the phone before he was entirely awake. Not his most graceful maneuver, and fuck, did his leg hurt—everything hurt—but he'd managed to shut the thing up by answering it. "Hello?" His voice was unexpectedly hoarse.

Lavi jumped off the bed, his displeasure at being disturbed evident in the flick of his tail before he vanished under the bed.

"Eli?" Sam. The man on the other end was Sam.

"Yeah, it's me." He scrubbed a hand over his face and blinked. "What the hell time is it, anyway?" On the bed, Justin rolled over and looked at him.

Justin. Eli took one breath, then another. *Oh.*

"It's almost noon." Sam's voice sounded puzzled. Frazzled.

Memories of the previous night flooded back. Of terror, tears, and hope. Justin on top of him and—

Justin raised an eyebrow and chuckled.

Sam spoke. "Eli?"

"Sorry, I'm still waking up. Had a long night."

A pause. "Look, I don't mean to bother you... but I can't get ahold of Justin. He's not answering his cell and I'm really worried. Lots of accidents last night. Did you see him leave the party?"

"I..." Black hair, stunning blue eyes, and a thin and supple body. He'd felt so good moving inside Eli. There Justin was. In his bed. "Yeah. He's here. With me."

"What?"

Eli flinched away from the phone. That had been loud —enough to dissolve Justin into a fit of giggles.

"What the *hell*, Eli?" Another pause. "You took him home and *fucked* him?"

"Other way around. Kind of. Tried to give him a lift to Oakland because he was going to walk home... but I spun the car out. I think. That part's hazy. We ended up here. And he fucked *me*, if you must know."

Dead silence on the other end.

"Technically," Justin said, "you had me fuck you. There's a difference." Amusement was written in his smile and wrapped around his words.

"Oh, hush, you." How he loved the man lounging in his bed. Eli rubbed his eyes. "He's *fine*, Sam. Would you like to talk to him?"

Something like a choke came from the other end. "E— are *you* okay?"

He had to contemplate for a moment, which meant the answer was... "No. Not exactly." Yes, he ached from the past, and holy hell, was he fragile at the moment, but— "It's going to be fine, Sam. Everything. Just need to... piece it all back together. I—" Words ran out. Justin crawled to the edge of the bed and held out his hand.

Nothing to do but hand the phone over.

"Sam?" Justin said. "Yeah, I'm okay. I mean—" A pause. "He's pretty shaken up."

Eli leaned back in the chair and closed his eyes. Understatement of the year. At least Dr. Brohmer would be able to pay off her Christmas bills. He giggled.

"I—" Justin sounded chagrined. "I know. Believe me, I know." A pause. "He told me everything."

He had. Opened himself completely to Justin. Physically, too. That had been intense—being fucked. He'd forgotten how powerful that could be. Eli opened his eyes.

Justin sat cross-legged on the bed, playing with the edge of the sheet while he listened to Sam talk. He lifted his head and gave Eli a faint smile. "Oh, I'm sure he knows that. He's pretty aware of himself." Justin picked at the sheet more. "I'm not—there are things I need to tell him. But he's right, Sam."

Such blue eyes. The jagged black and red hair, mussed with sex and sleep, was lovely.

"It's going to be okay."

Eli exhaled. Yeah, it really was.

"Right. I'll tell him. Thanks, Sam. Bye." Justin turned off the phone and set it on the bed. "Sam says if the roads are shit tomorrow morning, stay home. Because he won't be in, either."

"Wonder how bad it is?" Eli levered himself up and hobbled to the window. When he peeked behind the shade, a sea of white greeted him, dotted with several neighbors clearing their drives and walks. A few ruts in the snow in the street marked a car's passing, but nothing like a plow had touched the road. Thin clouds hung in the sky, bright with the sun that tried to pierce them.

"How much?" The bed creaked.

"A foot? Maybe more? I can never tell. Enough to cause trouble. No plow."

Two soft *thump*s, then the warmth of Justin's hand pressed against his back. Eli's breath caught and he shivered.

Justin raised the blind, letting the light spill into the room, and studied the scene. "That's not as bad as it could be. Bet they'll have it cleared by tomorrow."

"Pity." There was something magical about the white scene outside and the warmth of Justin behind him. To have it interrupted with something so mundane as work seemed wrong.

Eli's chest hurt, but the pain was—different. Not overwhelming despair or guilt. Like the clouds above, something sweeter seemed to be breaking through the haze.

He hadn't felt anything but anger and fear at snow in so long.

Justin drew him away from the window. "Eli, is there someone I should call?"

That was a bit like a bucket of cold water. Good. Too much focus inward and he would spend all day contemplating his navel. He sat down on the edge of the bed. "Do I look that bad?"

Justin scratched the back of his head. "You look distant. Scattered."

Eli shrugged. "That's not far from the mark. But it's not —" He searched for the right words and came up a bit empty. "I'm a bit out of it, but I'll be fine. I'll call my therapist tomorrow." He took Justin's hands in his. "I didn't lie to Sam. It's going to be fine."

Justin nodded. "Why don't you catch a shower, and I'll make coffee?"

Something of the fire that usually burned in him came back. "Are you telling me what to do, Mr. White?"

His grin was utterly perfect. "And if I am?"

Eli stood and pulled Justin into a kiss—one just long enough to shift Justin's breathing. "I'll take a shower. You make coffee, and we'll see, shall we?"

"Yes, Eli."

Music to his ears. "Good."

WHILE ELI SHOWERED, JUSTIN BORROWED A PAIR OF sweats from the closet and headed to the kitchen. This time, the smell of freshly ground coffee brought a tangle of lust and guilt. The guilt he pushed away. There would be time and ways to deal with that later.

The water in the kettle boiled about the same time the shower upstairs shut off.

The glimpse of Eli's half smile, his voice changing from unsure, back to in control. One moment, Eli had been lost—the next? Justin thought Eli might bend him over and tan his ass right in the bedroom. That shift fucked with Justin's brain and heart.

When Eli entered the kitchen, there were still traces of the stress of the night before—the flashback, the aftermath, the confusion of this morning—but that lifted brow was familiar and it drove a spike of desire through Justin.

"Are those *my* sweats you're wearing?"

Of course Eli had noticed. "I only have my suit, nothing else... It is a bit cold in the house."

"I see." Eli took a seat at the breakfast bar, but his focus remained on Justin. It was the Eli he knew so well, the confidence, the razor edge that could mean passion or pain. Eli's sense of command had returned.

"I'm sorry." Justin pressed the plunger down on the coffee, then grabbed two mugs from the cabinet.

"You are not." Cool words, but the smile belied the tone.

Justin matched it with one of his own. "I apologize?" He poured the coffee and carried both mugs to the breakfast bar.

Eli nodded. "Better." Eli cupped the side of Justin's face. "And that's one, by the way."

He couldn't help the shiver. Nor another then Eli stroked his thumb over his jaw.

"Though neither of us is in the space we need to be for sceneing yet." Eli let go and hefted his coffee mug.

Reality crashed down around them. Eli was recovering from his flashback, and he... Justin sat down on the stool next to Eli. "I should tell you about Francis."

Soft, sweet voice. "When you're ready."

Being ready wasn't something that was ever going to happen. Only one thing to do. Justin took a sip of his coffee. "After I graduated from Stanford, I got a pretty decent job with ErazaTech."

A nod. "I remember."

From his résumé, of course. "Did pretty well, too. Got a raise and a promotion after the first year. By the second, I was well on my way to managing my own accounts." Justin fingered the lip of his mug. "I was also involved in the Scene. Got into it in college."

Eli finally took a sip of his coffee. "Boyfriend?"

"I was between boyfriends—but I had this friend Mitch. We blew off steam together and he noticed I tended to come a lot faster and harder when he held me down as he fucked me. Took me to my first party." He couldn't help the chuckle. "Blew my mind. And my load. Twice."

Eli snorted. "Amateur."

Justin curled his toes over the rung of the bar stool. "As you might expect, I threw myself into the Scene. Played with a lot of Doms. Watched others play." He'd loved those days. Pleasure and pain on the weekends, laser focus during the week. If he'd have kept at it, he wouldn't be living in a dank, mold infested apartment now. But what was done was done.

"I got invited to a different party by one of the Doms I played with—an exclusive party. Less college, more business. That's where I met Francis. He was..." Justin shook his head. "So focused. Intense. Or so I thought at the time. Turns out, it was cruelty." He met Eli's gaze. "You've always treated me like a human."

Behind those gray eyes Justin caught a glimpse of unrestrained anger. "You are." Sharp, strong words.

He knew that now. "The play we did at the other parties just scratched an itch. First time Francis topped me, I flew for hours. I'd never experienced pain like that—or true subspace. I had to have more."

Eli looked down at his mug and took a sip. For all the world, it looked like he was chewing on the words and swallowing them. Letting Justin tell his story—just as Justin had done for Eli last night.

Justin winced at the stab of guilt. "I went back. Over and over. Every time I could. Each time, I escaped into that oblivion and each time, it was harder and harder to break free of it. My work slipped. I became—distracted. What mattered was the next time I saw Francis. Felt his whip. Got fucked."

"Addicted."

That. Justin drew a finger around the lip of his coffee mug. "Yup." His gut twisted. "Then I gave Francis my cell number and he started calling. Taking me to dinner. Buying me clothes. Electronics. Anything I wanted." He took another gulp of coffee. "I liked that, the attention, but it was even more of a distraction. A month later, I had my first dressing-down at work. I was devastated, completely. Despite everything, I hadn't seen it coming. I was so *young*."

Again, Eli looked to be holding back his words.

"Yeah, I went straight to Francis."

"I'm betting he didn't mind at all." Spoken like steel spikes.

Justin would have chuckled, had it not hurt. *Why did it still hurt?* "Long story short, two weeks later, I wasn't working at ErazaTech anymore and I moved in with Francis. He had all my things put into storage. Said he'd provide for me." His own memory was far more bitter than the coffee. "He did. In exchange for pain and sex. A new shirt cost a blow job. He took dinner out of my hide and my ass."

Eli's eyes were a bit too wide. "I didn't... I wouldn't..."

"I know." Justin reached across the breakfast bar and pried one of Eli's fingers off his coffee mug. "Believe me, I know that now." He gave Eli's shaking hand a gentle squeeze. "But with Francis... that's how it was. I didn't understand at the time. I thought he cared, that it was a game."

He let Eli go. "Little by little, Francis took over my life. First it was what I wore. Then what I ate. Then when I got up, what I did, who I talked to, where I went... until he controlled every moment of my day. Every minute was for him alone. Most of the time, I was naked but for his collar. My world revolved around the pleasure he took and the pain he gave. Hell, he wouldn't even let me read." Justin ran a hand through his hair. "The worst thing was, for a while, I enjoyed it. It was different and extreme. But when I wanted it to stop, or wanted a breather, it... didn't. He didn't. No safeword. No way to leave. I... didn't know what to do."

"You wanted a dominant/submissive relationship. You ended up in a master/slave one." Eli stood and paced to the other side of the kitchen. He placed his hands on the counter, back to Justin, but fury was written in the tightness of his stance. "It's a good thing he doesn't live here. I'd have his balls."

"I wouldn't want you to do anything."

Eli dropped his head. "I know that." He exhaled. "I'm going to make an omelet. Would you like some?"

That was an odd question. "Yes, but..."

"I need to do something about this." Eli's voice was quiet, but his arms shook. He raised his head. "I know I *can't*, but I need an outlet. Please let me make something for you."

Eli had the same need for control that Francis had. But how Eli handled it? So very different. "Do I get a choice of fillings?"

"Of course." All at once, Eli both relaxed and stood straighter. "Limited to what I have in the fridge."

In the end, they both settled on sausage, onions, peppers, and some brie Eli found in the cheese drawer.

"Thank you," Eli said. "I find cooking beats homicide any day."

Justin laughed, but the lighthearted mood evaporated instantly. "I suspect you're not going to like the rest of the story."

"I already know I won't." Eli started chopping vegetables. "But I want to hear it anyway."

Justin cleared his throat. "We never set any ground rules. So yes... I'd become a twenty-four-seven slave without wanting to—or even knowing what that meant." Shame twisted and broke free, squeezing Justin's heart until he couldn't breathe. He bent over and pressed his forehead against his knees.

An instant later, Eli was there, *kneeling* before Justin, one hand lifting his head, the other brushing his bangs away. "Just, it's okay. You don't have to tell me any more."

"Your leg..."

"Fuck my leg. Don't worry about my leg." The pain and concern in Eli's expression... entirely for Justin.

Eli understood the pain of the past. "I want—need to get this out." Justin wiped the tears off his face. "And the onions will burn."

The kitchen already smelled of caramelizing onions and sausage. Eli frowned, but climbed to his feet anyway, almost concealing the wince. "You're not going to accept 'fuck the onions,' are you?"

Justin hiccupped a laugh and shook his head.

"Figured." Eli returned to the stove and pushed the vegetables around before pouring egg on top.

A deep breath steadied Justin. "We did go to parties sometimes. I enjoyed those. Even though I was forbidden to talk to anyone, I could listen and see someone other than Francis."

Lavi walked into the kitchen and jumped up onto the breakfast bar, his fur soft under Justin's fingers. "I disobeyed the whole no-talking rule quite a bit. Francis was controlling, but he got squeamish about damaging me, especially around others. I'm enough of a masochist that I thought I could handle any punishment he doled out." He'd been wrong about that. Pain? Yes. But there were other ways to punish besides flogging or whipping.

Eli added cheese to the omelet, his shaky, quick movements speaking for him.

"During the last party out there, someone I'd known from college told me my parents had been trying to find me. It had something to do with my sister." He could taste the panic of that moment, the way the world had frozen as the worst possible thoughts scrolled through his mind. Anger heated his gut. Lavi pressed his face against Justin's hand. "I'd had my mail forwarded to Francis's address. I *thought* he'd been giving me everything."

"He hadn't." Eli flipped the omelet—a huge mass of egg and cheese—onto a plate.

"No. I didn't say anything that night or even the next day. I waited until one of the rare times Francis left me alone in the house and snooped through his office and the trash. I found shredded letters. Pieced enough together and recognized my mother's handwriting."

Eli leaned against the counter and pushed his hair back with both hands. "You confronted him."

"Yeah. I was sick of the shit. The orders, the lack of free will. I couldn't even leave the house without him. I found a pair of scissors and cut his collar off. When he got back, I handed the collar to him along with the shredded bits of my mom's letter."

"And he freaked out?"

"Yes, but he didn't get angry, didn't yell. He... fell apart. Tears, apologies, the whole nine yards. Told me he loved me, that he was only trying to protect me. He thought I loved being taken care of." Justin picked Lavi up and held his warm, purring body against his chest. "I bought every word."

Eli blew air out from between his teeth and pulled two clean plates from the cabinet. The tension in his body could have held up a bridge.

"After talking things through, finding out what was happening with my sister, getting Francis's promise that things would change and that he'd let me go visit my family, we had sex. Some of the best we'd had in a while." Lavi squirmed and he let the cat jump to the floor. "I let him tie me up and flog me. He bound me like I'd asked you to."

Eli slid the large omelet between them and sat down. "Is that why you... ?" He rotated the plate slightly.

"I used to love being bound tight and hard against a cross. With cuffs I can move and it's not as fun. I... didn't realize he'd ruined it." Justin took a swallow of cold coffee. "He did flog me that night. Hard, and I loved every second. When he finished, he told me that every inch of me belonged to him. He'd clothed me and fed me and fucked me and he wasn't letting me go." Justin blinked away moisture. "Then he walked away and left me there."

"He—" Eli stood again, paced to the counter, then turned around. "He *left* you there? How long?"

"I don't know." Long enough to piss himself. Long enough to run out of tears. Long enough to not be able to move when Francis took him down and shoved him into a bathroom with the order to clean himself up. "I—" Maybe he shouldn't have told this story because he couldn't stop shaking.

Again, Eli was there, this time handing him a glass of water. "Justin, look at me."

Eli was so much taller than Francis. There was no rope here, only a giant omelet and two plates. Justin took a sip and cold liquid eased his throat. "A day or so later, I snuck out of Francis's bed, grabbed a change of clothes, and left. I

—sat in a park until morning, then went to my former office and begged a friend to let me use her phone. Then I called home."

That hadn't been pleasant. His father had answered, and lashed out with the latest news of his sister. He'd only stopped when Justin had started sobbing. "In the end, my dad wired me money they didn't have so I could fly home." He looked up.

Eli held out his hand and Justin took it. A slight tug had him on his feet and Justin stepped into Eli's arms.

"Thank you for trusting me with that."

"There's more." He could only whisper. So much more. Seeing his sister. Explaining what had happened to his parents. That phone call home a couple months ago.

"There always is," Eli said. "But there's also time."

There was now that they could talk again. Touch again. No traps here. "Now what?"

He felt Eli shrug. "There's breakfast to eat."

"Not exactly hungry." Though the omelet smelled fantastic.

"Neither am I, but it would be a shame to waste it."

Justin let go of Eli and sat. "We'll need forks."

A glimpse of Eli's stunning smile warmed Justin's heart. Yeah, maybe Justin's past was fucked. But the present? The future? Those might work out if he didn't screw up again. "I think I need to talk to someone."

Eli pointed at the omelet. "Eat before it gets cold." He took half and slid the other portion on Justin's plate. "I'll give you Dr. Brohmer's number. She'll likely refer you, but she'll recommend someone Scene-friendly."

So matter-of-fact. "I shouldn't be like this. I mean, what happened to me was nothing compared to Mercy. Or to you."

Eli laid his fork down. "Don't. Trauma doesn't work like that. There's no better or worse."

"But—"

"Justin." Exasperation. Eli rubbed the bridge of his nose. "What happened to me, as horrible as it was... was an accident. Yes, your sister went off to war. But what happened to you... Justin, it was deliberately done."

Air left his lungs. He hadn't wanted to think about that, but there it was. "I'm really fucked, aren't I?"

Eli's voice was as soft as his smile. "No. No more than me. Or Sam or Michael. Or likely anyone in the office. We all have our demons."

He poked at the omelet. "I'm tired of demons."

"I know. It's going to be okay, I promise." He pointed at the plate. "Now, please..."

Still that edge of control in Eli, but Justin needed a bit of that. One bite, at least, he could do.

Despite everything, once the food hit Justin's mouth, his hunger returned. The sausage and brie worked perfectly, and before he knew it, his plate was empty. So was Eli's.

The world felt more solid. "I guess we should think about shoveling." A foot of snow would take some time to clear out.

Eli slid off his stool and collected the dishes. "I'm waiting for the doorbell to ring."

"Doorbell?"

"Next-door neighbor's twins. Shoveling is rough on me."

Right on cue, musical notes sounded in the living room. "Are those real chimes?"

"Old house." Eli grinned and made his way toward the front door. "Where did my coat end up last night?"

Justin followed. "On the bench by the door." Bits and

pieces of clothing and a smattering of buttons were still strewn by the stairs.

Eli extracted his wallet from his coat and opened the front door. Cold air chilled Justin's bare chest and he found himself shying away, both from the cold and what it would look like to have him standing there, half naked.

He caught a glimpse of two teens, both bundled up in hats, gloves, and scarves. "Hey, Mr. Ovadia! Need your driveway done?"

"You two are the first to call, as always." A huge smile from Eli, one that made Justin's heart skip. He'd always assumed Eli was a loner, but there was a community here and Eli was a part of it. "Do the driveway, the walks, and clean off the car, and I'll give you forty each?"

The kids whooped and ran to start. Eli closed the door.

Justin rubbed his arms to warm them up. "That's really generous."

"Keeps them coming back. They mow my lawn during the summer, too. Help out when I need a hand. They're good boys. Smart. Do well in school. Their mother says they've been putting the money away for a road trip when they graduate." Eli bent and collected a few random pieces of suit and tux and put them on the bench. "I may help with their college expenses, depending on where they end up."

Hearing all that was like slipping and falling while standing perfectly still. "There's so much I don't know about you."

A bit of color rose to Eli's cheeks and he deposited more clothing on the bench. "Likewise." Then he met Justin's gaze. "But we can remedy that."

They could.

Eli tipped his head, and cocked his finger in a come-hither motion, then he made his way up the stairs. Well, there was only one thing to do. Justin climbed up after Eli to the second floor.

"I want to show you something," Eli said. At the end of the hall, he opened another door, one Justin had never been through, and stepped to the side. He gestured inside.

A staircase leading up. Dark at the bottom, but daylight filtered in at the top. Justin glanced at Eli, then climbed. He hadn't realized the third floor was finished.

More than finished, actually. He entered into a huge room with light walls and windows. Bookcases. A bed. A reading nook. An old-fashioned writing desk. A bathroom tucked off to the side. Even a tiny kitchen. Justin stepped farther in.

The stairs creaked and Eli sat down at the top. "I rarely come up here. I thought you might like it. Should have offered this months ago, but..." He rubbed the back of his head. "I'm not very good with the whole relationship thing, as you can tell."

"You want me to live here?" That pit of dread opened up again.

Eli shook his head. "I'm not asking you to move in." He shifted a bit on the stairs, stretching out his left leg. "But when you're here, this can be yours. Your own space. To study. Relax. Whatever." He paused. "Two flights are a bit much. I think the cleaners come up here more than me."

A meow sounded as Lavi bounded into the room. He sniffed the air. "His Royal Fuzzy Butt isn't allowed up here, either."

Justin approached the far side of the room. Each step felt like treading over eggshells. Part of him was excited—the other part wanted to flee. He took a breath. Eli wasn't trying to trap him—just give him space. "This'll be a good place to study." Warm and full of daylight. So very different from his apartment. He could do this. Be a part of Eli's life without that consuming him. Maybe, just maybe he *could* move in at some point. If Eli would have him.

Lavi jumped up onto the desk and peered out the window. Justin scratched between his ears. "I'll let you come up here, buddy." That tumble in his stomach wasn't terror, but anticipation.

He returned to the stairwell and joined Eli, sitting next to him. "Thank you."

"You're—"

Justin kissed him. Not hard, but enough to shut him up. Eli cupped his neck, his warm fingers raising goose bumps on Justin's arm.

Justin broke the kiss. "Please don't give up on me."

"I won't," Eli murmured. "If you won't, I won't." He stroked Justin's hair.

"Deal." He wasn't sure what Eli meant, but he wouldn't give up on himself and he wouldn't give up on Eli, either.

CHAPTER NINETEEN

By the time evening rolled around, the roads were free of snow and even dry. Eli glanced out of the front window. Pity. Justin's company had been delightful. Still, he understood the need to go home. Reevaluate. So much had happened in so short a span of time. *Maybe that's good. You think too much.*

Justin stood in the foyer, his suit packed in a garment bag. He'd changed the sweats for an older pair of Eli's jeans, cuffs rolled up, and a sweatshirt. The coat and gloves were Eli's, too. The least he could do. Justin had likely saved his life last night, if not his sanity. "Ready?"

"Yes." Eli buttoned his coat, gripped his keys, and fought the twisting in his gut.

When they reached the car, he hesitated. Icy roads, the lurch of spinning.

"I can drive," Justin said. "If you need me to."

He sucked in a lungful of cold air and opened the door. "When was the last time you've driven in this kind of weather?"

Justin's expression answered that question, even before he spoke. "Never."

Not surprising, what with growing up partly in the South and working in California. "Well, then." Eli dropped into the driver's seat. Justin sat in the passenger's seat. "I do need to do this. It's a control thing."

"Imagine that." Deadpanned, but with the smirk that made Eli want to bend Justin over his knee. Perhaps someday soon, once they both settled a bit. In the meantime... "Two, Mr. White."

"Promise?" Justin's voice turned gravelly.

"If you're willing. And when I decide." He turned over the car and backed out.

A quick smile from Justin. "Good."

Fear lurked at the thought of resuming that part of their relationship. The sight of Justin leaving haunted Eli, not like the accident, but still. Like driving on icy roads, he'd take it slow.

Eli forced himself to relax. Navigating to Oakland on dry tarmac, even in the dark, wasn't troublesome. As minutes ticked by, his muscles loosened. By the time they pulled in front of the row house that contained Justin's basement apartment, his heart beat at a normal rate and his palms weren't even sweaty.

Excellent.

"You memorized my address?" Justin's voice rose at the end of his question. He unclipped his belt.

Not so excellent, that. "No, just recognized it. My first place was two doors up. Also a basement apartment." That had been hell—and heaven. Moving into a shitty apartment, away from everything he'd known, changing his culture, practically overnight. But the *freedom*...

Justin stared at him. "You lived here? Why?"

"It was dirt cheap and close to campus?"

"But—" Justin bit his lip. "You didn't want to spend the money."

Eli released his seat belt. "When every penny feels like death? I didn't want to touch the money. I got a job on campus and this was what I could afford."

Justin opened the car door and climbed out. "Maybe," he said, "we should have talked more."

"Probably." He was wretched with that kind of thing, though. He followed Justin down the snow-covered back stairs, bracing himself with his cane. "But I never know when I'm oversharing once I get started. Michael threatened to gag me once when I started detailing my class schedule to him."

Justin fished out his keys and unlocked the door. "Did he? Gag you?" A flush on Justin's cheeks.

Interesting. Turned on at the thought of a gag, or at the thought of Eli gagged? He didn't answer but followed Justin into the apartment instead.

A moment later, Eli fought every instinct to drag Justin back out. The apartment—if you could call it that—was cold, dark even with the lights on, and smelled of mold and mildew. His skin crawled, but he kept silent. Justin needed the same freedom he'd required all those years ago.

His expression must have been readable, though. He'd never mastered a decent poker face.

"You're not happy." Justin hung up the suit on the back of a door—probably to the bathroom. There wasn't anything else it could have been. Justin shoved his hands into the pocket of the coat. "It's not as bad as it looks."

Yes, it was. A ring of mold lined the baseboard of the walls. "They never cleaned up after the water leak, did they?"

Justin twitched. "Um, they haven't finished repairing that yet."

Fuck. No wonder it was cold. Eli fiddled with his keys. "I... This isn't *good*, Justin. Not for your health." Or sanity. Maybe they should get in touch with Sam. He and Michael had a spare room and— He stopped himself. *No.* Eli took a breath. "Call me if you change your mind about staying here?"

Justin scratched his neck. "I do need to find something better, I know. But my budget..."

Now, there was something he could help with. "You know, I'm pretty decent when it comes to finances and getting the most out of a dollar. Perhaps I can help there?"

A smile curved onto Justin's lips. "I'm not the best with my own money. I'll probably take you up on that offer."

Good. That took the edge off the desire to remove Justin from this place. Eli stepped forward and tipped Justin's chin up. "I should go." He stole a quick kiss and let go, but Justin didn't and then kissed him back, harder and longer.

When Justin broke the kiss, he dug his fingers into Eli's arms. "I'm afraid when you walk out, you'll realize how awful I've been and never want to see me again."

Yes, it had been bad. But— "I understand, Justin. I really do." He blinked a few times to keep his vision clear as his mind clambered for purchase. "One of these days, you'll figure out that I'm a monster and—" Leave. Run. That had happened once already.

"You're not a monster," Justin said. "I know that now."

If only the voice in his head agreed. "And you're not awful." He touched his forehead to Justin's. "You're just a brat."

That got him a laugh. Justin loosened his grip. "Well, you have a solution for that."

Eli cupped Justin's chin and stroked his jaw. "I do, indeed." His tremble under Eli's touch sent a shiver of delight to Eli's core. "Don't you forget it."

"I won't."

The world clicked back into place. The apartment was a horror, they were both a bit fractured, but everything was *right*. Eli stepped back. "I'll see you in the office tomorrow. Call if you want a ride and we can rescue your bike."

"Yeah. That sounds good." Justin looked lost, but also determined. "Tomorrow."

It took effort to turn, to walk away, but Eli managed. His fingers shook a bit against the wheel as he drove back home, and the house felt big and empty. But Lavi was there, all purrs and demanding meows, and the couch was still comfortable.

Eli made himself a cup of valerian root tea, lay down on the couch, let Lavi crawl up onto his chest, and closed his eyes.

Usually he despised winter. He might change his mind about this one. Time would tell.

———

MONDAY MORNING, JUSTIN MELTED AGAINST THE passenger seat of Eli's car. "Oh God, you turned the warmer on."

"I thought you might appreciate it." Eli waited until Justin had clipped his belt before pulling out from the curb.

"You have no idea. It's freezing in there." He stretched his fingers out in front of the vents.

Eli bit his tongue to keep from speaking. Still not the time or the place to harp on Justin's living conditions. He thought about finding landlord's name and calling around until the situation got fixed, but Justin would resent that. He *was* a grown man, after all.

And Eli didn't own him. Just wanted to protect him, which had its own pitfalls. He tightened his grip on the wheel.

"I know. You don't like it." Justin dropped his hands to his lap. "It *is* hideous in there."

"But it's yours," Eli said. Anything more would be too much. His chest hurt from conflicting desires. Rescue Justin. Let him be. The second was the correct choice, whether Eli liked it or not.

"Except it's not mine, it's the landlord's, and he doesn't give a shit." Justin ran a hand through his hair. "I needed space, but..." He trailed off and glanced out the window.

"Sam and Michael have a roo—"

"No. If I'm going to move in with someone, it'll be you or no one."

For a moment the world stopped, then Eli hit the brakes to not ram the car in front of them. Thank goodness they were nearly there. His breath was gone and his limbs tingled to his feet and hands.

No idea what he looked like, but whatever his expression, it caused Justin to chuckle. "I'm not ready to move in, don't you fear."

"It's not fear." He found a snow-free parking spot near the office—one without a chair stuck in the middle of it—and pulled in. Fear didn't taste like light and laughter and woodsmoke in the air. Fear was a bitter, awful thing.

Justin grinned. "Could have fooled me." He unbelted and got out of the car.

Eli followed and they walked in silence up the street. So many words in his head, so many plans and ideas, all the things he wanted to tell Justin. Hopes he wanted to unbox, shake out, and share.

Everything was so raw. So new. "Would you like dinner tonight? Maybe order a pizza?"

Justin blew out a puff of air, passed the office door, and pulled open the one to Grounds N'at. "I have class tonight."

Right. Monday. Eli shook his head ruefully and entered the warm shop behind Justin. "I forgot."

"Well, I'm going to have to bum a ride to campus and back from *someone*. Maybe we can pick a pie up on the way home?"

The world stuttered again, tripping over the word Justin had mouthed. *Home.* "Sure. We can do that." Though his heart beat double-time, Eli ordered coffee anyway. *Home* continued to rattle in his head while they waited for Brian to make their drinks. When Justin took his hand, the word lodged itself in his throat.

He needed to be careful. They both did, but he had no way to ask Justin to slow down. Nor did he want to.

Two coffees and a flight of stairs later, they walked into the office and split only when they had to go separate ways to reach their desks.

Eli shed his outerwear and stared at his desk. Friday, he had loathed being here. Saturday, he'd vowed to quit. And now? Everything had changed.

Well, not *everything*. He wasn't at all surprised to hear his door click closed. The only question was whether it was Sam leaning against the wood surface—or Michael.

He turned and found Sam.

"Please tell me I'm not losing either of you."

"You're not losing either of us." Eli sat down in his chair. "But it was a near thing."

"I know." Sam leaned his head against the door and

closed his eyes. "Now tell me we won't be going through this again in a couple of months."

"I don't think so. We're... We understand each other better now." He paused. "You were right about past trauma."

Sam blinked his eyes open. "Figured I might be. Not like I have any experience with that."

Sam's own past had nearly kept him apart from Michael. "We're going to take things slower. We both took so much for granted, and I should have noticed—"

"You're not a mind reader, E."

Eli fought with the idea, but Sam was right. "I know."

"Good. 'Cause if you start with the 'Doms know everything' shit, I will kick your ass."

Warmth touched Eli's face. He was, on occasion, guilty of that line of thought. "I suspect Justin might get there first."

"As he should." Sam pushed himself off the door, and opened it. "You two really are ideal for each other." A moment later, he disappeared into his office.

Justin must have heard Sam's last words, because he sat openmouthed and ruddy-faced at his desk. Eli enjoyed that sight before waking up his computer. If he was going to stay at this job—which he was—he had quite a lot of work to do.

CHAPTER TWENTY

ELI'S ATTIC WAS A PARADISE COMPARED TO THE SHITTY basement apartment. Now it felt like heaven. Justin stared at the computer screen. Done. His group had finished their capstone project.

Well, at least until the committee looked at it. But for now? It was complete and entirely cleaned up. Ready to be turned in. He closed his eyes and waited for the heady vertigo to stop. So many hours, so much research, so many arguments, negotiations. He croaked out something that felt both like a laugh and a sob as his head tried to touch the clouds that floated somewhere above the roof in the icy January air.

Celebration time. Justin flicked his eyes open and pushed away from the desk. More and more of his belongings dotted the room. Books, art that had escaped the flood. A photo of Mercy. Sometimes he even slept here, especially on nights Eli tossed and turned due to his leg. Or he did, due to nightmares.

Most of the time, he woke in Eli's bed.

They ought to get the rest of the stuff from the Oakland

apartment. It had been almost a week since he'd gone there. All his mail came here now.

Time to admit he'd moved in with Eli. Justin eyed his laptop. Ends and beginnings. He stood and headed downstairs.

One of the best things about living with Eli was learning his little quirks, from the annoying—he squeezed the toothpaste from the center of the tube—to the endearing. On the weekends, Eli read in the afternoons, usually some history book or another. Except Eli's reading always turned into a nap on the couch, book splayed out at his side and Lavi curled up on his chest.

Like everything Eli did, he slept with intensity, so Justin could sneak up on him, even when walking down two flights of stairs in a creaky older house. Justin took a seat next to Eli's sock-covered feet.

No reaction whatsoever from Eli. Lavi, however eyed him though half-open lids.

"Sorry, bud. You're not gonna like the way I wake your dad."

The cat rotated an ear backward.

Justin ran his finger, nail first, up the inside of Eli's right foot.

Eli arched his back and practically levitated into the air. Lavi took off, clearing the coffee table in a blur of white-and-black fur, and the book by Eli's side hit the floor with an audible *thump*.

Nice. Very nice.

"Justin!" Eli's voice pitched about an octave higher than normal, his eyes wide, and so far from his unflappable demeanor. Justin grinned. That was one of the delights of this round of dating—seeing behind Eli's mask.

Eli grabbed Justin's shirt and dragged him forward. "You little... fuck!" He gulped air.

Justin giggled.

"You're so asking for it!" A mixture of surprise and annoyance, in Eli, but also a hint of joy.

"Yeah," Justin said. "I am." He shifted enough to press his hardening length against Eli's thigh.

Eli loosened his grip. "So you are." His voice fell back into his normal range and he pressed up against Justin. "But just what are you asking for?"

"Anything you'd like." They hadn't set foot in the playroom since the day Justin had walked out. Not together, anyway. Sometimes Justin walked in when Eli wasn't home, to look and remember. He wanted that again. Eli's punishment. The pain and oblivion. The joy.

Eli stroked his cheek. "You're going to need to be more specific."

He couldn't say it yet. "What number am I up to?"

Eli's focus turned inward for a moment. "Seven. After that little maneuver?" He refocused. "Ten or eleven. I haven't decided just how upset I am yet."

Eleven, hopefully. Justin's heart sped up. "I want that." Eli had to understand what Justin meant.

Fingers grazed Justin's lips. "Want what?"

Same conversation as always. Justin laid his head against Eli's chest. "You know. You've known."

"I do." Eli stroked his hair. "But I want you to say it. Words have power."

Like safewords. The echo of his own voice sounded in his mind.

This had to end. He'd finished his capstone. He was going to move in. If he couldn't ask now, then when?

"I want you to whip me. Or cane me. Or both. I want

you to tie me up and—" He pushed himself up. "I want you to punish me."

Eli raised a brow. "Punish you for what?"

"For leaving you." He'd planned to say *For waking you*, but the truth slipped out.

Eli's expression softened. "Oh, Just." A whisper of words. "I'm not mad at you for that."

"I know you're not." His throat tightened. "But I'm mad at me. And I need..." No more words came. He could only search Eli's face and hope he understood.

It wasn't right, this need. Hell, his therapist told him none of what had happened was his fault. But he'd feel a lot better if he could get the guilt out of his head.

Or could drown it out—drown Francis out—with pain and joy and Eli's approval. Their pleasure.

In the soft voice Eli used when he whispered *I love you* when he thought Justin was asleep, Eli spoke. "Then eleven it is, Mr. White."

He melted into Eli's arms. "I love you, too."

Eli kissed his forehead. "Upstairs. Now."

So many memories haunted Justin in this room. Good ones—and one bad one that had shattered everything. He shivered, but it had nothing to do with being naked. Thank God Eli's back was turned. Last thing he wanted was for Eli to pull back. The Dom mask was in place, but there were enough cracks that the Eli who fretted and worried peeked out from beneath the leather pants and the linen shirt and the sly grin.

Eli's nervousness was heartening. Justin wasn't alone.

They both wanted this and desperately didn't want to fuck it up.

When Eli turned back, Justin held out the leather collar he'd collected from the attic.

Eli regarded the offering, then met Justin's stare. "Put it on me."

Heat flooded Justin, from his soles to the crown of his head. "What?" You didn't collar a Dom.

Eli tipped his head back, exposing his neck. "Humor me tonight."

Would it even fit Eli? Only one way to find out. Justin slipped the band around Eli's neck, threaded the leather through the buckle and tightened. Yes—a bit loose, but better than too tight. By the time Justin lowered his hands to his side, his head was wrapped around a proverbial pole.

Warm fingers cupped his face and Eli kissed him, lips and tongue opening and claiming his mouth until Justin moaned. When Eli broke the kiss, he whispered, "Think about it."

He had been, his brain reeling from the implications and the kiss. Justin's collar on Eli's neck claimed Eli. As surely as Eli claimed Justin. Equals, despite Eli's orders and Justin's submission.

Never, ever, in a million years, would Francis have let leather touch his neck like that.

"It's different."

Eli's grin was full of teeth. "That it is." Another quick kiss. "Up against the cross, Justin."

This tremble, he didn't mind Eli seeing. He obeyed, pressing against the cool leather and raising his arm out. Familiar sharp scent and stretch of muscle. Eli's breath on his back. "I'm going to use rope, like before."

"Good."

A kiss between his shoulder blades. "If it becomes uncomfortable, let me know. Talk to me. Yes?"

Eli wore leather around his neck, a band Justin had placed there. "Yeah." Blood pounded in his ears. Did Francis lurk in his mind this time? Please, no. He'd had more than enough of that man. Of his ghost.

When the rope crossed Justin's flesh and pulled his arm tight against the leather pad, it was Eli who hummed in his ear. Loop after loop. First his left wrist, then his right. Justin's cock hardened with each touch, each breath of Eli's against his skin.

When Eli knelt—with a slight grunt—and pulled Justin's leg over to be bound, Justin groaned.

"Good or bad?"

"Fucking hot."

Eli ran his leather-clad hand up the inside of Justin's thigh, just grazing Justin's balls. "You have no idea."

Every nerve in Justin's leg twitched. He rocked against the cross. "Think I have some."

The answer to that was a slap on his ass—enough to make him jump and whet his desire, but not hard enough to satisfy. Eli kissed his hip, right where his tattoo was.

"Tease," Justin muttered.

Eli finished tying one ankle and pushed the other over, spreading Justin's legs wide. "You're begging for twelve, aren't you?"

"I'm begging for more than that."

Another grunt as Eli stood, then a scrape of teeth at the nape of his neck. No pain. Eli hadn't bitten, but the warmth and wet enflamed Justin's blood and made it hard to breathe.

"Well," Eli said, speaking each word against his neck. "We'll see if you get what you want or what I want."

Or both.

Eli stepped back, but not away. He caressed Justin—arms, back, torso, scooping around to tease Justin's chest and nipples before returning to cup his ass and balls and thighs.

Justin squirmed against the cross, creating the friction that would drive him higher. Eli slid his hand between Justin's ass cheeks and brushed his hole.

Like lightning straight to his balls and brain. He pulled against the ropes and tried to pull air into his lungs. They'd fucked plenty of times since they'd gotten back together. Tenderly. Hard and furiously. Everything in between. But not like this, not while Justin was bound and helpless. "Please."

"Patience." Eli stepped back, taking his warmth with him. "First things first."

The first strike of the cane didn't register until the pain of it flooded into his brain. Which was about the moment the second blow landed against his ass. The cry that ripped from his throat was half pain and half shock. The third blow rattled his bones to his fingertips. Then Eli paused.

Fuck, he'd missed this, the burn, the way it spread into his head, the way his skin tried to crawl away. His balls ached for more. Justin pushed back, waiting for the next strike, dreading it and wanting it.

The fourth strike fell sharp and hot against his right shoulder blade, stealing his breath and hazing his vision. The fifth mirrored the fourth, and sparked starbursts before his eyes. Then Eli repeated both blows, and fuck, did it hurt.

Right on the edge between what he liked and what he could endure. And beyond that? Bliss. Pure bliss.

The next blow struck slightly lower and took away his ability to count. The rest fell like fire and turned his throat raw from sobs and pleading and cries. More. Less. He didn't know and Eli didn't stop.

Time bent and the agony flamed upward, pulling him toward heaven. Blow after blow until he hit the top and screamed as the world around vanished into one single pillar of fire.

He was pretty sure he didn't pass out. Still, it took a while for the world to creep back in. When it did, it was a wonderfully achy place, full of bright light, freedom, and skin that felt like ice and fire at the same time.

"Eli?" His voice sounded like broken glass.

"I'm here, love." A warm kiss to the back of his neck. "I'm going to take you down."

Justin's ankles came free first, before he could even formulate the words for a protest. "We didn't fuck."

Eli stood again, so quickly. Or maybe time was still screwed up. He couldn't tell.

"It's all right." Eli untied Justin's left wrist.

"But you didn't get anything." That wasn't fair, for Eli to do all the work, give all the pleasure and pain.

"But I did." Eli kissed top of Justin's right shoulder. "You gave me more than you can imagine."

"But—"

"Shh." Eli freed the other wrist. "It's okay. You're in no shape for anything else."

Justin slumped against the cross. Tired, so very tired. And light and... "But—" Eli picked him up, and for a moment, Justin was back in the night they'd first played. How long ago that seemed. "I'm sorry for everything."

"I'm not," Eli said. They were in the hall, then in the bedroom. A lot fewer steps than in that big mansion. "Some things, yes. But not everything."

Yeah, come to think of it, a lot of their time together had

been good. The bad bits? They were fixing those. *He* was fixing those. When Eli set him down on the bed, the sheets turned Justin's back into a pile of stabbing pins. He rolled over. "Did you use that stupid little cane?"

"The carbon fiber? As a matter of fact, yes." Humor in Eli's voice.

Justin cranked his head and looked up. Eli still wore his collar. His shirt was unbuttoned now, torso covered with a sheen of sweat, but his face—his face was radiant, full of a wide, natural grin, Joy spilled into his eyes and into the tiny crinkles in his forehead.

"That explains a lot."

Eli snorted. "I'll be right back."

When he returned, it was with the familiar tub of slave. Justin groaned when the cool cream touched the flaming stripes on his back. "I finished my capstone." It came out as a whisper.

"Thought you might have."

"Why?"

"Ends and beginnings."

"Beginnings and beginnings."

Eli laughed. "That, too." He brushed Justin's cheek with a kiss. "Go to sleep, Just."

There was an order that was easy to obey.

CHAPTER TWENTY-ONE

THE DAY DAWNED FOR ELI LIKE EVERY OTHER HAD recently. Justin slept next to him, his warmth and presence keeping Eli calm and grounded.

Thirty-four. Today he turned thirty-four.

He wouldn't celebrate for another six months—he'd moved his birthday the year he left home because there was no happiness in celebrating life two days after mourning death. Eli exhaled and shifted, waking both Lavi, who had been sleeping on his feet, and Justin.

Lavi made a soft meow of protest and repositioned himself, dropping hard enough to make his point. *No moving, human.*

Justin rolled over and propped himself up on his arm. "Hey," he said. "You okay?"

"I'm fine. I'm..." Worry marred Justin's face, creased his brow. "You know." Knew what today was.

"Yeah. Sam told me."

Eli closed his eyes. *Damn it, Sam.* "I would have preferred to let you know myself."

"I know. I said as much. He should have left it up to

you." Justin leaned over and kissed Eli's shoulder, the warmth of his lips melting away the anger in Eli's heart. "I guessed it was this week, though. You've been out of sorts."

A polite way of saying he'd been a moody fuck the past couple of days. "I should have said something, but I don't like thinking about it." He couldn't help thinking about it. Eli rolled toward Justin, dislodging Lavi in the process. "I'm sorry."

His Kitty Highness marched up between them and flopped down. Justin absently scratched the fuzzy interloper behind the ears. "You'd have told me in your own time."

Lavi stretched, purred, and rolled onto his back. Eli stroked under Lavi's chin. "Please don't do anything special."

"I won't. Not until July." A grin full of teeth. "All bets are off then."

The chuckle bubbled up naturally. "Looking forward to it."

"Also, it's my night to cook." There was a bit of a glint in his eye, a twitch to that smile.

Dinner... He could handle dinner. That was routine and normal. "So it is." Expectation formed and shoved the morass of the past out of the way. He didn't bother to ask what Justin was making. That was always a surprise. Sometimes a good one, sometimes... less so as Justin struggled with new dishes. Still, they ate and laughed and... His breath caught and his heart rammed against his ribs.

It was his birthday, and for the first time since the day he walked out of his parents' house, he wouldn't be alone.

"Eli?" It was Justin's *are you okay or are you not?* tone.

He pulled Justin close for a quick kiss, much to Lavi's consternation. "I'm fine. You just... make the day bright."

Justin's smile was the only gift Eli needed.

Dinner was an excellent meal of eggplant stuffed with a mixture of lamb and spices. Brownies for dessert. With those, a salad, and rice, Justin had outdone himself. The kiss Eli gave Justin after lingered just long enough to leave them both breathless.

"Nothing special?" How he loved to see that flush on Justin's neck. They cleared the dishes from the table.

"It was pretty easy, to be honest." Justin placed the last of the flatware into the dishwasher, closed it, and leaned against the counter. "Trick is soaking the eggplant in water with lemon."

Eli stole another brownie from the plate. "Feel free to make it again."

Justin chuckled. "Had a feeling you might say that." His smile leveled out when Eli picked up both baking pans and headed for the sink. "You don't have to—"

"Cook doesn't clean."

"But—"

But it was his birthday. He didn't need the reminder. As light and good as the day had been—the best since the accident—the weight was still there. No phone calls. No cards. No family. "But nothing, Justin. Besides, you have homework."

Justin's shoulders dropped, but he retreated to the living room anyway.

It didn't take Eli too long to clean what wouldn't go in the dishwasher. He set the machine to washing.

From the couch, Justin looked up. "Movie?"

Eli leaned against the doorway between the rooms and

shook his head. His skin itched and mind buzzed—too many memories and feelings threatening to trickle up and overwhelm him. He glanced back at the clock on the stove. 7:13. Still early enough. "I think I need to walk."

A thoughtful frown from Justin. "Do you want company?"

"No," he said, his throat tightening around the words spoken and unspoken. "Not tonight."

Justin's smile was sad, but at the same time, warming. "I understand."

Maybe he did, too.

"But take your phone? In case you end up in Polish Hill or Swissvale or downtown or somewhere else miles from here? I'll come get you."

That stung a bit, but he sometimes wandered a bit too far on his walks. "Ordering me now?"

"In this?" Justin drew himself up out of the slouch on the sofa. "Yeah. I am."

That Justin could? That Eli let him? Made all the difference. "Good." Eli pushed off the doorframe.

Coat, scarf, gloves, cane—and phone—later, Eli stepped out into the cold night. The dry air stole his breath for a moment, but it also felt clean. Pure. Pouring into his lungs and purging out the chatter and thoughts that wanted to turn this good day into a pit of morass and misery.

Maybe someday, he could reclaim this day from the past. Eli put one foot in front of the other, and set off down the street. Cold and clear, no snow blocked his way. Stars hung like splinters of glass in the sky, glittering between buildings and trees, despite the effort of the street lamps to blot them out. A perfect night. Peaceful.

In his mind, he told himself he was walking at random,

with no destination in mind. Yet somehow he ended up here, again, like every other birthday.

Staring at the front door of his parents' house.

They hadn't moved. Nor had the house changed much from the outside. Sure, the plants—all dead now but for the rhododendron—were a bit different. But the door remained the same. The windows. Even the lacy curtains glowing with light from within.

His fingers itched to touch the mezuzah affixed to the doorjamb while he recited the blessing. Strange, that. He had one on his house—bought in Israel, no less—but rarely ever thought of it. When was the last time he had the parchment checked? Why was he even thinking of this now?

Eli stared at the door.

Every other birthday, he'd walked away in anger, content with his break from the past. This time, the anger wasn't there. He had Justin. He had a future. Friends.

Family? Eli clutched the phone in his pocket. Maybe. Maybe he had a family, too. He could only hope and wait and see. The past, though... He'd let that rule his life for *years*.

Time for a change.

Eli took a breath of the clean night air, blew out a puff of cloud, and strode to the door. Before he could reconsider, he rang the bell.

Too many heartbeats and a dry swallow later, his father opened the door. His lips parted as if to speak, then flattened into a hard, unforgiving line. His father's grip on the side of the door had turned his knuckles white.

"Jaco, who is it?" Eli's mother joined him at the door. Same openmouthed gasp, though she didn't close her lips.

"May I come in?" The tightness of his throat hadn't lessened, but he spoke anyway.

They both hesitated for a moment, but then his father nodded and opened the door and stepped to the side.

Neither looked pleased. Hell, he wasn't happy, either. But enough was enough. Sixteen years since he'd left. Eighteen since the accident. Eli opened the screen door and entered the house that had once been his home. His refuge. He even brushed his fingers over the mezuzah.

It smelled the same, that hint of spice under the lemon cleaner his mother used. A gentle smell of wax. The years melted for a second, reforming to when he had been happy here. When he'd watched his mother light the Shabbat candles. When he'd thought nothing could ever harm him. The constriction in his throat slid into his chest. "I think it's time we finally talked about the accident. About Noah. And about me."

It was his mother who nodded. "Why don't you come and sit down? I'll take your coat."

He shoved his gloves and scarf into his pocket before handing it over.

His father eyed his cane, then gestured to the living room. He made it three steps into the room before what was on the coffee table stopped him in his tracks.

Photographs. Of him. His exhale was a little loud, with perhaps too much sorrow in it. But he was here for a reason —and the boy depicted in those photos, the boy he had been —was part of that. He forced himself to finish the walk to the couch, to sit down. He propped his cane up against the armrest.

The photographs spanned years, from his birth to his bar mitzvah and beyond. Even to high school graduation, when he'd cut his hair close and shaved his face completely.

Eli touched a photo of a dark-haired, smiling boy holding a stuffed dreidel. He couldn't have been more than three.

"Your second Chanukah."

"I don't remember being this young." Everything before the accident seemed like a dream. Improbable. Someone else's life.

Another photo had him riding a bike, his legs already too long for the frame. Again, the smile. This time, the curls were covered by a kippah. A pang in his chest, followed by a deep ache in his head and his bones. "I can't ride anymore."

His mother joined them, carrying a tray of cups. Tea.

"It's herbal. The one with the calming weed... oh, what is it? There's a bear on the box."

Eli set the photo down. How long had they been talking in Ladino? Had he been? He couldn't tell.

He answered in English. "Chamomile."

She nodded and set the tray down next to the photos and retreated to her chair.

Silence. Eli took one of the mugs and sipped, the warmth of the brew easing the pain in both his throat and chest. He studied his parents, their long, worried faces. He shared his father's eye and hair color—though his father now sported more white than black. His features, though, he found mirrored in his mother. Hers were softer, but the same length and angles looked back. He was a product of these two, but also of himself and of time.

"I am not the man you wanted me to be. I will never be that man." Eli paused. "And I'm not sorry for it."

They both shifted, looked at each other, and back at him. Fingers gripped mugs tighter.

"None of it was the fault of the accident. If that hadn't happened, I wouldn't be who I am now, but I don't think I'd be all that different. Not in the ways you hate me for."

His mother exhaled. "We don't hate you, Eli."

Hearing his name from her felt like being stabbed with many, many needles. He tried not to flinch. "No," he said, the words like pebbles in his mouth. "You hate what I've become. You want this boy." He touched the photo of the two-year-old. "Or who you hoped he'd become, back when he was young and innocent." He touched another picture, him at his bar mitzvah. "Or maybe this one, set to become a pillar of the community."

"Can you blame us?" His mother looked into her mug.

"I can. I have." Completely. Utterly. "Because you hate me for every unreasonable expectation you ever had."

Both of them started. His father made to rise.

"Don't," Eli said. "Hear me out this one time. You'll never know if you're justified in believing I'm the wretched and ungrateful son who does not honor his parents if you throw me out now."

An odd look from his father, but he settled into his chair. His mother's hands shook.

"I'm gay. I've always been gay. I'm going to be gay for the rest of my life." They surely knew this, but it still felt good to say it out loud.

His father worked his jaw, but remained silent. His mother set down her mug and folded her hands into her lap. "That boy Noah—"

"Noah had nothing to do with it!" He nearly slammed the mug onto the table. The sudden welling of anger shook him. He set the cup down gently and wiped his mouth with the back of his hand. "Noah didn't turn me gay." Hell, Noah might have been bisexual. He'd mentioned girls a few of the times they'd fooled around in some of the more secluded parts of Frick Park. No way to know now.

"He took advantage of you."

"Oh, Mom." *So, so not the case.* "If anything, it was the other way around."

His father rose at that. "We don't need to hear about your... exploits."

Exploits. He mouthed the word. Ladino again. Understanding came so easily. Speaking less so. So in English, then. "Not exploits. I'm being forthright." He tapped the fourteen-year-old version of himself. "You should have figured that out when dealing with this one."

His mother stared at the photo and her shoulders dropped. "You did have a way of asking for what you wanted." She turned to his father. "Do you remember, Jaco? When he talked you into that video game thing?"

His father grunted. "I remember a twisted logical argument about hand-eye coordination and how gamers were better at math and if I wanted you to get into Carnegie Mellon, you absolutely needed a PlayStation."

Eli's face warmed. "I *did* get into CMU. Twice."

"Twice?" That from his father.

They didn't know about the second time. Why would they? "After I graduated with my BS in business admin, I went back for my MBA. Graduated with honors that time, too."

"That's... good, Eli."

He shrugged. "I wanted it. I got it. I've never been afraid of hard work. It's the easy stuff that bores me."

Another nod from his father. "You've done well?"

"Reasonably. I've lost a few positions over my..." How should he phrase it? "My insistence on the proper way to manage things. But I'm a chief financial officer now, and that's the perfect place for such a quirk."

"You're an executive?" His father sat up and even looked a bit proud. "At thirty-four?"

"I signed on last year. A small consulting firm, but Sam is well known in the industry. We're growing."

"Such a coup."

"Yes, it is." He picked up his mug and finished the tea. "Not bad for your sexually deviant monster of a son."

They both recoiled. His mother looked mortified.

"I've heard the things you've muttered. I'm still involved enough with the community that I eventually hear your complaints." Back to Noah again. "He didn't abuse me, and he certainly didn't rape me. I *asked* him for sex."

"You were fifteen!"

"I was five days shy of sixteen! He'd *just* turned eighteen. Hell, he was born late enough at night he was probably *still* seventeen when I fu—"

They'd both gone crimson. Eli sighed and rubbed his forehead. "Yes, your son has a sex life. Even if I were straight, I'd still have one."

"You don't need to share it." His father spoke through a clenched jaw.

"In this case, I do. You sued Noah's parents. He was barely in the ground when you—" His throat tightened again. The sharp pain, the ringing in his ears. *I will not flash back now. Not here.* He waited a few seconds until his heart rate slowed, until his vision wasn't hazy. "Why did you do it? I can't change the past. I've had to live with what you did for more than half my life. But I want to know why you put Noah's blood on my hands."

Both his parents shrank back, both stared at him, his mother covering her mouth with her hand.

Had they only now realized what they'd done?

"I loved him," Eli said. "As much as I could at that age. Then you made me the instrument of his parents' punishment for a crime they didn't commit, that *he* didn't commit. I've been the one paying for it since. All because I trusted you. Trusted Rebbe Coen."

"We... thought we were doing the right thing. Protecting you."

He wanted to scream, *From what?* but swallowed the words, kept his voice neutral. "That wasn't the result. At all."

"We never intended to hurt you. We just wanted you to have a normal life."

"You wanted me to be straight. To turn back into the studious, religious boy I'd been before every adult I had ever trusted, ever loved, betrayed me." He shook his head.

"We didn't..."

"Yes, yes, you did. I may have been hopped up on painkillers, but I remember what you said." *Such an ungrateful son. How could you do this to us? We didn't raise you to be an animal.* At least *now* they had the wherewithal to look chagrined.

"I don't expect you to accept me or love me." That hope died years ago. "But I want this"—he gestured between them—"to stop. The snide remarks. The chatter. All of it." He held their gazes, each in turn. "You're adults. Act like it."

He had expected his father to rise, to order him out of the house, but that didn't happen. Tears fell from his mother's eyes. "We do love you, Eli."

The despair that lurked deep, the anger and the pain surged out of his heart and tangled his head in razor wire. "If that's true," he said through a throat that burned, "you've had an exceedingly horrible way of showing it for the last eighteen years."

"What do you want us to do?" His father's voice carried the same layer of anger and pain.

"Leave me alone." Eli reached for his cane and stood. "Or *actually* love me. One or the other."

They both rose as well. Shakily, slowly, but they stood. "Do you even care which?" His father's anger had deepened, brought out his accent more.

"If I didn't, I wouldn't be here." He walked to the hallway and pulled his coat out of the closet. "The question is, do either of you? You know how to find me." He donned his coat, scarf, and gloves and opened the front door. "Thanks for the tea, Mom."

"Eli—"

He walked out into the night and pulled the door closed behind him. Time to go home.

———

THE FRONT DOOR OPENING STARTLED JUSTIN AND HE flinched, sending a tablet and a pen crashing to the floor next to the couch. Lavi opened an eye and flicked his tail over on the far end of the sectional.

In the front hall, Eli unwound his scarf and chuckled. "Did you fall asleep?"

He must have, given that his book was resting, spine up, on his chest. *Jesus.* He knew better than to study while lying down. "What time is it?"

Eli hung his coat up and checked his watch. "Nine forty."

Holy hell. Eli had been gone for more than two and a half hours. And he'd been out... nearly as long. "Quite a walk." He picked the book off his chest, fetched the fallen pad and pen, and placed all of them on the coffee table.

"Not really." Eli pushed Justin's legs out of the way and

sat down on the edge of the couch. "I had a chat with my parents."

Those were the last words Justin had expected. Eli was smiling, bright-eyed, ruddy-cheeked. Not traumatized. "How—" He choked on the word. "How did it go?"

Eli stroked Justin's calf. "Better than I expected. For me, at least. I'm sure it was horrible for them."

"Well, good." Served them right.

Eli lost his humor. "I've always had this hope—stupid as it is—that someday, they might come to their senses. I'm not a horrible person. I gave them one last chance."

"They ought to be proud of you. You're perfect."

Eli's laugh was short. He leaned over and kissed Justin. "Flattery gets you nowhere."

"On the contrary." Justin stroked Eli's cheek, then pulled him closer for another kiss. "It got you here."

Eli huffed and sat back. "How's the studying going?" He eyed Justin's notepad, which was entirely free of notes.

"Good. Except for the part where I took a nap." He shrugged. "I'll read the chapters tomorrow."

"It's not even ten yet." There was Eli's raised eyebrow.

"I'd rather go upstairs with you." He ran his hand up Eli's side. Muscles quivered against his touch.

Eli's smile was pure evil. "And if I gave you incentive to do a little work first?"

That was completely different. "What are we talking here? A fuck? A blow job?"

"How about whatever you want to do to me?"

The bottom fell out of Justin's world. Not Eli the Dom talking. Yet... they were negotiating. "You... serious?"

"Very." Eli caressed Justin's neck. "What's that worth?"

Everything. Anything. "A chapter?"

Eli snorted. "I am not *that* cheap."

Yeah, he didn't think he'd get away with that. His stomach somersaulted. "Two, then? That's like a hundred fifty pages."

"Is that what you'd planned?"

He'd planned three. But two would put him where he needed to be. Still, the presumption chaffed a bit. "I'm not a child, you know."

"No, you're not." Eli leaned in and brushed his lips against Justin's, lingering long enough for Justin to smell the cold night air that hung in his curls. "You're the love of my life."

The world tumbled, like a boat rocking on the sea. Or maybe that was him. Eli offered everything, in one sentence. "Two chapters." It was fair—the work he needed to complete.

Eli grinned. "I'll be waiting." He stood and headed upstairs.

Justin pulled his book, notepad, and pen off the table. Two chapters. Notes. Then Eli.

You're the love of my life.

Careful notes, because he would not disappoint Eli or himself with sloppy work. Then on to graduation. After that? He knew exactly what he wanted after that.

He damn well would be the love of Eli's life, no matter what Eli's parents—or his own—said.

CHAPTER TWENTY-TWO

MERCY HAD SAVED ELI A SEAT WITH JUSTIN'S FAMILY for the MBA graduation ceremony, but it was Justin's mom who dragged him over to join them. "He wouldn't want you lurking in the back of the room."

They'd warmed to him over the past few days. Surprising, but heartening.

"Did you know the hoods are plaid?" Justin's mom waved her hand. "It's... odd."

Eli coughed a laugh. "Carnegie tartan is the school color. At least the collar is something that matches." Other masters programs were not as fortunate. The MBA was tan, not pink or orange or light blue.

A hand fell on his shoulder. "Hey, E." Sam's voice.

He turned and found Michael as well. "Have you met Justin's family?"

They hadn't. A round of introductions later, Sam and Michael settled into the seats behind them. Just in time, too. A hush fell over the audience and the first speaker approached the podium.

Eli scanned the group of graduates—they would be

seated in alphabetical order—and yes, there was Justin. As if he sensed Eli's appraisal, Justin looked back and smiled.

AFTER GRADUATION, ELI HUNG BACK AS JUSTIN'S parents and Mercy moved forward. A delight to watch Justin beaming in his cap and gown, suit and tie peeking out from beneath the robe. Vivid blue to match his eyes—the first tie Eli had bought him. An unexpected ache tightened Eli's chest as he watched Justin's father engulf his son into a hug and his mother kiss his cheek. Mercy, resplendent in her uniform, mock-punched Justin in the stomach.

He hadn't had that when he graduated—either time. Yes, Michael had been there and a few other friends, but no one else. He looked down at the cane beneath his palms. Some pain never left.

"Eli? What are you doing?"

He tore his gaze off his hands and found Justin in front of him, the edge of his smile shifting into worry. "Are you okay?"

"Yeah, I'm fine." Close behind Justin were his parents, arm in arm, with Mercy at their side. She winked at him. "I didn't want to ruin your time with your family."

"Ruin... ?" Justin stepped forward—too close—and caught Eli's tie with one hand. The other wrapped around the back of Eli's neck and before he could even breathe, Justin kissed him. Hard. Deep.

Eli's world tumbled so fast he had to grab on to Justin with both hands to stay upright. His cane fell somewhere— it bounced on his foot, but that barely registered because Justin was doing things with his mouth that should be illegal in the state. Probably would have been, had he been kissing

Eli anywhere else. Warmth and desire and love swept through Eli, leaving him dizzy and totally out of control of the situation.

For once, he didn't care.

When Justin relented, a round of applause broke out. A different heat rose, straight to his cheeks, but he was far too breathless to say a word. He could only stare at Justin.

"You can beat me later for that," he murmured so softly no one else could possibly have heard.

Eli swallowed and tightened his grip. He would. Quite soundly, too. "What was that for?"

"Because you're being an idiot." Justin smoothed down the tie he'd gripped and tucked it back into the vest of Eli's suit. "You *are* family."

"But I'm not—" A gleam in Justin's eyes stopped Eli in his tracks. The air was so charged.

Then Justin took hold of both Eli's hands.

Oh shit. "I swear to God, Justin, if you make me cry in public..."

So of course he dropped to one knee. "Eli Ovadia, will you marry me?" From somewhere, Justin produced a ring. Matte black, with a thin line of silver cutting through the middle.

Heat prickled from his toes to his head—even his lips tingled as he stared down at Justin. *You are family.*

"Yes, of course." Somehow he pushed the words out his mouth, then Justin was in his arms and the round of applause was far louder and longer this time. He caught sight of Michael and Sam, both of whom looked far too pleased with themselves. Bastards.

This time, he was the one who pulled Justin into a toe-curling kiss—one that forced a tiny moan that only he felt and heard.

When they broke apart the second time, they were surrounded by well wishes and hugs and laughter and—

Eli caught his breath. This—this was what the opposite of heartache felt like. So much joy Eli though he might crack apart from the lightness and fullness of it, or burst into flames, or... live.

He laughed and let the tears come as they may.

EPILOGUE

One year later

WHEN NOAH'S PARENTS ENTERED THE SYNAGOGUE, Eli's heart skipped a beat. They were older, but somehow still the same. Between them, he could almost see how Noah might have looked as an adult.

They shook hands with Rabbi Berkowitz, then caught sight of him.

"Eli!" Mrs. Feinberg folded him into a hug that crushed his ribs. "Look at you! So handsome! And where's this man of yours?"

Before he could introduce Justin, Noah's mom hugged him, too. Noah's father shook Eli's hand and clapped him on the shoulder. "You should have seen her when we got the invite. We're both very happy for you, and I think Noah would be, too."

There was that pull of guilt. Eli let it hurt. A necessary pain, even on this day. Nothing would change his past. "I'd like to think so."

A few more pleasantries and Sam stepped forward to

lead them to their seats. They were the closest thing he had to parents on this day.

He'd seen his parents a few times in the past year. No insults, but nothing else, either. He'd sent an invitation anyway, as a courtesy, but there was no RSVP.

He hadn't expected any.

Eli turned back to the door in time to watch his father and mother enter and the world tilted sideways into chaos. He grabbed Justin's arm, because the cane was not going to be enough to keep him upright.

They were here. They'd come. A Reform synagogue. A gay wedding—his wedding. They were *here*.

"What... ?" Justin trailed off.

Rabbi Berkowitz clasped Eli's father's hand, paused, and leaned in a bit. Whatever they said to one another, it was lost in the throbbing in Eli's ears. His mother turned and gasped. His father did likewise—and straightened.

Pride. Anguish. *Oh, Dad.*

He stepped forward. "Did you think we would miss our own son's wedding?" His father's voice was rough and thick, his English full of the musical dips and swells Eli had so loved as a child.

He had to blink a few times to clear his watery vision. "I wasn't sure you still had a son." Yes, that hurt them; those words made them flinch. "But I'm grateful you do, and I am glad you're here." Maybe, maybe they could find a path through the pain and hurt and all the shit they'd done to him.

Such a journey needed to start somewhere, and Eli wasn't alone anymore. He *had* a family—one of his own choosing.

Justin held out his hand. "I'm Justin White, Eli's fiancé."

His father hesitated, then shook Justin's hand. "Jaco Ovadia. This is... this is Eli's mother, Reiza."

She took Justin's hand. "I thought my son was lost. I was wrong. Thank you for finding him anyway."

Justin folded his other hand around hers. "He and I... We were both a bit lost. We found each other, brought each other home."

Eli's chest didn't need to be any tighter. He forced himself to breathe, though that became quite hard when Justin let go of his mother's hand and she turned to him, her eyes full of tears. "Eli." Just that and no more, but it carried the weight of the years that lay broken between them, the missed opportunities, the joys that never were, the sorrow that was, and the fear he knew so well.

He wouldn't turn his back. Not when they'd come this far. "Mom." He handed Justin his cane, then stepped forward and wrapped his arms around her.

She sobbed once, a sound that both broke and mended his heart. There would be more tears. Probably yelling, too. Anger lurked in his heart and mind, justifiable, given everything. But this—he could not deny that love lay in her. When he pulled back after several long moments, he saw it in his father as well.

"Thank you for coming." Now his voice was heavy and his vision far too blurry.

"Eli?" Michael stepped forward, a formidable figure in his tux. "Shall I show your parents to their seats?"

"Please." How they would deal with the sudden appearance of one of the grooms' parents, he didn't know. But that's why there were wedding coordinators. And best men.

Michael offered his arm to Eli's mother. "I'm Michael

Sebastian, Eli's best man." He led Eli's parents toward the inner doors.

Once they were safely out of sight, Eli wiped his eyes. "This is not how I thought I'd end up crying at my wedding."

Justin's own eyes were moist. "I can always stomp on your foot during our dance if you'd like a different kind of crying."

The absurdity, the ridiculousness in that flipped Eli's brain over until it settled down on one thought alone. "God, do I love you." That smart mouth, those blue eyes.

Justin smiled. "I hope so. This is a lot to go through for a casual fling."

Eli smacked Justin's ass with the back of his hand, hard enough to make him yelp. "Nothing casual about it, Mr. White."

"Good." A bit breathless and blushing slightly, Justin was captivating. He stepped closer and stole a quick kiss. "And I love you, too. More than ever." He stepped back.

A polite cough caught their attention. Rabbi Berkowitz stood at the doors. "We're all set, whenever you gentlemen are."

Eli nodded, and the rabbi vanished past the double doors.

"Are you ready?" Justin's warm fingers smoothed down his lapel.

"Yes." He'd waited his life for this. He took Justin's arm in his and walked forward.

———

JUSTIN DIDN'T TRAMP ON ELI'S FOOT WHILE THEY SLOW danced. His husband. That was what the vows and the rings said. The stomping on the glass. He kissed Eli's neck and took pleasure in the shiver that resulted.

"Stop that." No malice in those words at all.

Justin stroked Eli's back. "Why?"

"Because you're turning me on, and no one needs to see that." Eli's smile was as bright as the sun.

He nibbled at the spot again. "It's our wedding. I'm allowed to turn you on."

Eli ran his fingers through the back of Justin's hair—they both still wore kippot. "When we get home, I'm putting a very different ring on you."

Now it was Justin's turn to shudder. Fear and excitement at *that* thought. "Promises, promises."

Eli chuckled, and tipped Justin's head up for a quick kiss. "Have I ever not delivered?"

"No." To Justin's great delight.

As the last strains of the music faded, a crowd formed around them—with two chairs.

Uh-oh. He'd heard about this. "Eli?"

Eli shook his head, but his grin was wider. "I didn't plan this—honestly."

Justin recognized the man that came forward—Noah's dad. "What is a wedding without a hora, Eli?" He pointed at the chair. "Sit."

For the first time, Justin watched Eli obey an order without a quip or a frown. He sat and looked up at Justin, one eyebrow raised.

Oh God, he was going to have to do this, wasn't he? From out of the crowd, his sister's voice carried. "Don't be a wuss, Justin!"

He sat, the music started, and up they went, rocking back and forth, high above the heads of the dancers. Justin clung to the underside of his chair and tried not to fall off while those dancing him around aimed for the opposite.

Nearby, Eli's laughter rang out—his head was thrown back and that look of unrestrained joy took Justin's breath away and stripped Justin of fear. He reached out his hand and Eli took it, grinning from ear to ear. Awe and love bubbled out of Justin and into the laughter he could not hold back. Too soon, the dance was over and they were set back down. Somewhere along the line, they both stood and ended up breathless in each other's arms.

"You okay?" Eli gripped his arm.

Justin's heart hadn't quite forgiven him yet. "That was the most horrifying, wonderful—" He sucked in a breath. "Yeah. I'm fine."

Eli kissed him and they both stumbled back to the head table to rest and let the guests have the dance floor. Justin grabbed a glass of water while Eli stretched out his left leg. They never stopped holding hands.

His *husband*. *Holy shit.* Justin giggled.

"What?"

Everything. Justin set down his glass. "This is not what I expected when I handed Sam my résumé."

Once more, Eli laughed, his eyes mirroring the joy. "Nor I, love. Nor I."

Love. Yes. He squeezed Eli's hand. His. Theirs. Together.

It really didn't get any better than that.

THANKS FOR READING!

Dear Reader,

Thank you for reading *Just Business*! I hope you enjoyed Justin and Eli's story.

You'll see Eli again in *Due Diligence*, the next book in the Takeover series. He and Fazil are off to Seattle to help a floundering company get into shape.

Fazil's happy for some time away from Pittsburgh, until he runs into Todd, his first boyfriend, and the man he ghosted on fifteen years ago. Fazil also discovers he's not as much of the hero of his own story as he thought...

Yes, Eli's wrong about Fazil being straight.

If you're enjoying the kink element of the Takeover series, you may also enjoy my *Twisted Wishes* series, or the standalone novel *Cinnamon Roll*, though most of my backlist contains consensual kink of some kind.

To find out more about my books and new releases, you can follow me on BookBub, join my facebook group or sign up for my newsletter.

Thank you so much!

-Anna

ACKNOWLEDGMENTS

Once again, I would like to thank my fans, friends, family, co-workers, and fellow writers for their constant encouragement and support. I'm still amazed yinz read my books, n'at.

I owe a mountain of chocolate to Jennifer Udden for helping me wrangle an out of control manuscript into a reasonable draft, and to Cindy Hwang and Kristine Swartz for much fine-tuning, and to all the other folks who helped along the way. There's so much more that goes into creating a book than just the writing of it.

While Grounds N'at doesn't exist, my great thanks to all of my favorite Pittsburgh coffee shops for giving me somewhere to write for hours on end. Brian's shop is a bit of a love letter to all those wonderful and unique independent coffee shops.

Finally, while I was writing *Just Business* and pondering Justin and Eli's HEA, same-sex marriage became legal in Pennsylvania. Thank you to all who made that possible. Happy Ever After should be for all.

ALSO BY ANNA ZABO

Close Quarter

Close Quarter

Slow Waltz (a Close Quarter short story)

Takeover

Takeover

Just Business

Due Diligence

Daily Grind

Twisted Wishes

Syncopation

Counterpoint

Reverb

Standalone Works

CTRL Me

Outside the Lines

Weave the Dark, Weave the Light

Cinnamon Roll

ABOUT THE AUTHOR

Anna Zabo writes contemporary and paranormal romance for all colors of the rainbow. They live and work in Pittsburgh, Pennsylvania, which isn't nearly as boring as most people think.

They can be easily plied with coffee or a chance to see the Pittsburgh Penguins.

Anna has an MFA in Writing Popular Fiction from Seton Hill University, where they fell in with a roving band of romance writers and never looked back. They also have a BA in Creative Writing from Carnegie Mellon University.

Anna uses they/them pronouns and prefers Mx. Zabo as an honorific. They can be found online at annazabo.com.

 twitter.com/amergina

instagram.com/amergina

bookbub.com/authors/anna-zabo

amazon.com/Anna-Zabo/e/B00A7LA6OC